THE GOLDEN SPURS

by
David Ewens

Grosvenor House
Publishing Limited

The right of David Ewens to be identified as the author of this
work has been asserted in accordance with Section 78
of the Copyright, Designs and Patents Act 1988

The book cover picture is copyright to David Ewens

This book is published by
Grosvenor House Publishing Ltd
Link House
140 The Broadway, Tolworth, Surrey, KT6 7HT.
www.grosvenorhousepublishing.co.uk

This book is a work of fiction. Any resemblance to
people or events, past or present, is purely coincidental.

A CIP record for this book
is available from the British Library

ISBN 978-1-78623-232-8

About the Author

David R Ewens worked for many years in the English further and adult education sector. He lives and writes in Kent.

Also by David R Ewens
in the 'Frank Sterling' series

The Flanders Case
Under the Radar
Rotten
Fifth Column

Acknowledgements and disclaimers

This is a work of fiction. Names, characters, businesses, places, events, locales and incidents are either the products of the author's imagination or used in a fictitious manner. Any resemblance to actual persons, living or dead, or actual events is purely coincidental. In particular, episodes and characters relating to the Ashmolean Museum in Oxford, and the 1302 Museum and Begijnhof St Elisabeth in Kortrijk, are entirely fictional. My actual experience of these institutions consisted of nothing but courtesy and excellent, professional service. The novel involves reference to Belgian and specifically Flemish nationalism and politics, but not in a way that Belgians will directly recognize.

Thank you to my partner Ruth Gould for her unstinting support, advice, patience and willingness to visit oddly chosen places by awkward modes of transport.

Thank you to @stadKortrijk for permission to adapt and use its tourist map, and for advice on the book covers. Thank you to Mukdupmaps for map adaptation.

Thank you to my reviewers for their welcome and helpful comments and insights: Gill Fairbanks, Maggie Fieldhouse, Terry Monaghan, Carl Parsons, Peter Taylor-Gooby and Eleanor Waller. Special thanks to Walter Willaert, both for his generous encouragement and for his expert input on Belgium and Flanders, and to my editor Joanna Booth. Any faults with the novel can be laid at the door of all these contributors. The accolades can by mine.

Reading and research

The following books were invaluable in helping with the plot, the background and other aspects:

Clarkson, W. (2006) *Kenny Noye: Public Enemy Number 1,* London, John Blake Publishing

Fegley, R. (2002) *The Golden Spurs of Kortrijk,* North Carolina, McFarland and Co.

Johnson, Robert A. (1986) *Inner Work,* San Francisco, Harper

Singh, S. (1999) *The Code Book: The Secret History of Codes and Code-breaking,* London, Fourth Estate

Sounes, H. (2009) *Heist,* London, Simon and Schuster

Map of Kortrijk

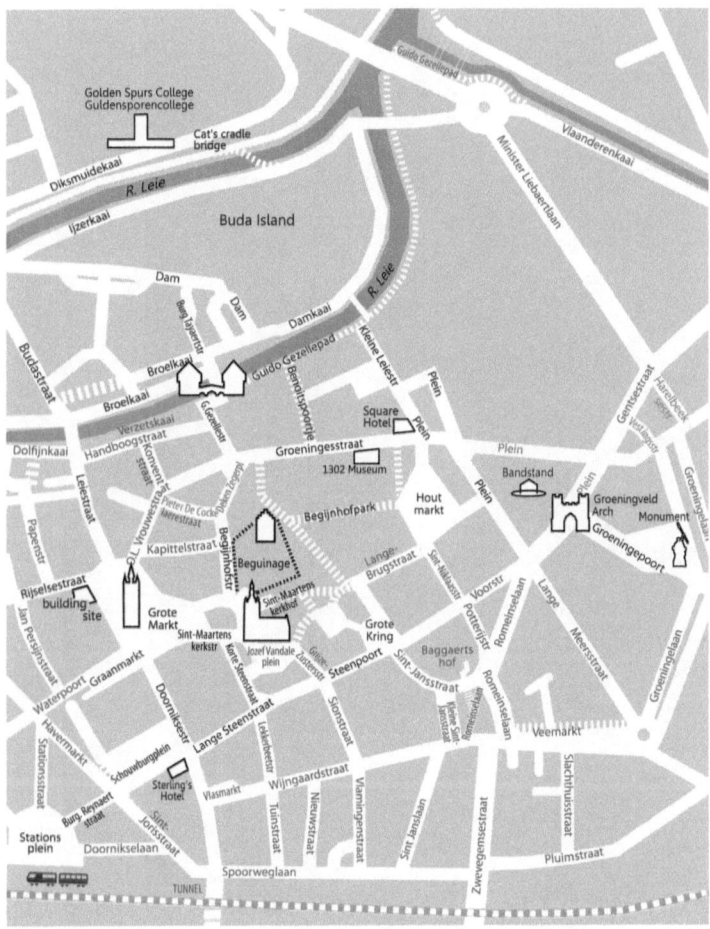

Chapter 1

No. *Impossible, or at least, highly unlikely.* Frank Sterling, private investigator, looked down from his office window onto Market Street.

A gaggle of people had entered the square – tourists from abroad, it looked like. The clues were in the clothes, the average age, the herd-like motions, and the habit of stepping into traffic while looking in the wrong direction.

On the men, it was all polo shirts with thin horizontal stripes of garish colours that hardly matched; the trousers that were not quite trousers and not quite shorts. The feet adorned with socks and sandals, and heads topped with floppy hats and baseball caps. On the women, the themes were similar.

The blouses were flowery and not striped. The hats were wider-brimmed and made of straw rather than canvas, and dresses outnumbered shorts. But the overall impression was the same. Some white beards, wide girths and arms both plump and wrinkled accounted for the age calculation. The discreet, polite parping of horns, in short bursts, from patient local drivers reinforced all the other deductions.

Sterling's own local knowledge rounded off the picture. It was Friday, and market day. A few coaches from West Flanders and the Pas-de-Calais, parked out of sight down by the quay, were inevitable. It would be Sandley in the morning; Canterbury (cathedral, lunch and even more shopping) in the afternoon.

But none of that was either impossible or highly unlikely. It was the young figure among the milling tourists, turned out in black, skinny jeans and bolero-style mauve jacket, with glossy red hair bunched in a ponytail, that piqued Sterling's interest. He knew her, surely, or someone who looked very like her. But what was that someone, if it was her, doing at 11 am on a warm July day in Sandley?

Sterling pressed his forehead against the cool glass as if an extra inch would get him a better view. The young woman was clearly popular in the group. He could not see her face as she spoke animatedly with the people around her, but their smiles and laughter told their own story. If it was her, how long was it since he'd seen her – two years? – more? – less? If it was her, from that distance and angle, some things had changed, but some were still the same. He remembered the roll and tilt of her head when she asked and answered questions, and the habit of touching the forearm of the person she was speaking to if that person was familiar enough – exactly what was happening down there.

She was engaged with her companions but trying, politely, to disengage. She put up an arm, her forefinger erect – 'Hang on a second, I've got to check something' – and turned around. Sterling's heart gave a lurch. The "impossible", or at least "the highly unlikely", was neither. Christina Van de Velde was there in the flesh in the centre of Sandley. Not only that, she was casting her eyes over the buildings towards him – not the restaurants and shop fronts, but at the level of the second floors, as if…

Sterling waited. He put his hand up in the manner of someone taking an oath. He would be a shadowy figure in the window, but it was just a matter of time. When the girl spotted the library sign, she looked up a little further. She squinted and did the head tilt. Her arm mirrored Sterling's in a shy greeting and her pale, freckled face transformed itself from searching frown to delighted smile. Then she crossed the road, looking the wrong way first, and started making her way to his office.

Sterling glanced around. The desk behind him was old and cheap but large enough, with a telephone on the right and a computer in the middle. To the right of the desk, the two-drawer filing cabinet was filled with more case files than ever before but, at the age of 37, and out of the police for three years, he wondered how full it would be when he reached the big 4-0. He wasn't even sure he'd still be in the game.

There was a chair for clients in front of the desk and against the wall a sofa for any associates. The editor's lamp on the desk with its green shade and faux-gold stem brought him luck, he was sure of it. Prints of hop farms and scenes from the Stour and Medway adorned the walls, just enough to avoid a completely bare look. A globe on a little table in the corner between the desk and the window was a reminder of the world beyond Sandley.

Sterling abandoned his inspection. If he knew Christina Van de Velde, the content and décor of his office didn't really matter. The point was, it was ready to receive her, and so was he.

As the footsteps pattered on the landing from up the narrow staircase, Sterling moved to the door, opening it before the knock came.

'Frank,' exclaimed Christina, arms wide and smile gleaming.

'Christina,' said Sterling. He hung back, pleased as he was to see her. He struggled with women. He liked them, and they liked him, but his mother had left him when he was a few months old, and his father had brought him up. He reckoned the issues stemmed from there. Demonstrativeness made him shy. The young woman didn't seem to notice. She wrapped herself around him and pressed her cheek to his chest. Sterling looked down on the lustrous red hair. Her perfume triggered excitement, confusion and regret. He responded with a hug of his own.

Christina broke the embrace first. Her hands grasped his arms just above the elbows, and she looked up into his face. 'Not much change, Frank. Still the handsome man I remember.'

Sterling coloured. 'You're looking good yourself, Christina.'

The girl made a small moue. 'Perhaps. Nothing stays the same. I expect I've filled out a bit.'

It was true. In the two years since their adventure together in Flanders, she was still slender, but more womanly than the girl she had been then.

'So,' said Sterling. He paused for a moment. Maybe it was a bit presumptuous. He took the plunge. 'Norway has got a little wider.' He was referring to the strawberry birthmark that ran up from Christina's belly.

She laughed, and a flush spread up from her pale neck into her face, somehow enhancing the green of her eyes. During Sterling's Flanders case, they'd had a, well, what? Not really a one-night stand. Not really a fling.

But certainly a night of passion after shared danger. 'Yes, Norway is bigger. Do you want to see?'

'I'll take your word for it, Christina.' He swept his arm towards the sofa. 'Take a seat, Madam. I'll put the kettle on and we'll have some tea. I can probably rustle up some biscuits.'

'Ah yes. Tea. Of course. You English must have your tea. Nice office, Frank. I thought it might be like this.'

'Yeah. It suits me. I'll be Mother.'

'You'll be Mother? How can that be poss...?'

'It's just an expression. The person who pours from the teapot is usually "mother". I'm surprised you don't know that, since you spend so much time with the English, making them tea and toast, in that hotel of yours.'

'I missed that one. Hotel Sultan is OK. Ypres is OK. My mother...' – Christina looked sideways at Sterling – 'is OK.'

Sterling nodded. Mrs Van de Velde had been formidable and protective of her pretty daughter, not entirely successfully. 'Right. Good. What brings you to Sandley, Christina, apart from the opportunity to see me?'

'I've been wanting to visit and see how you are for some time, Frank, and a coach goes from the Grote Markt to England every two weeks for retired people, so I have taken the day off. The others are going to Canterbury in half an hour, but if I stay here the driver has said that he will come back for me later. It depends what your plans are. You might be busy.'

Sterling took a sip of his tea. A couple of things were rumbling on. There had been a spate of apparently staged rear-end crashes in the district. An insurance company involved in a couple had asked him to investigate (were they scams or were they genuine?). There was an inevitable infidelity case instigated by a businessman's wife. Humdrum and sordid stuff. The kind of work he'd known he'd have to take when he left the force but which he'd hoped would be extras when business was slack, and not his bread and butter.

'I'm not that busy, and even if I were, I'd make time for this – and you.'

Christina smiled and looked into her tea. Then the smile faded, and a frown creased her forehead. Sterling waited, letting the silence in the room stretch. A pipe on the landing rattled and gurgled. Sometimes it signalled that Angela, his friend the head librarian on the ground floor, or her assistant Kerry, was filling the kettle. Neither could work out how Sterling knew there might be refreshments when he turned up shortly afterwards, and he let the air of mystique around him run on. 'Must be an ex-copper's instinct,' Angela said to Kerry, 'or he sniffs it from upstairs.' Outside a small-engined motorcycle, almost certainly a moped, whined noisily through Market Street. Sterling imagined a lad who'd just turned sixteen trying things out.

'It was exciting, wasn't it, Frank?'

'What, you getting kidnapped and dumped in a cellar? Me getting tied up and tortured with cigarettes? All the other stuff? I'm not sure "exciting" is the right word. You were plucky, that's for sure,' Sterling reflected. It was the girl's determination that had given him backbone.

'I miss it,' she mused.. But life's been good. I've always been happy in the business. In my hometown.'

It was true. She was a small-town girl, happy with her lot. Marriage, kids, an ordinary life... they'd all stretched out before her, and she'd seemed perfectly happy with that. Sterling tried to remember the name of Christina's then-boyfriend. He was an optician in Kortrijk, one of the towns east of Ypres, along the railway line that ran almost next to the French border before it veered off north to Ghent and north-east to Brussels.

'But now...?'

'Now, I don't know. Things have changed. That's why I've come. One of the reasons.'

'Right. Well, I'd better top you up. Then we can get down to business.'

Christina held out her cup, and Sterling replenished hers, and then his own.

'It's Guy,' said the girl.

Guy, that was his name. Sterling had been a mixture of jealous and contemptuous at the time – Guy, an optician in Kortrijk. 'When was I in Ypres, Christina? A couple of years ago? You were together then. You're still together now, still engaged?'

'Yes. We started going out a year before that, so we have been together for three-and-a-half years.'

'A long engagement. Have you named the day?'

'Named the day?'

'Sorry. Another expression. Have you got a date for getting married?'

Christina's eyes brimmed. 'I keep asking. I keep suggesting. He laughs or changes the subject. His eyes look away into the distance. He gets angry. He says there's plenty of time. There are things to do first. I feel that my life is slipping away. I need more now – something different from the hotel and all the old habits.'

As she fell silent, Sterling mulled things over. He really liked this girl. He admired her too. But what was happening here? Was he meant to be a relationship counsellor? That would be hopeless. He saw life as too black and white to be any good at that. Had she come over to have a semi-independent shoulder of a friend to cry on? He wasn't sure he was very good at that either. Did she want advice? *Finish it. Move on.* Sterling was good at running away, or perhaps more accurately drifting away, but he knew that it wasn't always, or even often, the best way to go – especially for other people. There was another possibility. He and Christina had got on brilliantly in their time together, in every way. Was she looking to rekindle the spark they'd both allowed to die?

She dabbed at her eyes with a square of Belgian lace she'd produced from her jacket and then continued. 'I didn't mean to cry, Frank. I don't want to sit on your sofa while you be my therapist. I don't want sympathy. I don't want you to tell me what to do. I'm not looking for love – much as I like you and think about you.'

She was a mind-reader. Sterling spread out his hands. *What then?*

Christina smiled at the confusion. 'I thought it would be obvious. I want to hire you, Mr Private Detective.'

Chapter 2

'I get it,' said Sterling. He wasn't sure that he did, but he knew he was about to find out. 'Tell me.'

'Over the last six months, Guy has changed. He's spending more and more time in Kortrijk and less time with me. He comes back late on the train and sometimes doesn't come back at all. He's given up his phone. It's as if he's cutting off his connections with modern life.' The girl's flush made the freckles that cascaded from her nose and over her cheeks disappear. 'We hardly have sex anymore,' she whispered. 'I don't know what's happening.'

Sterling rubbed his palms together and looked at the floor. He could take things sideways on or he could take the direct route. In his experience, blunt was always best.

'You don't think he's got another girl in Kortrijk?'

'You don't waste time, do you, Frank?' The girl bit her bottom lip and her eyes brimmed again.

'I know you a little bit, Christina. You wouldn't thank me if I beat about the bush, would you?'

'No, if I have understood those words. Maybe it's a girl. But I don't think so. He asks me to give him time, and that everything will be alright in August. I can't wait till then. I need to know what's going on now.'

'I think I would too. But if you're determined to go down this road, aren't there private investigators over there in Belgium – people who speak Dutch and know the area? It would be less expensive.' Sterling chose not to say that more likely than not this was just another bread-and-butter infidelity case, made more difficult by his connection with and fondness for his would-be principal. There was the matter of his fee as well – charging the girl to deliver what would likely be bad news.

'I've thought about it all, Frank. I could probably get someone in Ypres, but it's you I want. I trust you and you'll do a good job for me.' Sterling saw a tiny smile flit across her face. 'You needn't worry about getting paid either. My mother has agreed to do that.'

'Your mother?' Sterling chuckled. 'I never thought I'd hear that. How come? I didn't think I'd ever be in her good books.'

'She wasn't so against you. She knew you cared about me. It's just that things got…' - Christina struggled to find a suitable word – 'shaken up when you were around. The point is that my mother is just as interested as me in finding out what is happening. She has tried very hard and put in a lot of time.'

'Investment. She has invested time and effort in Guy.'

'Yes, that's it. Also, you don't have to worry about not speaking Dutch. I have got someone who can help you. My grandfather.'

'Your grandfather? Doesn't he know Guy?'

'No. It's my father's father. My father is long gone, and my mother and that grandfather don't get on. He's always been apart from my family, a … stranger. I'm the only one who has contact these days. He lives in Comines. He was a teacher but now he's retired. I asked him and he agreed.'

'Christina, you seem to have thought of everything. Do I have a choice?'

'Not really. I knew I could rely on you.'

Sterling put his hand on the girl's arm. 'I'll get answers, but they might not be the answers you want. Will you be ready for that?'

'Yes. I want my life back. I can't live in this...'

'... limbo,' suggested Sterling.

'Limbo,' repeated Christina. 'I'll remember.'

Sterling went to his desk and retrieved a pad and pen. 'Right. Tell me some more about Guy and anything else that will help us find out what's going on.'

'Where should I begin?'

'Anywhere. I need to get a feel for what Guy is like.'

'OK. Well, he is twenty-seven, the same age as me. Guy Verstraete. I met him in a pub in Ypres, a little way along from the hotel. I was with my girlfriends, and he was with his own friends. It's a surprise we didn't know each other before because Ypres isn't such a big place, but we went to different schools. He wasn't like many of the usual boys in the town – full of themselves and noisy. He was serious and steady, although he could make me laugh as well. We got talking. He was going every day on the train to Ghent for his optician's training. It made sense, he told me, because when he had... to spend time in a real opticians' shop... I don't know the words...'

'Placements,' murmured Sterling.

'When he had placements, he could go into the shop in Ypres. Anyway, he is like me. He is happy to be at home with his family.'

'Tell me about his family.'

'His father has a photography shop in the Grote Markt. His mother works in a pharmacy. He's got two older brothers who don't live at home anymore. They are all kind to me. Guy and I started going out. We got on well. You know me a little bit, Frank. I don't want much from life. He finished his training and got a job in an optician's shop in Kortrijk. He could continue to take the train, but he didn't have to go so far. So, I am in the hotel, and he is in the optician's. We are saving to be married and get a place of our own. He is ordinary and so am I.'

'What kind of things do you do when you aren't working?'

'On Sundays after lunch, we sometimes go and watch the football at the stadium outside the town. Sometimes we go cycling. We go out with friends on Saturday night. Everything was good.'

Dull, more like. But what business was it of Sterling's? Anyway, where were the fireworks in his own small-town life? 'Tell me some more about the last six months.'

Christina shrugged. 'Guy changed, like I said. On Mondays and Wednesdays, he'd walk down from the station to the hotel and have dinner with me and my mother and my other grandfather. On Tuesdays and Thursdays, if I wasn't working, I'd go over to his house and we'd eat with his family. On Fridays, we'd go out. He'd often work on Saturdays, so I would too, in the hotel. Obviously, each week was different, but the pattern was like that. Then it changed. He'd phone me to say that he had been held up in Kortrijk on some of the days. Then he would pretend that he was going home when I was doing an evening shift, but I'd find out he hadn't gone home at all. That was around the time he said he wasn't going to have a mobile phone anymore. Everyone had managed without before. Now he was going to manage without. "What about me?" I said. "Do what you like," he said. I was very upset.'

'Understandably. It doesn't seem very kind, and from what you've told me, out of character. I'm getting an idea about Guy. Does anything else stand out? Hobbies, odd behaviour?'

Christina was silent and looked at the hands in her lap. 'I don't know if it's important, but Guy was interested in politics. I don't care about them much myself, but he was – this is difficult for me because of the words – a nationalist, like his father and my mother's father. They are all in the *N-VA*'. Sterling could see her lips making the translation. 'The New Flemish Alliance; in Dutch, *Nieuwe Vlaamse Alliantie*.'

'I think I remember that one,' said Sterling. A year or two back, in Flanders where he and Christina had first met, Sterling had also met an Ypres bike shop owner – Martin de Groot – who had given him vital lessons in Flemish history for his case. De Groot had spoken about *Vlaams Blok*, which he'd translated as Flemish Bloc and later *Vlaams Belang* (Flemish Interest). The N-VA, as he remembered it, was more mainstream.

Politics. Like Christina, Sterling didn't pay much attention, whereas his father, a Customs man originally from the nonconformist Fens near Cambridge, was a devout socialist, trade unionist and internationalist. The results of that for his son were trips as a boy on May Day to Calais to listen to speeches and glug lemonade, along with sneaked gulps of beer, at Confédération Générale du Travail knees-ups, singing "*The Internationale*" with the comrades. Left was better than right. Rich people were too rich, and poor people too poor, but it had always been like that, and always would be, in his opinion. He made a note about Guy and his politics. It probably didn't matter, but he knew he had to be thorough.

By the time Christina's coach was almost due to return from Canterbury, three pages of Sterling's notebook were full. A warm mid-afternoon breeze riffled and drifted through the office through the top and bottom of the sash window. The faint rattle of the frame and the hubbub outside formed a backdrop to the conversation. In the middle of the meeting, they had fitted in a visit to the pub for a drink and a sandwich.

Sterling leaned back on the sofa and scratched an eyebrow. 'I think I've got everything. Anyway, if I stay at the Sultan, I'll be able to ask you things if I haven't.'

'Not everything, Frank. This last thing. The most difficult bit.' Christina rummaged in her small handbag and produced a folded A4 sheet. She took a deep breath. 'I made this photocopy and put the original one back in Guy's jacket after I went through his pockets.' She registered the shock on Sterling's face. 'I knew you wouldn't like it.'

'Well…,' he mumbled, buying time. It was back to that abandonment by his mother, and single-handed rearing, without explanation or condemnation, by his father. It meant that Sterling put women on pedestals. That is, when he wasn't doing the abandoning himself in pre-emptive acts of self-protection. Private investigators did sneaky things like going through pockets and operating on the borderline of decent behaviour, not pretty, spirited, honest, gracious young women like Christina Van de Velde – in fact almost St Christina of

Ypres, in his eyes. He wasn't sure he'd want a girlfriend who went through his stuff.

Christina frowned. There was a set to her mouth. 'I'm not going to say sorry for what I did and I'm not just going to let things happen to me. You know me better than that, Frank. Finding this shows that I was right to look. You're a detective. You'd do it. Why shouldn't I? Anyway, I wanted you to agree to help me before... it became difficult.'

'OK, let's see what we've got.' He unfolded the paper. At the top was an all-black lion and next to it what looked like a pike consisting of a staff with an iron ring and spiked point at the end. 'This is a black and white photocopy. On the original, what kind of lion was it?'

'What do you mean?'

'Did it have red claws and red tongue?'

'I don't think so. Both the lion and that other thing were black.'

'So, the nationalists' lion.' Again, De Groot's tutelage. Sterling knew all about the Flemish black lion, the one with red claws and tongue officially adopted by the regional government as its flag, and the all-black one retained by the rightists and fascists. 'Do you know what the other thing is?'

Christina shrugged.

Sterling suppressed a sigh. He was fond of her. He was glad to see her again. He knew how plucky she was. But she seemed to lack curiosity.

He scanned the rest of the sheet. There were four blocks of seemingly random letters in clumps of smaller blocks. In previous cases, there had been codes, some more rudimentary than others. He'd even seen a friend's daughter cracking a password using a computer program. But this was different.

'Can I keep this, Christina?'

'You're still on the case?'

'Of course. I said so, didn't I?'

'I thought maybe…'

'I'll come over next week, after I've sorted some things out here.'

'You could come now if you had your passport. I know the driver and the tour guide, and the bus company.'

Sterling kept a grip bag of essentials under his desk, ready for a quick getaway. When he'd got involved with an alleged terror group back in April, he'd needed it, but this didn't seem so urgent. 'Next week will be better. I may need to do some digging, and I was going to ask – is it OK if I share some of this information with my associates? They help with research and so on.'

'Mike, the man who rescued us from the farmhouse cellar?'

'Maybe him, maybe one or two other trustworthy friends.'

'OK, but not the personal stuff about… you know.'

'Of course not, Christina. I'll be very discreet. What time is the coach coming back? I'll walk you through to the Guildhall.'

They hugged at the door of the coach, beneath the interested, smiling gaze of Christina's travelling companions. 'See you next week, Frank. Thank you,' whispered Christina.

On the way back to his office Sterling unpicked his tangled feelings; over the zebra crossing at New Street, up No Name Street, across Delf Street and into Market Street. Pleasure in Christina's visit was there, and in the fact that he had a new case that would pay decently in an otherwise generally fallow period. Going back to

Flanders would be OK, quite familiar and not too far for the home bird that he was. But there was also, well, not dismay exactly, but maybe a sense of being disconcerted. Christina knew he'd be disappointed by her own sleuthing activities on her own boyfriend and what they said about her, so she'd got him on board before she'd told him that part.

And then there was the assignment itself. Much later, when Sterling's mind drifted back to Sandley, he recalled his original thinking – that the odds were it was just another matrimonial-style case with a predictable conclusion; that there was likely a girl from the New Flemish Alliance in Kortrijk, communicating in code for fun, like the nineteenth-century lovers who used the "agony columns" in *The Times*; that Christina would be sad to know the inevitable truth. He couldn't have been more wrong.

Chapter 3

At seven minutes past four, the pipe on the landing began to rattle. Sterling knew that Angela and Kerry did not stick to exact times for their tea in the mornings and afternoons – not just because they might be busy in the library, but also, though it was never spoken out loud, to wrong-foot him. He himself did not scuttle down each time the pipe rumbled out its message because that would make things too stale and obvious. This afternoon he stayed where he was at his desk. He was researching the background to Christina's case, and he knew he'd be meeting Angela later in the snug of the Cinque Port Arms for a drink and to do the crossword together.

At a quarter to six, he shut down his computer, closed the sash window up and down and slipped the catch across. Almost opposite, on the corner of Market Street and Milk Alley, Freddy Henderson the grocer was taking his stock back into the shop, stopping occasionally to greet a passer-by or engage in banter, usually with a woman.

'Alright, Frank?' said Freddy, with a crate of apples in his meat-slab hands, as Sterling passed up Milk Alley.

'Good, thanks, mate.'

Abutting the alley, the lush greensward around Sandley's principal church lapped up to the grey stonework. Across St Peter's Street, Sterling plunged into the dark gash in the wall, like a prize-fighter's mouth, that started Holy Ghost Alley. If you were a stranger, you wouldn't know it was there. Inside, the air was cool and funnelled through the narrow passage. He eased round the kink in the middle, the damp brickwork and vine-like vegetation earthy in his nostrils, and then emerged again into the evening sunshine by the Masonic Hall. A few metres up the high street was his destination, the Cinque Port Arms. There was an equidistant route from Sterling's office the other way, down King Street, left into Short Street and left again, but this one had special charm and mystery, and he savoured its familiarity.

Thinking about it, he knew that he was only really comfortable in Sandley. Even going to Belgium for a short spell would be a wrench. He wondered how he'd become so loth to travel.

Angela was in the snug with her back to the window, sipping a Martini, and with *The Times* cryptic opened out on the table. A pint stood next to it. Sterling squeezed in next to her and took a pull of Powder Monkey, his current favourite of the guest beers.

He looked at the grid. 'Made a decent start, then, Ange.'

'Long way to go. You arrived at a good time.'

For a while, they worked in a silence punctuated by talk of solutions or theories for solutions.

'I got a new case this afternoon,' said Sterling eventually.

'Anything interesting?' Angela didn't look up. She was concentrating on unjumbling an anagram.

'Maybe. I'm going back to Flanders.'

Now she did. She raised her eyebrows.

'I've just had a visit from Christina Van de Velde.'

'The girl in the hotel in Ypres? The one who was abducted with you in the Etchingham case when I sent Mike over to rescue you?'

The man at the bar, Mike Strange, looked up from pouring a pint, having heard his name, and Sterling toasted him with his glass. 'The very same. She came over on a coach trip this afternoon.'

'Anything you can share?'

'Actually, yes. She said I could consult with my associates.'

'The Frank Sterling empire,' murmured Angela. 'Networks nationwide.'

'Yeah, you, Mike and Becky. Quite enough when it boils down to it. You do the research. Mike and Becky for the muscle and the clandestine stuff.'

At the bar, Mike looked over again, some kind of sixth sense. Although he and his wife Becky were now publicans and ran the establishment with smooth efficiency, both had once been in a never-named branch of the security services, and their skills, discreetly supplied, had helped Sterling out in at least three previous cases.

'So,' Sterling continued, 'Christina, and her mother…'

'Her mother…? Didn't she have some beef with you at the time?'

'There was something, yes.' Sterling had never mentioned his brief intimacy with Christina and didn't intend to start. 'Anyway, she's on board now. She's bankrolling it, the hotel being a little gold mine. It's all to do with Christina's boyfriend.' Sterling gave an overview, and at the end took out the sheet of paper Christina had given him. 'She found this.'

Angela looked over the letterhead and the blocks of letters below it. 'It's not just what you private investigators call a matrimonial, then?'

'I think it probably is. This is just the kind of way lovers could communicate. I think Christina, out of disappointment or whatever, is clutching at straws if she doesn't think another girl is involved. But I agreed to look into it and I'll do a proper job, even if I don't think it'll take more than a day or two.'

'When are you going?'

'Next week. Train, ferry, train.'

Angela sipped her Martini. 'I'm on holiday next week.'

'Yeah? Doing anything with Mamujee?'

'No. He's got to go on an anti-terrorism course in New York. They don't allow any contact out at all while it's on, so he'll be incommunicado, sadly for me. Anyway, I wish you'd call him Panjit, like the rest of my friends. You've been to dinner with us more than once.' Angela had started going out with Assistant Chief Constable Mamujee when they'd met during Sterling's Earlsey Tech case a year ago.

'He's police brass, Ange – top brass for that matter. I've got trust issues. You know that. With the suits, it's politics first, then upholding the law, then the poor bloody infantry. That's why I left.'

Angela sighed. 'That may be true in general, but Panjit's not like that. His family's from Uganda. He struggled to get where he is. He's like us. He knows what it's like to be an outsider. Anyway, as Panjit's away, I was thinking, maybe you'd like an offsider for a couple of days.'

'Where do you get this jargon from?'

'Mixing with you, of course. I'd bring my laptop, so I could do research. I've got some language skills. I'd be good in a ruck, as you know. I love the library, but it gets a bit... well, dull sometimes.'

Sterling stared out into the wider bar. The fireplace was already stacked with coal and logs ready for winter – typical of the way Mike and Becky Strange ran their pub. Sterling wasn't a team player. He knew that. He liked to go his own way and not take anyone else into account. On the other hand, Angela was good company and clever, and she was right – she could handle herself. He hadn't known how well till she'd told him, during the same Earlsey Tech case when she'd met Mamujee, that she'd run a teenage gang in London. He'd watched her fling someone through the window of his office and in the process she'd saved Sterling from being stabbed.

'I can't pay you,' he said. 'You'll have to take your chances with accommodation and so on, and no question I'm in charge. As I say, it'll probably be just a boring old matrimonial, and we'll be finished in two days tops.'

Angela straightened up and beamed, the whiteness of her teeth enhanced by the ebony darkness of her skin. If she'd been a child she would have clapped her hands. 'Goody. An adventure. I've always wanted to do a bit of detective work. Your round, Frank. This calls for a celebration.'

'Hang on – your celebration, my round?'

'Your turn. Do it and don't argue.'

She had a point. Sterling returned with the second round. 'What do you make of what's on that sheet of paper, Angie? A code, obviously.'

'It's not like anything you've given me in the past – the Commonwealth War Graves Commission text

Gloria Etchingham started you off with, or those other things. In a way, they were more like riddles, and we did some of it just with Google. What that woman was doing at Earlsey Tech...'

'Jane Casterton,' interposed Sterling.

'Jane Casterton,' repeated Angela, 'that was a code system with a special code book.'

'And *The Thousand and One Nights* volume that Mohamed Husain used during all that drama down at Drangeness...'

'That too. But this is different. The key probably isn't in a code book with this one. It's somewhere else. Maybe Mike and Becky can help.'

Sterling and Angela had finished the crossword by the time the publican husband and wife team had enough support around the bars and kitchen to come over.

'New case, Frank?' said Becky. The pub made her and Mike a good living, but they missed the excitement of the old life and never shrank from the voluntary provision of "support services", as Mike, when he chose to speak, termed it.

'Yep, back in Belgium. My client – actually, you know her, Mike – Christina Van de Velde – filched a sheet of paper from the target and made this copy. Ange and I think it's a coded message. He pushed the sheet over the table.

'You know more about codes than me, Becky,' said Mike.

'Cryptography and cryptanalysis 101, really,' murmured Becky. She pushed her fine blonde hair behind her ears as she looked down at the letterhead and blocks of letters. 'I think you're right. Really, what else could it be? If it's a simple cipher, it won't be too difficult to crack. Did your client get it from a fellow Flemish person? If so, then it's probably in Dutch, and therefore beyond my limited capabilities.'

'What would you have to do to crack it, Becky?' said Angela.

'It's all ifs and buts. You'd have to make assumptions if you were an amateur code-breaker. To have any chance, it would need to be a monoalphabetic substitution cipher – that is, letters consistently substituted for other letters in a regular pattern. So, you'd do a frequency analysis, working out which cipher-text letters are the most frequent and matching them to the most frequently-appearing plain-text letters. In English, those plain-text letters are "e", "t" and "a". Each letter in each language has a particular "personality", and that's helpful, and some letters are more "sociable" than others. Some letters often link with others in frequently-appearing words – like "e" and "h" in "the", and "a" and "n" in "and". You can work out whether a common letter ("e" or "t") is the vowel or the consonant by where it's most frequently (or least frequently) placed. If there are gaps between blocks of letters, as there are on this sheet, that indicates length of words. If this was English, there are two one letter words – "a" and "I" – so you'd assume, if you have one letter blocks, that the most frequently used one letter is "a".

'There are other tricks or pointers. For example, if you have to speculate between "ee" and "aa" in English, "ee" is much more likely. That might not be the case in Dutch. For example, "Vlaams" is pretty common, isn't it – meaning Flemish - and isn't "kraal" originally a Dutch word? Once you've got so far, if you've done it accurately, the solution comes very quickly, and you shift back and forth from the actual cipher to filling in gaps in words and sentences through likely patterns in the language.'

'Like the crossword,' said Angela.

'Very much like that,' said Becky, 'or like a codeword puzzle in some newspapers. As well as mathematicians, linguists and computer scientists, talented cryptic cross-word solvers were in demand for cryptography and code-breaking, and in some cases part of the recruit-ment procedure was to solve a crossword in a certain time – twelve minutes was one amount I think.'

'Rules me out then,' said Sterling. 'You might have got in on a good day, Angie. But if this is Dutch, you can't help, right, Becky?'

' 'Fraid not. And I don't even know anyone who could. I could do some research and have a try, I suppose.'

'Not to worry. We've got plenty of other lines of enquiry.'

'We?' said Mike.

'Have we?' said Angela.

'Angela's got next week off. She's coming over to Belgium with me. What did you say you'd be, Angie? My offsider. And yes, there are plenty of things we can do without knowing what's on here. Obviously, it would probably help, but all in good time. Maybe you could take a copy, Becky. You've got loads of contacts in Europe still in the game I expect.'

Insouciant. Blasé. When it was all over, and talk turned to Sterling's early attitude, those were Angela Wilson's kindest words.

Chapter 4

At Sandley railway station at 9.30am the following Wednesday morning, the track stretched out in a long curve south and slightly east, full of promise and adventure. At least, that's how it seemed to Angela, who was animated and talkative as she lingered with Sterling under the awning, clearly glad to be away from the library for a few days.

Once in the carriage, among the commuting contingent on board – en route for jobs in schools, offices and workshops – Sterling looked out over farmland towards the sea. Pickers in little clusters were busy, with larger groups round the Heath Robinson contraptions where the weighing and sorting took place. He'd had some picking jobs himself as a kid. It was back-breaking then and didn't look any different now. What he was doing was money for old rope in comparison. Spray sparkled up from a sprinkler fifty metres from the train.

After Deal, the countryside changed as the train sliced into the North Downs, cuttings and embankments ironing out its progress down to Dover. In a final picturesque flourish, a Victorian viaduct bore its load across and then down one of the long valleys stretching up from the sea. The townscape was all grey brick and slate amid a surprising number of trees bearing the verdant green foliage of the period just before high summer.

Sterling knew all the east Kent coastal towns from Margate down to Dover. He'd lived in every one of them, shifted from one house to the next by his wander-lust father in a restless search for... well, what? Sterling was never quite sure. He'd just had to make new friends and try and keep up with the old. There had been women in his father's life after his mother's early disap-pearance, but they were ephemeral, shadowy presences, kept at the front door or in the passenger seat of the car, or their fragrance occasionally filling the hallway.

There were no taxis at Dover Priory station. 'It's only twenty minutes' walk to the terminal,' said Sterling. 'We've got plenty of time. Fancy it?'

'OK,' said Angela. Sterling had his grip bag, which he swung along as he walked. The wheels of Angela's suitcase squeaked and grumbled over the pavement, the asphalt of the road, and occasional cobbles.

After crossing the ring road through the underpass and into the centre of the town, they passed through a gracious Georgian former residential district undergo-ing regeneration – all wrought iron railings and broad, solid doors at the top of bulky stone staircases. The last time Sterling had been in this district he had been running for his life from an armed gang. Then they were walking on the arterial road next to the busy, noisy traffic also heading into the terminal.

Approaching the doors for foot passengers, Sterling sensed Angela tensing up. 'Alright, Ange? It'll be flat as a millpond today.'

'It's not that, Frank.'

'What then?'

'You'll see.'

At Passport Control, Sterling was waved through. He looked around. Angela was not at his shoulder. Instead, at the booth a woman in black glasses and a serge-blue uniform, her dark hair tied back from her face, was conducting an examination of Angela's passport, the lack of a magnifying glass rendering it just short of forensic. A man, tall and rangy in the same uniform, had taken her suitcase aside and was poking through its contents on a separate counter. Even for Sterling, unthinking as he could often be, and mind ever focused on the here and now, all that might not have been surprising. What was more shocking to him was Angela – feisty, proud, spunky Angela – whose eyes could flash – literally – with passion, or anger, or humour – was now hunched, passive, smaller, dull... submissive.

For ten minutes, Sterling slouched on a nearby pillar, seething, but warned by Angela's small gestures to do nothing.

'What was that about?' he hissed, as they resumed their walk to the port bus that would take them to the ferry.

'You know all about DWI, don't you?'

'What's driving while intoxicated got to do with...?'

Angela's voice was harsh as she interrupted. 'Here's a new one.' Sterling could see her head tip from side to side and her lips move silently as she went through a silent rehearsal. 'GTPCWB.'

'I still don't...'

'Going through Passport Control while black. Like DWB – driving while black, when you get stopped and checked by the police ten times more frequently than white people. Still, better than the brick through the window of our flat in Clapham at Christmas in 1984 and its succinct little message – "Go home black scum".'

Sterling had stopped walking while he reviewed the initials. Now he hurried to catch up as Angela marched on. 'I'm sorry,' he said on the bus.

'Leave it for now, Frank. Let's get on the bloody ferry. I'm dying for a coffee.'

Later, takeaway cups in hand, they leaned over the guardrail at the back of the ferry and watched seagulls wheeling, squawking and swooping in the frothy, cappuccino wake.

'It gets wearing, the low-level discrimination and intimidation,' said Angela. 'You learn at a young age to avoid eye contact and suss situations out before you go any further. It could have been worse back there. If I'd made a fuss, it would have been more than a ten-minute delay. It could have involved a body search. Managing the hassle is a very understated skill.' She turned around and rested her back and elbows against the railing. 'Why did we become friends? And don't say it was because of your irresistible charm.'

Sterling looked towards England. Dover's white cliffs still jutted up into the empty, harsh blue sky. A young herring gull, its down still mottled-grey, flew gamely to the sea, imitating and learning from the older birds. 'You were sparky. Unusual. Looked me in the eye, despite what you just said. Clearly independent-minded. Willing to talk. Your house had been burgled – my last investigation in the job, in fact – but you weren't that fazed. Some people get really spooked.'

'That's from your side. I'd never been that keen on the police, as you know, being black and from the wrong side of the tracks in Clapham. But you were polite and professional. Friendly even. Clearly honest. I wasn't used to that in a policeman – or any man for that matter. I could even see a bit of sly humour in there. Someone a bit quirky. Worth getting to know. Here I was, fetched up in hick old Sandley Library, with mostly white faces, a lot disapproving, in the early days anyway, and you were someone I thought I could probably get along with. You recognised I was alone in a new place. Then there was the clincher, Frank.' She looked away from the soapy water and directly into Sterling's grey-blue eyes. 'You seemed – and later proved – you were completely colour-blind.'

They started talking again as the grey, blurred contours of France emerged from the summer haze, a low outline above the sea. Then the ferry was working forward parallel to the beaches and blocks of holiday apartments of Calais.

'I'm glad you're on board,' said Sterling. 'We'll make a good investigating team.'

Angela searched his face for tells. 'I suppose I'll have to try not to be too conspicuous – if we have to tail somebody, if there's cloak and dagger. I don't know Belgium. I've only travelled through. How diverse is it, anyway?' She waited for the wisecrack.

Sterling stared ahead, deadpan. 'We'll plan all that, if we need it, for when it's dark, Ange. Then you'll be camouflaged…' There it was. 'Ouch,' he muttered, as he felt the elbow to his ribs.

She had got a point, though. There were ramifications to her joining him that he hadn't thought of. If it came to it they'd need to be subtle.

On the shuttle bus to Calais town centre, Angela perked up. She seemed enthused despite the grimness of the heavily fortified port area swathed in a mesh of metal fencing topped with barbed wire; and then the residential areas, street after long street of dull brick houses and apartment blocks, bisected by concrete islands studded with plane trees and parking spaces.

Her sunny mood carried them on the train out of Calais and into the wide Flanders plain. Everything was new, and everything interested her. Between Bailleul and Lille she spotted, shoulders shaking with amusement, a giant mermaid sculpture on a smallholding by the railway track, a voluptuous fish-body with breasts like ballast tanks. Even the ticket collector aroused comment – dapper, with a neat, navy-blue cloth cap and a smart casual ensemble, aided by his dark good looks and slim frame. 'Now I know what they mean about French style,' she whispered as he moved down the train, turning in the aisle from one side to the other checking tickets and passes.

But as well as the good spirits, there was a short out-break of bickering just at the point where the journey was beginning to seem interminable. 'Why did we come this way, Frank?' Angela had said. 'We could have got the Eurostar from Ashford and have arrived already.'

Sterling's jaw had set. 'Because I wanted to, and I'm in charge.'

At Lille Flandres station – equilibrium restored by a sandwich and a glass of Orangina – they changed plat-forms for the train across the border to Kortrijk, and at six o'clock, beneath a still-sunny blue sky, they had reached their destination.

On the concourse, commuters, and other travellers caught in the rush hour, thronged and bustled at the Panos sandwich franchise and near the snack machines, or queued for tickets. Nearby, a huge shelter, dominated by black sit-up-and-beg bicycles, was dotted with students and schoolchildren.

'What's the address, Frank?' said Angela, her phone at the ready.

'We don't need your phone, Ange.'

'Why? Do you know where we're going?'

'No, but we can ask.'

'But neither of us speaks Dutch. I'll Google it.'

Sterling approached a young black woman sitting on a metal bench with her two young children. 'Excuse me.' He smiled and nodded. I'm looking for the Hotel Ibis.' He pointed to an address on the booking sheet. The woman frowned, suspicion settling over her features, and then realised that Sterling wasn't begging. She looked closely and smiled in recognition. Walking to the large glass doors, she pointed down one of the streets stretching out like radii from the railway hub. 'Go down there,' she seemed to say, making little chopping gestures with the edge of her palm – '*Rechtdoor, rechtdoor, vijfhonderd meter*' and then she indicated right, with a sweeping motion.

'Thank you,' said Sterling. He pressed his palms together and bowed. The youngest child, a little girl in a pink anorak and white skirt, giggled and bowed back.

'Now I know how you do it,' said Angela, as they struck out along the street indicated, the suitcase clacking behind them.

'What?'

'Get people to help you. You've got the knack.'

'When it boils down to it, people like to help. More often than not, they like to communicate. It makes them feel useful. Even better when there's a bit of an edge, or something out of the ordinary is happening. I know I should do better, but I'm not that interested in technology. It's all very fancy but it gets in the way of ordinary conversations.'

'And stuff like this,' added Angela, waggling her phone, 'is made in Chinese sweatshops, which is another reason for doing things the old way.'

Sterling shrugged. 'You said it. It might be true, but what can you do about it? You know me – waste not want not – but what we do makes no difference in the general scheme.'

'Still... Everyone can make a small contribution.'

The young woman at the station had been entirely accurate in word and gesture. Angela and Sterling, with the clanking suitcase, went down the indicated radial street, past what seemed like a cluster of nightclubs and pubs for young people, and into a square lined with typical Flemish buildings and crenellated frontages. Underneath the cobbles, there was a car park, and to the left an old statue tinged copper-green. A few moments later, after the right turn into the main street, the electric doors of the hotel whispered open and a receptionist whose name tag said 'Aurélien', with extravagant arm movements and excellent English disguised by a heavy French accent, registered them and went through his introductory spiel.

Originally, the plan had been for Sterling to stay at the family place, Hotel Sultan, in Ypres. It would have been cheaper, but he had changed his mind. If the action – if there was going to be any action – was in Kortrijk, he reasoned, then that was where he needed to stay. Christina, and probably her mother, who was bankrolling the case, had acquiesced. The arrangement was that all of them would meet at the Kortrijk hotel at 8 pm, giving Sterling and Angela time to settle after their arrival. Aurélien sashayed over to the lift with them, and with a flourish handed over keys to neighbouring rooms on the second floor.

In the corridor, Sterling and Angela paused. 'Right,' said Sterling. 'We've got about an hour to unpack and freshen up. The meeting downstairs will be interesting. I'll knock on your door when it's time.'

In his room, he went over to the window and looked down into the square he and Angela had not long crossed. He thought about Angela – how knowledgeable she was, her joy in the journey and how that was rubbing off on him, and even her fighting skills acquired as a teenaged gang-leader. She was an asset, no doubt about it. But he didn't forget the racism engendered by her colour, and the difficulties she herself had highlighted.

Then there was the assignment. It was vague, and it had a kind of sneaky undertone that had tipped Christina from the pedestal he'd previously put her on.

Taking everything into account, the journey across to Belgium was the easy bit. Sterling reckoned he'd got time for a short nap before everything got harder.

Chapter 5

As soon as Sterling came out of the lift with Angela, he saw Christina's red ponytail amid the angular modernity of the hotel's décor and furnishings. He saw her mother too, her hair a lighter, less glossy version of her daughter's, age washing the colour away. With them were two short, wiry older men wearing jackets and trousers in a muted European style, shades indeterminate even in the bright evening light.

Christina rose and smiled, holding Sterling just above the elbows and kissing him lightly on each cheek. Solemnly, she shook Angela's hand, their clasp delicate and formal, virtually fingertips only. Sterling had told her that Angela was coming with him. 'One of my associates,' he'd said.

'You know my mother, Frank.'

'Mrs Van de Velde,' murmured Sterling, and received a nod and a half-smile in return. Something about Christina's mother made him want to put his hands behind his back, click his heels and bow briskly from the waist. They'd never really hit it off after his first Belgian adventure.

'And these are my grandfathers – *Opa* Albertin and *Opa* Van de Velde – Yves and Willem. Yves speaks English, but I have to translate for Willem.'

The grandfather Albertin had bequeathed Christina her clear green eyes and delicate features. His own had a clever and appraising twinkle, the rest of his face arranged into a sardonic small half-smile. 'How do you do?' he said in perfect English, as he shook Sterling's hand firmly. When it was Angela's turn he placed his left hand over her right as he shook, bowing his head gravely. Sterling could see that tough, no-nonsense, proud Angela Wilson was charmed. *Another bloody Mamujee*, thought Sterling. *You're my offsider, Ange, remember.*

Sterling recalled where he had seen Willem before. He was the night manager-cum-porter back at Hotel Sultan when Sterling had been in Ypres, and he was as unengaged now as he had been then. His bequest to Christina, and indeed to his daughter, was their red hair, though his own was overrun by grey now, producing a light sandy effect. He shook hands brusquely, and Sterling could hear a quiet muttering, verging on chuntering, that seemed to indicate irritation and resentment. The old man – if late sixties really qualified as old these days – could barely take Angela's hand, and looked everywhere but into her face. The atmosphere crackled, and he was the source.

'Thank you again for coming over, Frank and Angela,' said Christina. Guy was her boyfriend. She was in charge. 'We're all here to help you as best we can. We all have an interest in what's happening to Guy. Opa Albertin can be with you all the time. As I promised, he'll be your guide and translator. The rest of us are...' she paused and searched for a word...

'Back-up?' suggested Albertin.

'Back-up,' repeated Christina, 'exactly.'

'Good,' said Sterling. 'And Angela is here to help me with research and other duties I might not be able to do by myself.' It sounded more plausible – and professional — than to say that she had a few days' holiday and fancied an adventure across the water. 'Why don't you do a summary for us, Christina, so we are all on the same page?' He noticed her frown. 'Sorry, so that we all know what is currently happening.'

'Guy, my fiancé ,' started Christina, and almost immediately faltered... 'is in some kind of trouble. For days every month, he disappears – no phone calls, no texts, no e-mail, no Facebook. Even more seriously, he's given up his phone and laptop altogether. He can get on the train at Ypres at 8.15 in the morning one day and I don't see him till three or four days later. He tells me not to worry and gets angry if I ask questions. "Be patient", he says. "It will all work out in a little while".'

'How do you know he gets off the train at Kortrijk?' said Sterling.

Christina stopped. Sterling let the question sink in. 'I don't know. I just think he does, that's all. He works here. Where else would he go?'

'Is he in Ypres tonight?'

'Yes, but he won't come back tomorrow evening if things are the same as usual.'

'Right, well we need someone to get on his train tomorrow morning, when the cycle of absence starts, and get off where he gets off. It probably is here in Kortrijk but there are presumably stations before the train gets here, and I imagine plenty afterwards. Yves, how well do you know Guy? Where do you live – Ypres? Could you be the one who follows him tomorrow?'

The temperature in the little leisure area in front of the hotel's plate glass window went down a notch. 'I can do that. I haven't met Guy yet.' Sadness crept into

his eyes and smile. 'I live in Comines, a few stops down
– in fact, the last stop before Ypres in that direction.'

Opa Van de Velde muttered in Dutch. 'Komen,' he
said clearly. 'Ieper.'

Imperceptibly, Albertin rolled his eyes, struggling not
to be provoked.

Christina launched into a translation of the conversation, but no one could have been in doubt that she
was making extra points of her own. The old man gave
back as good as he got. Mrs Van de Velde stared down
at the table.

Christina put up her hand. She turned to Frank and
Angela. 'I've just translated for Opa Van de Velde. He
heard Opa Albertin say "Comines" and reminded us
that it's "Komen" in Flemish, just as it's "Ieper" and not
"Ypres". *Komen*,' she gave the name heavy emphasis
and glared at Opa Van de Velde, 'is half in Belgium and
half in France. The Belgian bit is in the Walloon part of
Belgium.'

'An enclave...' murmured Albertin, 'and I am a
Walloon, not Flemish.'

Angela sat very still and rapt. The history lesson, if
that's what it was, and the undercurrents in the Belgian
contingent, were fascinating.

Opa Van de Velde erupted again. 'Guy... he's a good
boy. A very good boy,' rapidly reaching the limits to his
English.

Christina fired off another volley of angry Dutch.
This time the old man held his hands up and fell silent.
'I reminded Opa Van de Velde that we all agreed what
we are going to do, and he can't change his mind now.'

'OK,' said Sterling. Whatever the undercurrents, they
all had to focus on the job. 'So, Yves will be waiting at

the station in Ypres tomorrow morning and will follow
Guy. We all need to exchange phone numbers, so we can
communicate. If Guy gets out at Kortrijk, well and good.
If he doesn't, Angela and I need to get on the train.'

'What happens next?' said Angela.

Sterling leaned forward and clasped his hands. 'We'll
have to see how the cards fall. I doubt if anything will
work out the way we think it will. We've got everything
organised as far as we can – except for this.' He plucked
from his pocket the paper Christina had given him
much earlier, in Sandley. 'We've established that this is a
coded message, but as it's likely to be in Dutch, we
haven't got any further.'

Albertin put out his hand and Sterling handed him
the sheet. 'I don't know much about codes myself, but
I've got a friend in Comines – Komen' – he changed the
name of his home town in a clear gesture of conciliation
– 'who should be able to help.'

'Fine,' said Sterling. 'Good news. If he cracks it that
will probably be very handy.'

'She,' said Albertin. Angela smiled.

Christina translated the exchange for her grandfather Van de Velde.

With nothing left to discuss, the meeting broke up.
Christina, her mother and grandfather Van de Velde had
clearly arrived together, so left the same way. Mother
and Grandfather shuffled and looked away as Christina
enveloped Albertin in a brief, fierce hug, kissing him on
both cheeks, gazing into his eyes, and giving him a
single, brisk nod. Delicate, formal handshakes were
made with Sterling and Angela. As the Ypres group
walked off through the parting glass doors of the hotel,
Opa Van de Velde took Christina's arm, and she clasped
his with her free hand. He'd got her back.

'I'll be off as well,' said Yves Albertin. 'I'll see you tomorrow.'

Angela watched the old man slip through the doors and out into the late evening. 'What do you make of all that?'

Sterling shrugged.

'They love that girl,' Angela continued. 'But for old man Van de Velde, it's a painful love. He sat close to her. He was truculent, but he caved in when she came back at him. He didn't want to get on the wrong side of her. He's scared of losing her, and the fear will make it more likely. Maybe it's the same for Albertin about losing her, but being the outsider, he's got less to lose, and he didn't show so much. There's jealousy there. Rivalry – at least in Van de Velde. You've got to admire Christina. She treated them both equally. She made a fuss of Albertin when they were parting, but she left arm in arm with Van de Velde. What?'

Sterling was smiling – almost a smirk. 'Another reason I'm glad you came. Psychological profiling that I can't do myself.'

'You're teasing. You're just as good as me. Better. Learnt in the school of hard knocks.'

'Well, I agree with your summary, but I'm not sure if it's any use to us. Come on. I'm hungry. Let's go and find something to eat.'

A few metres from the hotel to the north was the main square, the Grote Markt, dominated by an ancient, solitary brick belfry tower in the middle, which looked as if it had been plonked there, rather than the newer buildings and structures growing up around it. After a meal in a pizzeria on the south side, popular given that it was almost full even past nine o'clock, Sterling and

Angela wandered around the square in search of a café for a nightcap. They could hear the high screech of swifts, and, looking up, the sky was still full of them, feeding as insects were swept upwards in spirals of warm air. Around the square, people strolled and chatted. A bevy of four young girls in denim shorts and T-shirts, brown arms, hair flowing and faces glowing, cycled across on bicycles like those at the station – sit-up-and-beg, classic Low Countries style.

There was a café on the eastern side, tables and chairs overflowing out onto the pavement under a long canopy. A waiter and waitress bustled and wheeled among the happy clientele. Old people, young people, groups and couples, families and friends, chattered and drank in the balmy air. It's possible to be lonely, or at least alone, in any number of ways – in a marriage, at a dinner table, in an apartment drinking a solitary cup of tea, on an empty bus. One man was managing it in a café full of carefree, jolly people enjoying the warm mid-summer. Among the throng to the right and left, in front and behind, sat Opa Albertin with a goblet of beer, looking with empty eyes out into the square.

'Yves Albertin, again so soon,' said Angela, plunging forward. 'Do you mind if we join you?'

Chapter 6

Albertin half-rose from his chair, a little startled but not displeased. 'Of course,' he said. Around him, people adjusted their chairs and tables to accommodate the new small group, some good-naturedly, infected by the cheerful atmosphere, some irritated at the disruption. Sterling nodded and muttered his thanks as he squeezed into his seat by the table. Angela had made the running. He wasn't sure if there was any merit in a further conversation with Christina's paternal grandfather – not yet anyway.

Angela caught the waitress's eye. 'What are you drinking, Yves? It looks interesting.'

'Tongerlo dubbel blonde.'

Angela looked at Sterling and then at the waitress, a small, pert girl with a strawberry mark like a vertical cricket bat on her left cheek. Angela pointed at Albertin's almost-empty glass and held three fingers up. 'Three more of those, please,' she smiled. The waitress hurried away, too busy to do more than nod.

'We thought you'd gone home, Yves.'

'It was such a nice evening, Angela, that I thought I'd have a drink before catching the train. It's – what expression do you use? – Indian country for me here, in a way. Kortrijk is a proudly Flemish, not Walloon town, but I am here, and I was thirsty... Besides, it's all Belgium.'

'So, what's the story?' said Angela.

'The story?'

'Well, the story and the backstory really. It was interesting back there in the hotel. And I'm certainly intrigued by how well you speak English.'

The drinks arrived. Sterling sat back and took a long pull. It wasn't bad for a lager. He could taste the alcohol, unlike in the characterless rubbish often served in England. He stayed quiet. Angela's direct, inquisitive, just-short-of-nosey style was a long way from his normal *modus operandi*, but she was doing no harm and there might be some good.

'How can I resist such an invitation from such a beautiful woman?' said the gallant Albertin.

Sterling had known the feminist Angela Wilson to give short shrift to such flattery, possibly interpreted as sexist, but the Walloon's age and apparent guilelessness worked in his favour.

'The backstory first then. I'm a schoolteacher, or I was. I retired from my school in Comines – I can say Comines now, can't I? – two years ago. I taught history, having got my first degree at the Sorbonne, by the skin of my teeth really, since I was there in Paris during the student uprising of 1968.'

'You were there?' Angela's eyes shone. 'With Danny Cohn-Bendit and all the others?'

'Yes, on the organising committee, as I was not an anarchist. Of course, like all such insurrections, from the Paris Commune onwards, it was like a comet in the night sky – a brief flash of light and then a return to obscurity. We argued; we were indecisive; we were arrogant; ultimately, we failed. After that, I went to England – to the University of Warwick – to lie low, as you say, and do a Master's. I stayed on in England for three more years, quietly, doing this and that and, of course, perfecting my English. My first language is French, as a Walloon, but unlike many of my Walloon friends and colleagues I was always keen to learn Dutch and it is truly my second language. It's a pity Willem won't accept that anymore. And English comes after that.'

'1968...' murmured Angela, listening to the rest but focused on that magic time. 'There's nothing like that anymore – nothing that tries to strike at the heart of government and capitalism.'

'I agree,' said Albertin. 'We've all subsided into making our livings, into consumerism and individualism. We take comfort in small things and try not to think about the world in general and all its problems.' His eyes drifted back over the square. 'I think I would have stayed in England if my mother had not fallen ill back in Comines. I came back and cared for her till she died, and after that never left my hometown again. I met my wife there, and we had our son, René, and René married Agnes – Christina's mother, and then Christina came along – the apple of everyone's eye. Luckily, she's got her head screwed on – otherwise, the family would have suffocated her. Willem...'

Sterling took another pull of his Tongerlo. He wasn't much interested in the minutiae of Albertin-Van de Velde family relationships. How was it relevant to the case? But Angela was fascinated. She fixed Albertin with her lively dark eyes. No one would have been able to resist, and certainly not a lonely old man.

'Willem...,' Albertin continued. 'We were friends, sometimes an unusual thing between French and Dutch speakers in Belgium. It started at a football match. I kicked him, actually, but in those days, he didn't bear a grudge. You saw him just now, but he wasn't always like that. After the match, we all had a beer together and the two of us got talking – in Dutch, which pleased him. He was cheerful. Easy-going. We spent more time together. He'd just got the hotel and I used to go over to Ypres from Comines on the train. We'd argue about politics and so on, but it was good-natured. After 1968, I wasn't active anymore, except a little bit in the local *Parti Socialiste*. Unfortunately, I think that provoked him to get involved with the Flemish nationalists. It would have been OK, I suppose, if he'd been involved with *Volksunie*, which was a kind of moderate Flemish movement, but somehow *Vlaams Blok* got their hooks into him – much more radical, right wing and in fact racist.

'At the same time, my son René met Agnes. We're talking about the late eighties now. René I don't know where we went wrong with him – if we did go wrong. He was a lovely boy – charming and, if I say it myself, good-looking. But there was something dark about him as he came out of his teens, and he never saw anything through to the end. Well, his courtship with Agnes promised everything. Both the families, Walloon and Flemish, were happy. They were married… and then, after two years, he was gone. He lives somewhere down near Marseille now, doing something or other. Coming to nothing.'

Albertin looked away. 'Willem never really forgave me – though I can't accept that I was to blame in the first place. Other things happened. I lost my wife not very long after my mother. Agnes… got on with things. Willem persuaded her to revert from Albertin back to Van de Velde, and she brought Christina up with that name as well. Agnes is the one who's really made a success of the hotel. But she hasn't borne a grudge. She just doesn't rock the boat. Christina though…'

A smile transformed Albertin's face, new wrinkles springing up on his forehead and around his eyes. 'History, personal and political, doesn't matter a jot to her. I've never known anyone more…' – he searched for a word – 'pragmatic. And loyal. From an early age, she kept up with me – made her mother bring her over to Comines to visit, told old man Van de Velde to mind his own business if he didn't like it. I just don't want her making the same mistake as Agnes, with this boy. That's why I'm on your team.'

Then he frowned. 'How is it I'm doing all the talking?' He looked from Angela to Sterling. Forgive me for saying, but you make an unlikely duo. What's *your* story?'

'Doesn't really matter,' said Sterling. Generally, he deflected talk about himself, and he saw no reason to change.

'We're friends,' said Angela. She saw no reason to hold back. 'When I came down from London a couple of years ago to Sandley, where we live, to take charge of the library, I was burgled almost straight away. Frank was still in the police, and he was on the case. He was my near neighbour too, it turned out. By the time it was over, we were drinking in the pub together. I'm a Londoner. I went to the London School of Economics, got a degree in history and modern languages and left to get some peace and quiet. Frank's always lived and worked in Kent – in most of the coastal towns – eh, Frank? – and left the police force to set up as a private investigator. That's how he met Christina and the Van de Veldes. Not working in a big organisation suits him.'

Go on, tell him everything, Ange, why don't you? My sole parent upbringing. Marriage and divorce. The disciplinaries in the job. My alleged hot-headedness. While you're about it, why don't you say why you really left London, when your gangsta past threatened to catch up with you?

Sterling's foot started tapping. First it was the challenges and the occasional bickering on the way over, and now it was telling a stranger all their business. He didn't mind Albertin. He seemed OK so far, if a little too glib. It was probably useful, on balance, that he was Christina's grandfather, and, as Christina had said, handy to have around with his three languages. But Sterling had learnt the virtues of letting other people do the talking, and here was his new offsider spilling the beans about their lives and friendship. He wondered again about the less positive aspects of having Angela tag along.

She snapped her fingers in front of his face. 'Lighten up, Frank. I'm doing a bit of team-building here.'

Sterling grunted. Albertin laughed. 'Don't worry on my behalf, Angela. I'm just one of the workers.' He looked at his watch. '*Zut* – damn – I'm in danger of missing my train. I'll phone you early tomorrow morning from Ypres station about Guy and tell you if he catches the train. If all goes to plan, I'll see you here at Kortrijk station at around 8.15am.' He rose and shook Sterling's hand firmly. Angela's hands he clasped as he kissed her on both cheeks. Angela's face glowed as she smiled. No doubt about it, Opa Albertin was a big hit.

She and Sterling watched as he slung his linen jacket over his shoulder and strode purposefully off across the square to the station in the fading evening light. He looked younger than a man in his sixties.

'What a charming man. He'll be an asset, I reckon.'

'He knows his place. That's the important thing.'

'What's that supposed to mean?'

'He knows he's an Indian, not a chief, unlike some people. I'm the chief.' He smiled to show he wasn't picking a fight. 'At least, I think I am. I was when we started out.'

Angela nudged him and laughed.

Chapter 7

Even though they were expecting the call, it caused a frisson. The ringtone of Sterling's mobile sounded with a tinny persistence around the hotel's breakfast area.

'Frank? Yves Albertin. Guy and I have just boarded the train. We'll be arriving in just over half an hour, at 8.45. He didn't get a ticket at the counter, which means he'll have used his season ticket, I think...'

Last night's conclave had discussed this. 'So, he'll be getting out here in Kortrijk. See you at the station, Yves.' The call ended. Sterling turned to Angela. 'We're on.'

Angela beamed. 'This is different from a Tuesday morning in Sandley Library. Exciting.'

Sterling pursed his lips. 'Maybe. There's a certain art to tailing someone, but it can be as boring as any other activity. As agreed last night, we'll tag him, the three of us. Yves will hand over to you, and I'll follow a few metres behind you and take over when the time seems right. I reckon you've probably still got some of your London street skills.'

'Like riding a bike,' murmured Angela. 'I was thinking that all this is a bit of a return to that life, without some of the components.'

'Crime, weapons...'

'Exactly.'

'It's 8.25. Let's stroll over to the station.'

The glass doors swished and they were in Doorniksestraat on the edge of the shopping district. After a few metres, they turned left into Burgemeester Reynaertstraat, which ran down the side of Schouwburgplein – Theatre Square – where the night before they'd discovered a car park underneath. This morning, a summer fair was in the early stages of setting up, trucks circling the cobbles like settler wagons in the Wild West, and young men in heavy industrial gloves shifting scaffolding and the more mysterious trappings of fairground construction.

As the road led out of the square, shops and commercial properties were replaced by the cafés and bars they'd seen the day before. But now there was a listless, apathetic air. It was early in the morning, and early in the week. Business would not really pick up in this locality till the weekend.

Sterling and Angela drifted across Stationsplein, the bike park right and centre like a silvery sea in the morning sun. Ten short minutes after they'd left the hotel, they were in position on Platform One, Sterling at the side exit into the square further down, and Angela near the doors into the station concourse. Glancing at Angela from his vantage point leaning against a pillar, Sterling knew she'd done her best. In any circumstance, she radiated charisma (a word he'd learnt from their crossword-solving hours together), enhanced by the style and brightness of her clothes. Now, in contrast, the black, loose-fitting linen trousers, grey T-shirt and dark flat shoes were neutral. She was wearing no socks, and her ankles looked barely lighter than the trousers and shoes. Her handbag was small, leather and brown, with a nod to North Africa in the patterning and frills at the edges.

But at 5'10" she was at least as tall as Sterling, taller with her mane of rich hair, and with her lively, intelligent face, it would be hard for any observer to dismiss her as an ordinary woman or traveller. Still, it might be equally difficult to identify her as the temporary assistant of an English private investigator on assignment in southern Belgium. Sterling shifted against the pillar and looked away across the tracks. The die was pretty much cast. He couldn't do much about Angela's aura now.

The station carried an air of urgency, with trains from every direction coming in to the block of platforms. It was, after all, just before nine o'clock during the morning rush hour and Kortrijk was a railway hub. The Ypres train was going on to Antwerp, but not via Platform One. He and Angela would have to be alert not to miss their quarry as he came through, but if Albertin was close by, he'd be a marker. Sterling looked again at the photo Christina had supplied to him and his team, a full-length shot of a young man in what Sterling thought was the typical continental garb he'd come to recognise – a dark jacket, fawn slacks, and brown Oxford brogues. He was handsome and probably just under 6', the shot capturing him with a half-smile and a faint echo of quizzical surprise as he approached the camera.

There were two walkways under the platforms. As the commuters emerged up the stairs or escalator from the one designated to Sterling, he straightened up and concentrated. There was only a dribble of humanity here, compared to Angela's, but seasoned travellers like Guy, as Sterling imagined him to be, might well choose the quieter exit, even if it was a few steps further from the town.

Planning and doing are always different. 8.45 came and went. The trains, sturdy, elderly box-shaped loco-motives with spindly cat's-cradle structures pressing for their power up to the overhead wires, obscured his vision, except on Platform One, where people climbed down from steep carriages. Sterling couldn't see Guy or Albertin. He began to feel uneasy. Angela flickered in and out of his vision as the throng of passengers filtered through the concourse, she too waiting. Then he saw her move, and a second later, he caught a glimpse of Albertin, who gazed across and nodded imperceptibly. He checked that Albertin and Angela had moved off into the concourse and, to avoid surveillance overkill, made his own way through the side exit into the square, intending to pick up the trail outside.

Surely something was wrong. Many people emerged from the station, but not Angela, Albertin or young Guy. Sterling cast his eyes over to the taxi rank. Perhaps Guy had taken a taxi, and the others were following. They'd all have had to be lightning quick though. Sterling walked briskly to the main entrance and peered through the plate glass beside and attached to the heavy glass doors. None of them was there either.

'What the f...?' Sterling muttered.

It wasn't a disaster because Angela and Albertin could phone him anytime it was convenient. But it was disconcerting and filled him with doubt. Was he losing his skills? He battled against the flow through the door and got out of the stream turning the concourse into a thoroughfare. The young man under surveillance and his trackers were gone.

There was a café to the left of the concourse as Sterling faced the platforms, its entrance next to the

Panos baguette bar. At the glass door, he immediately saw Angela sitting sideways on at a table just inside, making herself visible while carrying out her job. Sterling took a breath, pulled the cuffs of his shirt down inside his jacket sleeves and pushed open the door. The flotsam and jetsam of south Belgian railway travel had washed up here in a milieu that was overwhelmingly smoky brown. That section of humanity mingled with a listless portion of Kortrijk citizenry, almost without exception down-at-heel, who had nothing better to do and nowhere better to be.

On the walls were large, life-sized photo-pictures weathered and yellowed with age. In the nearest, a jowly, heavyset man in trilby and overcoat sitting on a high stool at a small, raised, round table attached to a pole, sipped an espresso, the smoke from a cigarillo in his pudgy half-clenched fist curling up and dissipating to nothing under a ceiling fan. Except for the cigarillo, the picture reflected the current scene. In the adjoining picture he had gone, and all that was left was a bleak grey view of rails stretching off into God knew where.

Sterling found himself a table on a kind of raised dais nearest the platforms and reached for the menu, trying to work out if it was counter or waiter service. His dilemma was resolved when a girl in jeans and short apron, ponytail swaying even as she trudged over, took up station by the table, her tray wedged at an angle on her hip. He pointed to a cappuccino on the card, and the girl, bored and unsmiling, nodded and turned away, the transaction apparently requiring no words. That problem attended to, Sterling looked surreptitiously around the deadbeat café.

Angela was still in position, and soon he spotted Guy Verstraete at a table that was not near the side door that led into the concourse but rather one that led out into *Stationsplein*. There was no doubt about it, Christina had chosen a looker. Guy, even obscured by his table, was slender, with a pianist's slim fingers and a swan-like, elegant neck enclosed in a small-checked blue and white shirt. His hair was a shock of thick, tight, dark curls artfully cut to frame his smooth, oval face with its straight nose, unblemished skin, and, judging from a distance, dark brown eyes. There was a sensitive, soulful look about him. Sterling observed the admiring glance of a young mother in another corner, absent-mindedly dandling her baby as the glance turned to stare. The young man's smart summer jacket and trousers enhanced his status as a young professional.

Beside him was a thin open briefcase with short vertical straps connected by a horizontal metal bar. Sterling recognised the vintage style. You flipped the flap and handle over in one direction, and then slipped the bar over the handle in the other. The bar fixed itself at the bottom of the handle, keeping the flap closed and the briefcase secure. It seemed oddly old-fashioned for a young man who seemed so *à la mode*, as Angela would say. Perhaps that was the point.

Guy was not alone. Opposite, with an espresso on the table in front of him, was a large, shambling man in an ill-fitting light suit. His untidy, white hair, creeping over his shirt collar, was receding from the front, and he made no attempt to hide it, the swept back style giving him the air of England's Swedish football manager back in the far-off 2000s, but without the urbanity. Although the history in the wrinkles rippling across his forehead, the bags under his eyes and his jowly cheeks put him at least in his late fifties, he was still near the peak of his powers. Sterling had seen some bruisers in his time, and he'd come off worst against a few of them. This man was a bruiser – not the kind Sterling would want to be on the wrong side of in a scrap.

The odd couple sipped their coffee with Guy referring to a sheet of paper he'd pulled from his briefcase. Even if Sterling and Angela had been closer, they would not have heard the conversation, still less understood the language. Angela was fluent in French and German – she and Albertin had babbled away in French for some of the time – but Angela had said that German and Dutch were too far apart for her. Guy made a few marks on the paper with his pen, which certainly wasn't a Bic, and then he and his unlikely companion got up to go. Sterling allowed himself to glance over at Angela. She rattled a few coins on the table and prepared to move off as well. She turned back at the door, ostensibly to check that she'd left nothing behind, and caught Sterling's eye. He waggled his phone and she nodded. The girl brought Sterling's coffee. Albertin had still not turned up. No worries. Angela was competent, and she could handle herself.

Chapter 8

Angela watched Guy and the Big Man set off out of the café just after nine o'clock, into Stationsplein. She checked that they weren't being picked up or taking a taxi and then followed casually as they went off side by side towards the town and down the same street she and Frank had come up earlier. But when they came to the main street the hotel was on, they carried on across the road and into the principal, all-pedestrianized shopping street. Angela made a mental note ready for feedback later – Lange Steenstraat. A few doors down was an optician's, and she thought it might be Guy's workplace. Perhaps it was, but he ignored it and carried on. A few doors down was a women's clothes shop. While Guy went in, Big Man lingered outside. Angela wondered if he was look-out or bodyguard? Five minutes later, Guy emerged from the shop, exchanged a word or two, and the duo moved on, Guy swinging his brief case with a kind of easy nonchalance as they went.

And so it carried on down the main drag for the next hour, with some of Guy's visits on one side and some on the other, Big Man always taking up station in a similar position outside each shop. Angela began to realise that he was less about being a look-out or personal protection and more about being intimidating. It didn't take much to imagine how his figure loomed in the window for those viewing within the shop. For the odd couple, progress was smooth and serene. In one or two places Angela was able to see Guy being greeted warmly by shop managers or owners, with smiles and handshakes from both parties.

It didn't all go smoothly. There was another, smaller optician's roughly in the middle of the high street, the nature of its business signalled by a pair of lopsided John Lennon frames to the left of the company name above three arches of granite blocks, windows right down to the pavement at the two sides and a glass door inserted in the middle.

The performance began again. This time, though, the combined levers of charm and menace jammed. Moments after he entered the shop, Guy was backing out, arms and legs tangled in the door as he struggled to open it inwards as he made his retreat. The rattle and hubbub carried down the street. A short woman, not even five-foot-tall, clad in black slacks and a red cashmere cardigan that matched her flaming pre-Raphaelite hair, followed closely behind, her forefinger jabbing into the young man's chest as she delivered a shrill diatribe. Her face was twisted with anger, his with a kind of startled bewilderment. The woman seemed unaffected by the Big Man's looming bulk. She delivered a volley of Dutch in his direction as well. Big Man looked up and down the street – checking to see if the commotion was being noticed – and Angela steered herself swiftly into a Benetton shop. It was a weekday and trade was thin, but one or two shoppers had paused to see what the fuss was about.

Angela was getting used to doing surveillance. From the doorway she looked down towards the optician's, and in the reflection of another clothes shop opposite, she saw Guy put his hand on Big Man's arm and tug him away. From the middle of the street, the tiny woman, arms akimbo, watched them edge away. Angela abandoned the reflection and peered directly out. Big Man looked back, a scowl smeared across his craggy face. The meagre smattering of people drifted away ('nothing to see here – move along'). The small woman returned to her shop and Angela resumed her shadowing.

About fifty metres along, the two men disappeared to the left. Angela quickened her pace and got to the corner of a small, scruffy square. It had the air of a space that had been tacked on as an afterthought, a concrete appendix. All it contained was a map of Kortrijk, a couple of scraggly trees and a bicycle stand that featured a bright all-yellow touring bike, yellow even down to the drop handle bars, the saddle and the tyres, which by itself added a dissonant splash of class and colour to the drabness. Angela was just in time to see Guy and his minder (if minder he was) enter a betting shop in the far corner.

She looked at her watch. It was 10.30, and a good opportunity to let Frank know what was happening.

*

The trouble with shadowing someone is that those who are not doing the tailing have to spend large amounts of time doing nothing, which in practice, without a specific base, means spending time in cafés, pubs or any other venue amenable to using up minutes. Sterling and Albertin were in the same establishment on the Grote Markt – Da Franco – where they had been drinking the night before. At the station café, where Albertin had turned up ten minutes after Angela had gone, he had launched into an exhaustive explanation about why he had gone missing. 'The big man with Guy – I've seen him about in Comines, and he's seen me. I was scared that he'd make me. I knew that if they hadn't left the station you and Angela would catch up with them, and I got that right.' Sterling again admired Opa Albertin's English, its smoothness and colloquialism, but something didn't feel right. Who would use 'make' for 'recognise'? Not, generally speaking, a Fleming.

His phone trilled. 'Angela.'

'I'm still with them. They've just gone into a betting shop in – hang on a second – Grote Kring, which is just off Steenpoort.'

'Good.' Sterling unfolded his map. 'How well do you know this town, Yves?'

'Not that well. I confess... since Willem fell out with me and so on, I've stuck to Walloon areas. I know the general layout.'

'There's a big church just around the corner from here...'

'St Martin's...'

'Getting around it looks a bit complicated. If we go down here – Korte Steenstraat,' – Sterling struggled with the unfamiliar words, and, for all he knew, the pronunciation, – 'we'll come out at Lange Steenstraat, turn left, walk down, and Grote Kring will be on the left.'

'Short Stone Street, Long Stone Street, Grand Circle,' translated Albertin. 'Except... because the Big Man knows me...'

'Right, I'll go. I'll catch up with you later. Will you pay?'

Albertin raised his hand in acknowledgement and farewell. Sterling hurried out of the Grote Markt and veered right, away from the huge doors of the church straight ahead. One thing was sure: he wouldn't be able to drink any more coffee that day. The small, pedestrian-only street came out as predicted into a larger one – the main shopping street – but further down than he'd been before. Two dozen shops later he spotted Angela on the corner of the scruffy square she'd described. She pointed.

'They're in that betting shop.'

'What have they been up to?'

Angela was just about to reply when she took his arm. 'They're on the move.'

Guy and the Big Man were emerging from the betting shop, sharing a joke or something that was causing laughs and smiles. They seemed to have recovered from the optician's verbal assault and their ignominious defeat in the face of much smaller opposition. Guy swung his briefcase jauntily as they set off through the other side of the square. They disappeared around the corner and out of sight, and Sterling and Angela hurried to the point they were last seen. Grote Kring led to another, smaller square, and the little and large duo, having just crossed it diagonally, were again about to disappear at the other side. Sterling's sense of direction, and the sun's position in the mid-morning sky, seemed to show that Guy and his companion were heading towards the Grote Markt, where Sterling had just been. The difference was that they were proceeding roughly along the hypotenuse of an imaginary right-angled triangle, whereas Sterling had reconnected with Angela along the other two sides.

His speculations were both confirmed and denied at the next corner. It was no longer possible to go in the line of the hypotenuse because the huge St Martins church was in the way, and the quarry had vanished again.

'What now?' said Angela.

Sterling pointed to the left. 'You go around the church that way, and I'll go around the other. One of us should pick them up. Don't go too quickly and bump into them. If that doesn't work, at least we'll meet each other.'

Angela nodded and set off. Sterling paused for a moment to orient himself and then went himself. A ramp with a handrail led downwards, the old brick church on his left and a new block of flats close up on his right, complete with entrance to underground parking. The day was warming up, and there was humidity in the atmosphere. Sterling felt prickles of sweat surface on his forehead and took off his jacket. The ramp merged into a tree-shaded, cobbled pathway next to the church, which in turn splayed out into another cool, leafy square. There had been a tributary off to the right, but Sterling could see out to a car park and there was no sign of Guy and the Big Man. Now the longest side of the church was on Sterling's left and a solid, white, gracious turn-of-the-last century tenement on the right, complete with shutters on every window. In front of the building at the far end were red parasols and matching chairs.

Angela emerged from the side of the church at the other end. She spied Sterling and they met in the middle.

'I popped into the Grote Markt for a quick look, but they were definitely not there.'

'No one this way, either.'

There was only one conclusion. Guy and the Big Man were gone, this time for good.

Chapter 9

'What now, Frank?'

'Let's just check at the café.' They walked down to the cluster of parasols where a small, slender young girl of Asian origin was waiting on tables. 'We're meeting a couple of men,' said Sterling, speaking English in Albertin's absence. The girl shook her head blankly, brightened and scuttled off inside.

Seconds later a young man, brown eyes, wispiness around his lower face that barely qualified as a beard, emerged through the café door and spoke. 'Can I help you, sir?'

'We're meeting a couple of men here, I think. If I've got the address right,' said Sterling. 'One, your height, curly hair. The other much bigger, bald, with white hair, what's left of it.'

The young man shook his head. 'No, sorry. No one like that has come in.' He gave a small bow, his serving tray hugged to his chest. 'Go inside and check if you like.'

Sterling did as invited while Angela waited outside. The café was fitted out in a style of quiet luxury. This was not one of the easy-come-easy-go cafés to be found in the main square. Here, well-heeled, sleekly dressed older men and women were having late coffee or early lunch. The men were in business suits, with meeting papers strewn among the coffee cups, the women fitted out from the more expensive shops, friends getting together for refreshment. Guy would have fitted in except for his relative youthfulness. The natural milieu of the bruiser with him was the station café.

Sterling nodded his thanks to the Asian girl and the young manager and shook his head at Angela.

'They must have gone somewhere.'

'Wherever it is, we've lost them for the moment. Let's just take a pull around the square and consider the possibilities. Then we'll review.'

Sterling was already convinced that there had been nowhere for Guy and his companion to duck into on his way around the church and into the square, and, accompanying Angela back around her route, came to the same conclusion. Even the big, heavy doors of the church were locked. They stood together in the tree-canopied square, looking towards the tenement.

Sterling's eye-casting stopped as he focused. There was a small, dark, vertical gash in the tenement wall between the two private residences next to the café. He pointed. 'There'.

'Surely that's just a side alley to the backyard where they keep the bins.'

'Maybe, but we won't know until we check, will we?'

They walked over.

'Won't we be trespassing?'

'Working in that library has made you really law-abiding, Ange. What's going to happen if someone turns up? It's broad daylight. It's not as if we look as though we're breaking and entering. We just say we got lost – or something.' Sterling ducked into the opening.

'It probably does just lead to a small backyard with a few bins.'

But the passageway wasn't a dead end. There was a section that clearly ran the length of the tenement from front to back, cut into the block and cobbled underfoot, with whitewashed brick at the sides and overhead. Then there was a kink, as if two sets of builders, having started at opposite ends and not quite come out dead in the middle, had improvised. At the kink, the walls and cobbles continued, but Sterling and Angela could look up and see the bright summer sky. Finally, a few metres further on, they came out into a small courtyard, utterly silent even though so close to the busy town.

'Wow,' said Angela. 'This is amazing. I reckon it's a religious institution.' Sterling remembered her double first in history and modern languages. The history bit was kicking in.

The courtyard led to a larger enclosure and they could see numbered doors in front of whitewashed cottages with the customary crenellated gabling. As they followed the cobbles, there seemed to be no standard shape to the little settlement but the dwellings seemed both to skirt the outside boundary and act as a barrier, the doors facing inwards rather than towards the town. A statue in a small grassed area dominated the centre and behind it a structure larger and newer than the houses grouped around the perimeter. Still in the Flemish style, it was un-whitewashed, and its red brickwork and large windows jarred with the general ambience.

Angela took Sterling's arm in both of hers and propelled him in an uneven exploration around the community within a community. Her eyes shone. Guy and the Big Man were forgotten as she pointed and exclaimed. Ever the pragmatist, Sterling did not resist. His copper's gut told him that their quarry was in here somewhere, and it would do no harm for them to be thought of as star-struck tourists. Their jagged circuit took them past a larger entrance and eventually back to the alleyway by which they'd entered.

'What about that building in the middle? It looked as though it might be open.'

Angela was right. As they approached the stone steps leading up to the entrance, the sliding doors opened and they found themselves in a museum-like centre with glass displays and a sequenced system of computerized multilingual screen guides.

'A *beguinage*,' exclaimed Angela. 'I should have known straight away.'

Sterling looked blank.

'The individual houses here make it unlikely that this was a convent or a monastery. From medieval times to the beginning of the last century, one of the only real options for lone women in European society, if they did not marry or if they were widowed, was to go into a convent or nunnery. Widows or spinsters, particularly if they had independent means, or maybe only if they had independent means, found alternatives in the Beguine movement. Beguinages, like this one, were set up mainly in the Low Countries. Beguines did not take vows but lived religious lives. Sometimes women who had no independent means lived as servants in beguinages. This one must be one of the oldest and best preserved in Europe.'

'A very good summary, if I may so,' said a soft, dis-embodied voice. 'Surprising also.'

Both Angela and Sterling started. 'Bloody hell,' muttered Sterling.

'A thousand apologies.' The voice was attached to a squat, plump man in a checked green and white cambric shirt whose round little belly protruded over brown corduroy trousers, hitched high by a pair of old braces. Small, dark eyes peered from behind a pair of gold, half-framed spectacles perched on a round, pink, unlined baby face. He walked a couple of paces from the lift in the corner of the exhibition space and turned specifically to Angela. 'You were so enthusiastic that you didn't hear the lift.' He giggled as the sentence finished.

Angela put her hand over her heart. 'Well, you and the lift were quiet.'

'Again, apologies. Heh heh.' The little man managed to say sorry without conveying any sense that he meant it. 'The renovations in here have only just finished and the exhibition has only just opened, so there are no squeaks and creaks – and you are among the first visitors.'

'And you are...?' said Sterling. His own heartbeat was only just returning to normal. There was something unnerving about this small man that kept him on the alert – and his heart racing.

'Pieter Van Leuven. Heh heh. I am the curator here in Saint Anna Hall – a beghard rather than a beguine.' The giggle again. 'Times have changed. In this community, there are women and men living their lives, some solitary and some not so solitary. Now there are even couples in...' the little man paused, finding the foreign phrase distasteful – '... the beguinage. Of course, we say *begijnhof* in Flemish. Your word is French and English, and since you're in Flanders and not in France or England..."

'"Beguinage" suits me fine,' said Angela. Sterling recognised the reaction. She wasn't going to be bullied by anyone on matters of vocabulary.

Unbidden, and with a giggle at the end of every other sentence, Van Leuven gave Sterling and Angela his own little tour of and commentary on what he called "the experience centre", highlighting the main parts and introducing his own embellishments, fixing his visitors with a fierce gaze. The emphasis was on 700 years of oppression of plucky Flemings – by the French, by the Spanish, by the Habsburgs, apparently by all and sundry, together with unwelcome influxes of migrants among the oppressors, diluting racial and cultural purity. He focused exclusively on Angela as he did his spiel, half warped version of history, half provocation, seemingly incited by her polite neutrality. Interspersed within the lecture, he fired off the occasional question in his soft, relentless voice; why had they come to Kortrijk? how had they found the beguinage? how long were they staying? what did they know of Flanders and its history?

Sterling trusted Angela to do the talking and responding, based on the detachment he knew she could muster in the face of the goading. He kept quiet and listened as she explained. They had had a few days off from their jobs in Kent. On a whim, they'd decided to go abroad, and Belgium was close by. They'd just popped over. Rijsel was close to Kortrijk, and so was Ieper. Brussel not far away. He realised that Rijsel was the Flemish name for Lille and remembered Ieper for Ypres. Brussel must be the Flemish spelling for Brussels. But while Angela was giving as little information as she could, and as vaguely as possible, she rattled out questions of her own. How long had Van Leuven been in the beguinage? Where had he come from? What was his background?

Reluctantly, Van Leuven was admitting that he'd only been in post for a few months and had come down from Bruges. His training was in museum curatorship. 'So, you approve of our little exhibition?' he finally said.

'Very much. And the beguinage. As a woman, this is exactly the kind of place I'd have liked to end up in if I'd been widowed or single.'

Van Leuven bowed and giggled. 'Well, I must get on.'

'So must we,' said Sterling. The beguinage was all very well and interesting – to Angela at least – but how did it help with the case, and what was Guy's connection to it? 'Thank you for your trouble and hospitality.' He offered his hand, and Van Leuven took it. Angela didn't trouble to offer hers.

As they went through the doors and down the steps, Sterling stole a glance back inside. Van Leuven was staring out. He raised his arm in a final gesture of farewell, his dark eyes glittering. Sterling felt a chill, even though it was coming up to midday just after high summer on a blue and cloudless day. He struggled to interpret the look on the little man's face. Dislike. Perhaps. Distaste. Perhaps. Suspicion. Maybe. Then he had it. Above all, loathing. A sixth sense stirred again in his copper's gut, just as it had when they first went through the alleyway. The beguinage, and Pieter Van Leuven, were connected to Guy Verstraete and the case. He and Angela just had to find out how.

Chapter 10

Sterling and Angela had found the main gate of the beguinage, just out of sight of the Grote Markt, and were walking towards the hotel. Near the belfry a young man dressed as a clown was juggling what seemed to be machetes. The blades glinted in the sunshine. He wailed and chuntered – 'Whooaah, oooohhh' – as they spun. A small crowd watched, the children open-mouthed and making their own little noises of thrill and fear. To a casual onlooker, the clown might have been hyping up the danger and his dubious competence, but the steely concentration in his eyes told a different story. He was a professional in full control.

'What do you think about it all?'

Sterling did not reply straight away. He stopped to watch the juggler. 'As far as the case is concerned, it's a jigsaw at the moment, and we only have a few pieces. But Christina is right. This isn't about a girl Guy is having a fling with in Kortrijk. It's something very different. And more serious.'

'That bastard – Van Leuven. Did you notice?'

'How could I not?'

'He didn't want to believe that someone like me – a black woman – could be so knowledgeable about medieval European history. The slant he gave to Flanders and the Flemish – nationalist in the extreme. Racist.

And he didn't want to touch my skin. The thought of a sanctuary for women occupied by someone like him. As bad as Opa Willem. Still, why should things be any different in Belgium than in Blighty?'

Sterling kept quiet. Angela knew what he thought about it. He'd seen how people had been when she'd first started at the library – before she'd won the users over and they could congratulate themselves for their lack of prejudice.

Aurélien was pleased to see them though, back at the hotel. He beamed and waved from behind reception. 'Mr Sterling. Miss Wilson. Can I do anything for you?'

Angela smiled back. Her rages quickly burnt out. 'Coffee, Frank?'

'If I have any more coffee today, it'll finish me off. Let's just sit at the window and I'll phone Albertin and see where he's got to. The fact we've been seen at the beguinage and Albertin knows the big man with Guy – by sight at least – and vice versa is going to make further surveillance difficult – if Guy and his mate did actually go in there.' There was no getting away from it, he and Angela were an unlikely pairing, and that made them memorable.

Albertin appeared at the hotel's plate glass window after Sterling's mobile summons. He too grimaced when Angela offered coffee. 'I had no idea that surveillance could be so boring and involve so much caffeine.'

The three of them sat silently by the window for a minute or two. The PI, the librarian and the Walloon, as unlikely a trio as you could meet, all engrossed in their own thoughts. Outside, shoppers passed, and dog-walkers, and people on local business from office to office. An old woman – black shawl, dark dress and clogs – stepped out of history, a nod to modernity only in the four-wheeled shopping trolley she pushed arthritically ahead of her as she creaked over the road to the bakery.

'Right. Do you want to summarise, Angela?'

She went through the main points, from tailing Guy from the station to the curator in the beguinage. At that moment, she shuddered. 'Oleaginous, with an extreme right-wing subtext.'

'Oleaginous?' said Albertin. 'My English isn't that…'

'Oily,' interrupted Sterling. Angela had taught him well.

'Anyway, after that, we came back here.'

'What about the Big Man, Yves?' said Sterling.

Albertin shifted in his seat and looked out of the window, not making eye contact. 'I've seen him around Comines occasionally, in a café in the main square. He's not there often, so I don't know if he lives there, but because I've seen him, I couldn't risk him seeing me, especially when I was following Guy.' He looked back to Sterling and Angela. 'It would have been awful if I'd messed things up before we'd even started.'

'Of course,' said Angela. She was a woman of strong passions and quick judgements. Opa Van de Velde: verdict suspended (a rare exception, awaiting more data). Van Leuven: a dreadful, odious man. Albertin: incapable of wrong – a leftist forever on the correct side of the barricades.

'OK,' murmured Sterling, neutrally. It wasn't about being cynical. It was about experience. 'So, theories?' It occurred to him that this was a big advantage of being in a team, and, not only that, leading it.

'Guy has got himself mixed up in a criminal gang,' offered Angela. 'There's a kind of protection racket going on, which is why he's been going up and down the high street. The Big Man is his minder, or muscle if things don't go to plan. Mind you, when that woman in the opticians had a go at him, the Big Man didn't do much. Maybe it was too public.'

'The betting shop?' said Sterling.

'Perhaps that's what got Guy started in the first place. He got into debt. He started hob-nobbing with the wrong people – and he still can't kick the habit. They went into the beguinage after the betting shop with the money they'd collected, or something. He'll do his work for four days, and then he'll go home to Ypres, as usual. Maybe he's just got time off from his day job as an optician.'

'Yves?'

'That sounds – what's your word? – plausible – to me. It's just that there seems to be a time limit on all this. Guy has been saying to Christina that everything will be alright soon, which suggests that things aren't going to last, and that doesn't fit with a... protection racket, which surely just carries on.'

'What do you think, Frank?' said Angela.

'I agree with both of you, mostly, except that maybe it isn't so much a protection racket but the two of them are collecting subscriptions. You can do that in the daytime. In most of the shops, you've indicated that there wasn't hostility. In one, you said the manager, or whoever it was, shook Guy's hand. It was only at the optician's half way down the street that the woman was angry and even came out of the shop. We need to go at it some more and we'll get a better picture.'

'What now, esteemed leader?'

Albertin's phone chirruped. 'Excuse me.' He got up and wandered into the interior of the hotel but returned quickly. 'That was the person I gave the coded message to. She's cracked it.'

Sterling looked at Angela. 'There's your answer – an afternoon trip to Comines – if that's where she lives, Yves.'

'That's right, but aren't we going to try and locate Guy, or make enquiries at that optician's where the argument was?'

Sterling had spent hours of his life on the job at stake-outs, often with his mate Andy Nolan, now a detective chief inspector with the Kent Police. Tedium followed by... more tedium. Only rarely was there eruption into any excitement. His mind drifted back to one famous occasion when, late at night, a well-known bad boy under observation had gone into his mother's house through the front door, straight down the hall, out the back and over the fence at the bottom of the garden. They hadn't known about it until the message came through that he'd been picked up loading cocaine into a van on the other side of town three hours later.

'Guy isn't going anywhere much now, I wouldn't imagine. If he is, it's probably more of the same. He's probably got his feet up in one of those little cottages in the beguinage with his mate. We can come back later, have a drink in the Grote Markt and see if they're around. A pony to a bluey they'll pick up where they left off tomorrow. The coded message is much more interesting. You can hang around the church if you want, Ange, but you'll probably get bored. And, if I'm honest, you'll be conspicuous.'

Angela smiled. As far as she was concerned, Sterling didn't do things the way she'd do them. She'd have been researching on her laptop on the train. They'd have gone by Eurostar from Ashford to Lille and then onwards, rather than by ferry and provincial train – route one, not meander. Sterling's investigation methods and priorities seemed completely lackadaisical to her. Where was the energy? Where was the pushiness? Why was everything such an amble? But the counter-arguments were compelling. In the short time she'd known him, he'd been remarkably successful with all his cases. His stubbornness, the way he let things shake loose rather than force them, his loner attitude, and his apparently casual approach, paid dividends.

She'd have been hanging round the beguinage, or talking to the red-haired optician, or worrying at things, probing and putting backs up, if she thought it would work. He was virtually suggesting an afternoon off. She shrugged. 'It's your gig, Frank.'

Albertin looked at his watch. 'There's a train in ten minutes.'

'Allons-y,' said Sterling. It was not far off the only French he remembered. He smiled at his little joke. The francophones didn't notice.

Chapter 11

Apart from the sign, which said "Comines – Komen" and thus nodded in the direction of both Walloon and Flemish populations of the divided country, the station itself could have been serving any number of border towns in this western corner of Europe. It had the same neat, muted red brick and angled gables, and the same low platforms, down to which you alighted via steep grilled steps that unfolded as the train doors opened. Sterling pictured Emma Jameson, the wheelchair user he had rescued during an earlier foray into East Anglia. He could hear her voice too. 'Fucking hell, Frank, what's this about?', and she wouldn't have spared the conductor a volley of abuse if there had been any nonsense about her eligibility to board.

Opposite the station front was a terrace of mixed-use residential housing, shop fronts and garages, all with decorative brick window arches, white brick and stone blocks among the red, again interchangeable with terraces in the towns the trio had just passed through, and in all likelihood the ones further down. A Jupiler beer sign illuminated the window of a bar.

Albertin led his companions to the end of the road as the level-crossing barriers rose in stiff-armed salute and turned left away from them and towards the town. He seemed somehow responsible for and apologetic about the quiet provinciality that enveloped them. 'It's not far. This bit's a little dull, but the square where we're going at the end is open and rather pretty.' To Sterling's mind, this was better than mooching about Kortrijk hoping to pick up the thread of their surveillance and, likely as not, be disappointed.

Ten minutes later, in a square that was neither prettier or more nondescript than the many squares Sterling had seen in his lifetime, he, Albertin and Angela pulled up at a doorway next to *Aux Artistes* café. Sterling wondered if it had been named after real artists – the Walloon school perhaps.

Albertin rang the bell and conducted a short conversation in French with a disembodied voice from a small intercom. The door buzzed and he pushed his way in. On the two short flights of stairs upwards, shabby but clean, were ledges with well-kept potted plants getting their light from windows to the front and back. A cyclamen was doing particularly well, its pink flowers in full, triumphant, exuberant bloom. Albertin gave a brief rap on the door at the top, which was already slightly ajar to welcome the visitors, and eased himself in, followed by Angela and Sterling. The transition was from down-at-heel to the cover of Good Housekeeping. The flat was small, with a mingled scent of furniture polish and air freshener, a deep-pile carpet showing the furrows of recent vacuuming, and a white dusting throughout of Belgian lace. A tiny, bird-like creature emerged from a room that overlooked the square.

'*Entrez, entrez,*' said the tiny woman, the timbre of her voice surprisingly rich and full-bodied in the light of her obvious old age. Rouge tinged her cheeks and scarlet lipstick on her flautist's lips. Her hair, recently permed, was chestnut brown, her forehead unlined and her eyes bright and inquisitive. She was ninety-five if she was a day.

The three visitors smiled and bowed, almost in unison, before entering the lounge. Albertin took one of the armchairs, while Angela and Sterling perched on a small two-seater sofa. Sterling was wishing he'd checked the soles of his shoes for dog muck, even after he'd brushed them on the mat outside the front door. He did not dare let his head go near the antimacassar behind him. The apartment was immaculate. The old woman took station in what must have been her usual armchair next to the window and nearest the television.

'Marie,' said Albertin, 'this is Frank Sterling and Angela Wilson. Angela and Frank, Marie De Haene.' There was more hand-clasping and head bobbing. Something about the old woman and her apartment demanded formality. 'Marie,' continued Albertin, 'actually worked for you near the end of the Second World War.'

'First at Berkhamsted with Rejewski, the famous Polish cryptanalyst, criminally underused by you English, without a doubt, and then Bletchley,' twinkled Marie. 'I could have ended up at Mechelen and then much worse.'

'Mechelen?' said Angela.

'"Malines" in French,' murmured Albertin. 'Between Brussels and Antwerp, and the Nazi administration and transport hub for the deportation of Belgian Jews.'

'Once I had got away from the Nazis in Brussels,' resumed Ms De Haene, 'good times. We were winning handsomely when I joined, so morale was high and we had fun.'

'So you were a refugee and a code-breaker,' said Angela. Bumping up against history brought out her star-struck qualities again.

'Part of a team of code-breakers,' said the old woman, 'but I picked up a lot.'

'That explains your excellent English, like Yves's,' said Sterling.

Marie smiled, with a trace of mystery in the look. 'Yes, like Yves,' she repeated. 'I am Flemish actually, but I am fluent in English and French.'

'But Yves told us Comines is a Walloon town,' said Angela. 'So, what...?'

'There's not much of what I'd call Belgian patriotism in this country. Most people have allegiance to either the Flemish areas or the Walloon ones. I don't. I consider myself to be Belgian first and last. Our disastrous Second World War king, Leopold III, caused Belgium endless difficulties, but his words still inspire me as a patriot. "*België verwacht van u dat gij uw vaandel eer zult aandoen. Wat er ook moge gebeuren, mijn lot zal het uwe zijn. Onze zaak is rechtvaardig en rein. De Voorzienigheid zal ons helpen. Leve België.*"' She turned to Albertin.

'Belgium expects you to honour her flag, whatever happens. My fate will be yours. Our cause is just and pure. Providence will help us. Long live Belgium.'

'Good, Yves. Maybe there's a Belgian patriot somewhere in you as well. Anyway, I had the opportunity, as a Flemish person, though with a Jewish grandmother, to live in a French-speaking part of the country, and I took it. Besides, there are always enclaves, Flemish or Walloon, in these border towns. There are people here with whom I can speak in my own Flemish dialect, and I am always happy to practise my French. And my English for that matter. Yves and I met through our shared languages.'

'It's much more complicated than it seems at first sight, this business of Belgium,' said Angela.

'But you learn fast,' said Albertin.

He never misses an opportunity for flattery, mused Sterling as Angela smiled and accepted the compliment with cast down eyes.

'So, this code,' said the old woman. She reached for a pair of half-moon spectacles and the sheet of paper Christina had provided. 'Perhaps you know this already, but it's of a Flemish dialect used in the Bruges area. Once I had worked out the language and taken into account the peculiarities of the dialect, it was easy to break – certainly, it was no Enigma, or it would have been impossible with my meagre resources. It's monoalphabetic, so you look for patterns based on the language being used.'

'Just as a friend of ours back home guessed,' said Angela.

Marie De Haene nodded. 'I'm interested in the history of cryptography and cryptanalysis, and I can tell you that this is so, well, rudimentary as to be… medieval. Things have got a great deal more complex than something like this. I'd even go so far as to say that modern codes are virtually unbreakable. Code-making has outstripped code-breaking if you like, though not quite to the extent that I can leave out "virtually". Just as something appears to have become impossible, someone or something else comes along. An Artificial Intelligence revolution has already started. Maybe the unbreakable will no longer be so. Anyway,' – the old woman dragged herself back to the matter in hand' – 'as I said, this code is simple and medieval, and I think that's important.'

'How so?' said Angela.

'Two things.' Ms De Haene had gone from welcoming host to steely professional. 'Firstly, I am not sure that the code-maker thought that his code would fall into the wrong hands,' – her eyes twinkled – 'that is if you are indeed the wrong hands. There's a playfulness about this in a way. It's not just a code but a kind of style. Just as in the war, when the women listening to Morse code could identify the transmitters by their particular habits, and also tell when a regular transmitter had been replaced – sometimes for counter-espionage purposes – code-setters betray styles. It's almost as if this is between friends or close associates. Secondly, the medieval aspect indicates a medieval mindset. It's so old-fashioned to have a coded message on a sheet of paper when there's so much more modern technology can provide. Fundamentally, this is old-fashioned – a code for the 1500s and not for the twenty-first century.'

Sterling leaned forward. 'This is all very interesting, but...'

The old woman put up her forefinger. 'There's some more before we get to the actual message, all quite important if you can bear with me.'

Sterling leaned back. He could sense that it wasn't ego, or the opportunity to show off, that was motivating the cryptanalyst, and after all, they weren't short of time.

'The lion, and this small picture here... The lion first...'

'Its claws and tongue aren't red,' said Sterling. 'It's not the lion of the current official Flemish flag but the flag of the Flemish nationalists.'

'Good,' said Ms De Haene. 'Impressive. Many Flemish people are not aware of that.'

'I've got a friend in Ypres. He gave me various insights. But I've no idea what the other thing is.'

'It's a *goedendag*, a weapon developed and used by Flemings. Goedendag actually means "good day", and the name only appears in French historical sources, not Flemish ones. The Flemings' own name for it was...' she paused to rummage for a translation – '"a pinned staff". You see the shaft, basically with an iron pin at the end, for thrusting into armour and horses. We'll come back to goedendags in a moment. Now for the message itself. It's a kind of action plan, or set of instructions according to my translation, as follows:

- Retrieve the Kortrijk Chest by any means possible, but no later than Sunday 10 July, and bring it to the usual meeting place.
- Complete the collection of tithes and subscriptions, and pass them to the treasurer, no later than Thursday 7 July.
- Receive your final instructions at the general meeting on Sunday 10 July, at the usual time and place.'

'What's the day and date today?' said Albertin.

'Thursday, 7th of July,' said Angela. 'The second thing must be what we were witnessing this morning. Everything's obviously hotting up. But what about the rest of it?'

Sterling clasped his hands over his knees and leaned forward again. Marie De Haene's eyes were sparkling more than ever, and he noticed a quiver in the frail and delicate frame in the armchair opposite.

'What's your take on this, Marie?'

Ms De Haene glanced over at Albertin. 'Don't you see, Yves? Don't you get it? Think, man.'

Albertin looked blank.

'You Walloons,' said the old woman vehemently. 'You never take any interest in the Flemish side of things. I know I consider myself a Belgian, rather than a Flemish, patriot. But it would help a bit if the Walloons played their part... Anyway, my take, Frank, is that this is something very strongly to do with Flemish national-ism, and what is rapidly approaching is the anniversary of the Battle of Kortrijk in 1302, later known as the Battle of the Golden Spurs.' Again, she did calculations in her head. 'Next Monday, 11th of July.'

'Of course,' said Albertin.

'Of course,' the old woman mimicked with a wobble of her head. 'Now it makes sense.'

'We have our own anniversaries,' said Albertin, almost primly.

'Yes, when you kicked the bishops out of Liège. Big event.'

Albertin smiled and shrugged. 'Why argue? I know we're basically on the same side.'

Angela interposed. There was the alluring prospect of another history lesson. 'You were going to come back to goedendags, Marie.'

'Yes, goedendags.' The old woman took a breath and composed herself after the small spike of agitation. 'The goedendags were what the Flemish foot soldiers used so effectively against the French knights in the battle. The Flemish artisans and weavers from the great Flemish cities – especially from Bruges — wouldn't really have stood a chance against the horsemen, but the battle was fought on marshy ground outside the town, and the horses and knights in their heavy armour got bogged down. The goedendags did the rest. After the battle, the golden spurs were taken from the feet of the dead French nobility and displayed in a Kortrijk church.'

'Wow,' said Angela. 'Amazing. We don't get that in our history books. But why were the Flemish fighting the French anyway?' said Angela.

'It's very complicated. Perhaps a longer story for another time. But briefly, at that period the Counts of Flanders were mainly under French influence – vassals if you like, although retaining some independence. The Flemish cities, prosperous through trade and wool man-ufacture, wanted their own independence, and it didn't always matter who from, the Counts or the French. In the years before 1302, the interests of the Counts and the cities were aligned against the French.' Marie gave Sterling a sly glance. 'Of course, the English, who sup-plied the wool, had an influence too, often a mischie-vous one. Anti-French interests in the cities were almost always pro-English. But even the little I've said so far is a simplification. For example, not everyone in the Flemish cities was against the French.'

Albertin turned to Sterling. Unlike Angela, Flemish history didn't captivate him. 'What's next, boss?'

'We're not quite at that point, yet,' said Sterling. Boss. It had a strange ring to it. This whole case, with a team that he had not selected, but which had eerily coalesced around him, was helpful but unnerving. He wasn't used to sharing his thoughts at such a prelim-inary stage. 'Firstly, we obviously know that Guy

Verstraete received the message, but we haven't dis-cussed who might have sent it.' He looked at Angela.

'That oily little man in charge of the exhibition in the beguinage – Pieter Van Leuven – you reckon, Frank?' Angela and Sterling had told Albertin of their encounter with Van Leuven, and now Angela quickly updated the elderly cryptanalyst.

'He's got at least some of the credentials, including a heavy dose of extreme nationalism. It seems likely that Guy and the Big Man disappeared into the beguinage when we lost them. We'll keep Van Leuven in mind.'

'He seemed a stunted, bitter little character.'

'So was Hitler,' said Marie, 'before he found his path, and we know how badly that turned out.'

'Secondly, bringing the discussion back...' said Sterling, 'Marie, what's the Kortrijk Chest?'

Ms De Haene did a mock-pout. 'You English are just as bad as the Walloons. With you, it's all William the Conqueror and the Battle of Hastings, or the Spanish Armada.'

'No idea what you're talking about,' said Sterling, working to keep a straight face.

A brief look of shock flitted across the old woman's features before she realised and laughed. 'I suppose I should get off my high horse – isn't that what you say? Well, the Kortrijk Chest is exactly that, a large wooden box with a panel on the side showing the Battle of Kortrijk. It's said that the engraving was done by a Fleming and that almost certainly he was present at the battle. But sometimes the chest is called the Oxford Chest, because it's ended up in the Ashmolean Museum there. Actually, it was found in about 1905 on a farm owned by New College, Oxford, whose tenant used it as a feed bin. Only the panel is fourteenth century. The rest is much newer. I imagine that it could be considered by some to be a symbol of Flemish independence, which is probably why your Guy is being sent to get it.'

'Well,' said Angela, 'he's not just going to be able to waltz into the museum and ask to borrow it for whatever purpose. Even official loans of art and artefacts can take years to arrange. That means...' She tailed off.

Sterling got up and looked out over the square. Marie had a wonderful view. An old man emerged through the heavy doors of the church. A gardener on her hands and knees was tending the flower display, a splash of yellow and orange in the mini-roundabout that split the road three ways. Her trowel glinted occasionally as it emerged from the beds. Sterling was hopeless at flower names. He turned back to his team and the code-breaker.

'You know, this whole thing is completely wacky, and has been right from the start. It should just have been a sad little case about infidelity, particularly sad because Christina wouldn't have deserved it. But it's a lot more than that and weird as it is, I reckon we'll get to the bottom of it. We need to split up. Someone will have to go to Oxford straight away to investigate things there.'

'That will have to be me,' said Angela.

'Agreed,' said Sterling. She'd done exactly what he'd wanted. 'Yves and I will do the kind of stuff we did this morning. Old Guy's a busy bee what with one thing and another, so we might not see him and the Big Man, but something else is probably happening. It will be helpful if we find out who "the treasurer" is, and what he's treasurer of. The last instruction... if this is about

Flemish nationalism, don't we need someone of that background who is plausible enough to help us find out about the "general meeting"?'

'Well,' said Marie. 'I'm Flemish, but I'm not a nationalist, and I'm certainly too old for the kind of rushing about that you might have in mind.'

'I hope you now think of yourself as part of the team,' said Sterling. 'Perhaps your role can be research and coordination. But I wasn't thinking of you.'

Angela was puzzled. 'Who then?'

'Opa Willem,' said Sterling.

Chapter 12

'Willem,' said Albertin. He puffed out his cheeks. 'I don't think he'll be much help.'

'Why not?' said Sterling. 'He fits the bill perfectly. He's got a nationalist background, so he and Guy share the same political interests. He obviously wants the best for your granddaughter. He probably gets on well with Guy and that will come in handy. You're no good, if you don't mind me saying so, for this particular task.'

'Even so,' said Albertin. Now he was shaking his head. Momentarily, his mask of easy suavity had slipped. 'Can we trust him? He wasn't exactly – how do you say it? – a barrel of laughs when he came over to Kortrijk.'

'You're jealous, thought Sterling, *just like Willem himself, only you've been trying not to show it.*

'It makes sense, Yves,' said Angela. She had picked up the vibe too and had put her hand on his arm. A smile played over the old woman's face.

Albertin nodded briskly and emphatically, regaining his composure. 'OK. If Willem has to talk with other nationalists, that's certainly something I can't do. My Flemish dialect is good, of course, but there are some words I can never pronounce properly, and that will show me up.'

'Shibboleths, Yves,' said omniscient Angela. 'Exactly.'

'Right,' said Sterling. 'Here's the plan. It's 2.30pm. I'm going to go over to Ypres to see Willem and

Christina and to enlist Willem's help, hopefully. Angela, if you set off back to Kortrijk now, you'll probably be able to pick up your passport and stuff and get over to Lille for a Eurostar to St Pancras and on to Oxford. Yves, what do you want to do? You can come with me to see the Van de Veldes or go back to Kortrijk to see if Big Man at least is around this afternoon. It would probably be a long shot...'

'... and remember,' said Albertin, 'the Big Man knows me. I think my time is better used by staying here in Comines and maybe seeing if I can find out his name and so on. I can rejoin you tomorrow in Kortrijk, Frank.'

Sterling nodded and got up from the sofa. The others followed him. 'Thank you very much for your help, Marie. It's been nice to have met you. We've got your phone number and we'll be in touch.'

'Well, I'm not going anywhere, and I'll be happy to conduct more... research.'

Angela weighed in with her own thanks. 'Yves is lucky to have you. You both seem to have had colourful lives...'

'Very colourful.' The old woman's hand fluttered.

By a quirk of the seating arrangements, Angela and Albertin were nearest the hallway and went first. Marie's hand went from fluttering and grasped Sterling's sleeve, pulling his face towards hers. Her eyes fixed on him. 'Yves's more colourful than mine,' she whispered. Then she winked and let him go.

Sterling acknowledged the intimacy and indicated that he'd registered the information. 'Thank you again for your help,' he said. 'Goodbye.' He eased the front door shut and caught up with Angela and Albertin clattering down the stairs.

'I'm down this way,' said Albertin, in the street. 'You can find your way back to the station?'

'Easily,' said Angela. She gave him a quick peck on the cheek. 'See you in a day or two, hopefully.' After Albertin had ambled off, she turned to Sterling. 'We're going opposite ways at the station, Frank. What's my brief?'

'What do you mean?'

'Well, you're sending me off to Oxford. What do I do when I get there?'

Sterling stepped into the road and sharply back onto the pavement, forced to by the furious jangling of a bicycle bell. A young girl in jeans and blouse swept past, her fine, blonde hair blowing back in the breeze, eyes rolling, head shaking. Crossing roads in Belgium, he couldn't get the hang of which way to look first, just like the tourists in England. 'It's Thursday today. Van Leuven, or somebody, wants the chest by Sunday. That's the window. That's when something is going to happen, if it happens at all. So… get to Oxford and go to the Ashmolean. Go and have a look at the Kortrijk Chest. See if you can get an appointment with someone in the museum's administration and warn them about what might happen.'

'What about the police?'

'What about them?'

'Well, shouldn't I warn them as well?'

'You've listened to me talk about the job enough times in the pub. What do you think?'

Angela reflected. 'The receptionist at the police station or the person on the switchboard, both civilians, will ask a few questions and pass the message on. If it gets to a real police officer, it will get a quick review and be filed somewhere, probably on the grounds that the backstory, a coded message in Flemish, is too outlandish to be taken seriously.'

'I taught you well,' murmured Sterling. 'You'll probably get the same reaction from people in the museum, but you might have more chance there. Anyway, do what's best. Do what you can. Respond to circumstances.'

'It's a bit vague, Frank. Really, I don't want to mess up.'

'You'll be all right. It's the F. Sterling way. Works every time.'

'In the end, then, we don't want anything to happen to the Kortrijk Chest, and we don't want it to go anywhere, right?'

Sterling stopped and thought. 'Actually, if there is some action, I don't know if I'm fussed. If you come back here and tell us the Chest has gone, then in a way we're on the right track. All clear?'

'As mud,' said Angela. They resumed their trudge, and at the station entrance hugged warmly. Soon they were waving goodbye to each other as Sterling's train pulled out towards Ypres. It was Angela's bad luck, on this one-track line, that hers was the forty-five minute wait for it to return and take her back to Kortrijk.

*

The last time Sterling had been in Ypres, he'd come by car and parked in the main square, the Grote Markt. He'd been to Poperinge, the last town down the line, by train, but that was in the other direction. He knew the station was close because there was a build-up of dwellings and population. On his left, there was a large, abandoned barracks, with small deer foraging in the vegetation between the blocks. From the station, it was a fifteen-minute walk to Hotel Sultan, the thriving business that supported three generations of the Van de Veldes. Rebuilt after its obliteration in the Great War and sustained by British and Commonwealth tourists, Ypres was different from other southwestern Belgian towns – livelier, more attractive, more diverse and clearly more prosperous.

Mrs Van de Velde was at reception. 'Good afternoon, Mr Sterling. Christina isn't here at the moment.'

'Mrs Van de Velde,' said Sterling. He didn't think that things would ever be less than strictly formal between them. 'I know. I phoned her half an hour ago. It's not her I've come to see this time. I understand that Willem is in, though.'

'My father? Well, yes...' She dialled a number and spoke for a few moments.

'He'll be down in a minute. How is the case going?'

'A lot of progress. We should be getting to the bottom of it in a day or two.' Sterling went over to the window and looked out on the square. Her mother, and presumably her grandfather, were the moneybags, but he regarded Christina as his principal, and he'd sit down with Christina when he was ready.

'*Meneer* Sterling?' Old man Van de Velde's voice was gruff.

Sterling remembered that Christina's grandfather had very little English. Mrs Van de Velde would have to be involved after all. 'Can we sit down on the sofa over here, the three of us,' he said.

'Are you sure?' said Mrs Van de Velde. Her laugh was almost identical to her daughter's. 'The last time you sat on that sofa, the police came and took you away. Maybe the sofa is bad luck.'

Sterling smiled. Perhaps she had a sense of humour after all. 'I got out of it, though, didn't I? And it all worked out in the end.'

'I believe it did. It would be better if I got a chair. Then I can face you and my father.'

'Willem,' said Sterling, 'we've seen Guy in Kortrijk and we don't think there is a girl involved.'

Daughter turned to father and translated. The old man replied. 'That's good news,' she translated.

'But we think that Guy is involved in something political in the run-up to the anniversary of the Battle of the Golden Spurs next Tuesday, and we think you might be able to help us get to the bottom of it.'

'*De Slag bij Kortrijk*,' said the old man after the translation, with some extra words.

'He's saying that it's called the Battle near Kortrijk, not the Battle of the Golden Spurs. He says that it was called *De Guldensporenslag* only from the seventeenth century, hundreds of years after the battle.'

God, this is hard work, Sterling thought. He nodded. He remembered that Marie had said roughly the same but mercifully without any touchiness. 'I stand corrected. Kortrijk, not the Golden Spurs.' The old man nodded back, satisfied, and started to speak. 'He still knows a lot of people in the movement, as he calls it,' translated the daughter. 'What do you need to know in particular?'

'The coded message that Christina gave us. Yves's friend cracked it. There's a meeting coming up this coming Sunday, 10th July. All we know is that it's at "the usual time and place". We could do with knowing when and where, and, better still, what it's about. Can Willem help?'

The question was asked, and a conversation in Dutch ensued, at times heated. Finally, Mrs Van de Velde turned to Sterling. 'Nationalist politics can be dangerous, I said to my father. So can crossing the road, he said to me. He's said that he'll help you as much as he can – for Christina. He'll ask carefully around. He has some friends in Kortrijk too. His idea, now that the anniversary is coming up, is to say that he wants to get involved again, wants to help. It might take a little while.'

'Thank him for me. If we get something it will be useful, I'm sure.'

Christina's mother wrung her hands abstractedly. 'Don't you think it's maybe time that you asked Guy himself what's going on?'

'I thought that wasn't on the agenda. The time to do it might be soon, but we lost him this afternoon so there's no opportunity now anyway.' Sterling got to his feet. 'No cops this time, Mrs Van de Velde.'

'No,' she smiled. 'Not yet, anyway.' She looked directly into Sterling's eyes. 'In future, please call me Agnes…, Frank. Christina will be back soon. Would you like to wait for her? Have some coffee?'

Sterling smiled but shook his head. 'I need to get back to Kortrijk shortly,' he lied. If he saw Christina, he'd get distracted. She'd want to know about every part of the investigation, and she'd be harder to resist than her relatives. There was another thing. It wasn't just the opas she had a hold over. He shook hands with father and daughter.

'Thank you again, Willem… and Agnes.'

'*Het is allemaal voor Christina,*' said Willem, his voice husky.

'It's all for Christina,' translated the daughter dutifully.

'My feeling exactly,' said Sterling softly as he stepped out of Hotel Sultan and into the square. For once, he hadn't needed the translation.

Chapter 13

From Comines to Kortrijk, where she collected her bag from the hotel, and through the decaying industrial hinterland from Kortrijk and eventually to Lille Flanders station, Angela worried about her assignment, and specifically its lack of focus. But along the wide, graceful Avenue Le Corbusier, connecting Lille Flandres to Lille Europe, her mood changed, and the usual shenanigans at Passport Control failed to shake it. She thought it might partly be because she was going back to England in style and not on the hick, interminable cross-country route, and uninhibited by Frank's funny ways.

She used her phone on Eurostar to find somewhere to stay in Oxford – a bed and breakfast in Summertown. How straightforward that was, compared to the Frank Sterling approach, which almost certainly would have been to wait till he got there. By the time she had arrived, after a post-rush hour transfer across London to Paddington, a train from Paddington to Oxford and a taxi ride to Summertown, she had decided what she'd do at the Ashmolean the following day. She got an unconditionally warm welcome from the bed and breakfast owner, an elegant, delicate-featured woman with expensive make-up and thick, grey hair pinned up with an elaborate Japanese-style wooden pin. Angela's room was too chintzy for her taste but clean and comfortable, and she settled in for an early night. There was no point in phoning Frank. He'd probably not answer, and she had nothing much to report. Panjit was on his anti-terrorism course and still incommunicado, which was lucky in a way. If they'd spoken, he would have asked questions she wouldn't have been prepared to answer.

The landlady in the morning was ready to gossip. Angela had been to one of the Oxford colleges, Oriel, for an interview during her A Levels. She'd got an offer too, but the pull of London had still been too strong in that moment of her life. She let that be known, said she was back for a business meeting, and then shut down the conversation. The truth bordered on the exotic and the romantic – a medieval code; a wooden chest carved with a European battle scene ending up at the Ashmolean and under threat of seizure; and a mission to... well, do something, anyway – you could hardly make it up. Taking her cue from Frank, the least anyone knew about her and her mission the better.

After breakfast – fruit, muesli and wholemeal toast rather than anything close to the full English – Angela and the landlady parted on good terms. 'Somebody will be here at midday when you come back for your case. You know where we are for next time' were her parting words.

From Summertown, Angela walked down into the city on a warm sparkly day, marred only by the tangy taste in her mouth, and itchiness in her nostrils, generated by snail-paced traffic. She'd checked the opening time – 10am – and, after half an hour of brisk walking, pulled up outside the Doric columns and arch of the museum just as there were signs of life – keys applied to heavy glass doors, and sandwich boards getting propped up outside. She took a breath and wiggled her shoulders. Time for action.

In the atrium, staff were moving into position. An attendant at the doors, short and thin, with dark skin and puffy eyes, looked her up and down and stepped aside. She judged that her bag wasn't big enough to trouble with a locker. She took a guide and put a fiver in the heavy duty transparent plastic contributions box. She knew all the ploys. Such boxes were rarely emptied, and it was already stuffed with cash to let new arrivals know how generous their predecessors had been and to encourage matching largesse.

She picked up a floor plan from a nearby stand, thinking that she'd like to see the Kortrijk Chest, the object of such interest, before she took her next step. She sat down on a bench near the reception counter and leafed through the slick document in her hand. If a visitor wanted to learn about China up to AD 800, it would be easy: go to Level G, Gallery 10. Music and Tapestry: go to Level 2, Gallery 39. Medieval Cyprus: go to Level 1, Gallery 34. But the Kortrijk Chest – depicting a medieval Franco-Flemish, or, on a grander scale, a European battle of 1302 – was a greater challenge. There was no gallery for Medieval France, or Medieval Flanders, or even Medieval Europe. Angela searched and searched and found nothing.

She went up to the information desk – reluctantly – aware of her height, her blackness, her presence, in every way memorable. A prim young woman, small nose, mean mouth, chin sloping down into her neck, dragged her eyes reluctantly from the computer screen.

'I'm looking for the Kortrijk Chest,' said Angela. 'I can't see it in any of the galleries.'

The young woman said nothing. Her eyes returned to the screen as her fingers jitterbugged over the keyboard. There clearly weren't hundreds of daily requests for directions to the chest, or pilgrims paying homage, and this member of staff did not seem familiar with it. Miss Prim looked up. 'It's normally described as the Courtrai Chest. I couldn't find Kortrijk to begin with. Level 2, Gallery 41, England 400–1600. It's in with the Alfred Jewel.' She turned back to the screen. Angela had been dismissed.

Her assertive self would have tarried and engaged, made eye contact and insisted on courtesy. Her passion for librarianship and polite, informed, intelligent service would have compelled her. Her assistant Kerry and team of volunteers knew exactly what her standards were. Her library was popular and thriving. Here, there were issues of culture and leadership. But as she was on a mission, she recognised the advantages of off-handedness and anonymity. Quietly, she turned to the stairs and made her way to Gallery 41. The Alfred Jewel, inscribed with the words "Alfred ordered me made" in an ancient language, and originally attached to a rod to make a text pointer, was delicate and magnificent. Larger but less magnificent was the Kortrijk Chest in a neighbouring cabinet. Angela dragged her eyes from the jewel and studied the chest, about the size of a two-drawer filing cabinet on its side, with dark, almost black wood, and intricate carvings, on one panel, of Flemish foot soldiers with goedendags and French knights on horseback. Truthfully? It was difficult to imagine, impressive as this was, that it was an object of desire for a band of Flemish nationalists.

Aside from her mission, her professional interest was piqued. There had been a curation module in her master's degree in librarianship, and that made her realise what a strange place it was to put the chest, separated from the Alfred Jewel in time by many hundreds of years and more significantly in geography by the English Channel. There was a strong textile trading connection between the great Flandrian cities and England in the thirteenth and fourteenth centuries, but in curating terms that was a tenuous link at best. In the end, the problem remained. If not in Gallery 41, where did the Kortrijk Chest belong? There was no obvious answer.

Immediate objective accomplished, she went back downstairs to find Miss Prim. A flicker, tiny but definite, passed over the young woman's features as she noted Angela's presence back at the desk. The middle of her forehead, just above the eyes, puckered into a frown. 'Yes?'

No, Angela thought. *Not a "Yes?" full of insolence and impatience. Instead: "Hello again. I hope you found what you were looking for. How can I help now?" That's what I should be on the other end of.* She bit her bottom lip. 'I need to see someone in authority. A curator. The duty manager.'

Miss Prim looked her up and down.

Angela folded her arms and fixed her with the Wilson stare. People were known to quail at ten paces. 'It's important, and if I don't see someone shortly, the consequences for you will be serious.'

The young woman's neck reddened and the flush spread upwards seamlessly to her cheeks. She picked up a handset from under the counter, dialled from a keypad and swivelled away. Her fine, dark hair fell over her face as her head bent down and she spoke softly into the 'phone. She turned back to Angela. 'What's it about?'

'May I ask what it's about?' Angela replied, in an angry attempt at customer care training. 'No, you may not. Just tell who you're speaking to get out here and stop messing me around.'

Hair flopped over face. High revolving chair swung away. Voice petered to nothing again. Visitors around the atrium sensed something – atmosphere, incident. The small security man looked over, dithering. Should he leave his post and come over, or should he let things ride? Obscurely, or maybe not, Angela thought of The Clash and a song from way, way before her time, about staying or going.

'Someone will come out in a minute,' said Miss Prim.

'Thank you,' said Angela. 'I'll be on that bench over there.'

Ten minutes. Fifteen. Angela was fuming. You wouldn't treat a dog like this. She was about to go back up to the desk and deliver a broadside, when a tall man emerged from the door behind the reception desk. Sandy hair, thinning. Narrow face stuck on a stringy neck and skinny torso. Patterned bow tie. Brown corduroy jacket. Blue slacks. None matching. His eyes followed the receptionist's to Angela. He paced over on long, bandy legs and loomed over her. 'Michael de la Vere, assistant curator. You asked to see "someone".' Brisk, a mixture of bored, arrogant and patronizing. 'And you are?'

Alarm bells started ringing. If something happened here, Angela would be vulnerable. She'd paid cash at the bed and breakfast, and Frank had given her euros for the journey over – "legitimate expenses" – he'd called it. 'Michelle Smith,' she lied. 'This is a bit public...'

Was there a hint of an eye roll? She folded her arms and crossed her legs.

'Follow me.'

'Please...,' Angela muttered. The place needed a programme of wholesale customer-focused re-training. Official and petitioner went behind reception through the door, into a narrow passageway and then into a small meeting or interview room, barely larger than a cubby hole. A table separated two plastic chairs on which they settled, facing each other. The tatty, windowless, stuffy room was in sharp contrast to the airy splendour of the atrium and galleries. Visitors didn't usually get to go in here.

'It's a busy day today,' said the assistant curator. 'We're expecting artefacts for a new exhibition. What's your problem?'

'It's not "my" problem, Mr de la Vere. It's potentially yours. I'm part of an investigation team and during our case my associates and I came across a message indicating that one of your artefacts might be a target.'

De la Vere leaned back in his chair. His body conveyed what his mouth, for the moment, did not. Disbelief. 'You're an investigator?'

'Temporarily, yes.' While on a week's leave from the day job as librarian at Sandley Library.

'Right. And what is the artefact in question?'

'The Kortrijk Chest.'

'The Kortrijk Chest?' De la Vere eyes went up and right. He couldn't remember what it was or maybe where it was.

'Depicting the Battle of the Golden Spurs in 1302. It's in with Alfred's Jewel.'

'Oh yes. That chest. And how did it become a target?'

'We cracked a coded message from people we think are Flemish nationalists, who seem to want it back.'

'You cracked a code...? Flemish nationalists...' De la Vere snorted. 'It's a bit, well, you know, far-fetched. The Alfred Jewel is worth a fortune, but that... Anyway, do you know how many cock-and-b... Do you know how many notifications we get about threats to our collections?'

Angela sprang up, the chair skittering back and knocking against the wall. Gradually, the smouldering anger that always lurked just beneath the surface of her psyche from her teenage gang days, had faded. Her academic and career success, and her integration into the Sandley community, had mellowed her. But now the anger came roaring back, and she was about to give it full rein in the face of this arrogant popinjay. Then she stopped. She didn't hear anything, and she couldn't see anything, but a sixth sense conveyed an alert.

De la Vere's reaction, a cocked head, stillness, listening, indicated that she wasn't the only one. 'Excuse me,' he muttered. Abruptly he got up and left the room, leaving the door open. Almost immediately, she got up and followed him down the corridor to the atrium. Neither of them had been wrong. The scene that greeted her was utter chaos. Visitors milled around, wailing, shouting and screaming. Staff, their credentials bouncing from their lanyards, were vainly trying to restore some calm and order. An alarm that had started a few seconds ago whump-whumped with monotonous, ear-battering persistence. De la Vere was nowhere in view. There was probably a behind-the-scenes emergency protocol he was masterminding from somewhere in the back office. Credit to Miss Prim, she looked as though she was effectively tending the security man on the main glass doors, from whose nose blood was dripping. A scarlet splash supplied thin rivulets down the glass door, which had a spider's web dent. The man looked dazed.

Angela knelt down beside them and offered her little pack of tissues. 'What happened?'

'A raid,' said the young woman. The drama and excitement had loosened her tongue. 'Four men. Dark clothing. Balaclavas. They must have come in as visitors and then changed in the cloakroom or somewhere. They came lurching down the stairs with a big dark box, shouting and making a racket, waving baseball bats. Eddy did his best, but one against four... I think his nose is broken.' Eddy looked up. Resentful. Eyes, deep brown, that said I'm just a security man on the front door. I check bags and put a damper on rowdiness. Foiling armed raids is not in the job description.

'Any other casualties?'

'I don't think so. It all happened so quickly.'

'There was a van in the road,' offered Eddy. 'They put whatever it was they stole in the back and scarpered.'

Angela nodded. Slowly, order was returning. The whump-whump stopped abruptly, replaced by a ringing silence punctuated by small noises – someone sobbing, the clatter of a walking stick clattering down the staircase, a murmur of shocked, eerily whispered conversation. One or two tourists had their phones out. A small corner of Facebook would shortly be in a frenzy. Angela's sense of vulnerability returned with a wave of anxiety.

Miss Prim was using the paper tissues to stem the bleeding from Eddy's nose. Angela stood up quietly and slipped away in a small exodus from the atrium and down the steps outside. Her brain was whirring. She was lucky she hadn't given de la Vere her real name, but CCTV footage would show her entering the museum and going via reception upstairs to Gallery 41 and the Kortrijk Chest, coming back down and engaging with museum staff. She could see the newspaper and TV reports: blurry but identifiable pictures of her and the phrase, somewhere in the text, 'police want to speak urgently with this woman, who was in the museum at the time of the raid.'

Already some hot-shot local radio journalist would have got wind of the story. 'Reports are just coming in of a raid on Oxford's Ashmolean Museum. Police and ambulance services are racing to the scene. We'll have updates for you as soon as we know more...'

Angela had come to alert the Ashmolean to possible hostile interest in the Kortrijk Chest and lo and behold it had come violently to pass exactly as she was meeting de la Vere. If she was picked up for questioning, some bright spark detective would immediately jump to the wrong conclusions.

In her head, she rapidly played through the imaginary interrogation.

"It was a brilliant plan. You're the accomplice. You divert the attention of the duty officer from the actual raid."

"OK, so why would I mention the Kortrijk Chest rather than make a complaint or use almost any other diversion? Why would I even bother **being** a diversion – in full view of CCTV cameras and introducing myself to an assistant curator? Why would I go up to the gallery and look at the chest beforehand?"

"Ah, well – the plan was brilliant but the execution was stupid – or maybe there's something you're not telling us… Do yourself a favour here, Ms Wilson…"

She'd get out of it eventually, since she was completely innocent, but she knew from Frank that "helping the police with their inquiries" would be a long drawn out performance. Not only that, but she'd have to reveal all the details of the case, and Frank wouldn't be pleased about that. Nor would the principals in Ypres. She owed the Ashmolean nothing, especially not according to Frank's moral code. De la Vere had had his chance. He had been just about ready to blow her off, and apart from the raid itself and Eddy's broken nose, there had been no other injuries or even fatalities.

She needed to get her stuff from the bed and breakfast, but even that would be tricky. The local Oxford radio station had been on at breakfast, so the landlady, if she was still listening as she went about her morning chores, might already know that something had happened. There was surveillance pretty much everywhere Angela had been. Her only consolation was something that Frank always said, from his own experience on the job. The police might seem effective and efficient in the immediate aftermath of a major crime, all cylinders firing, blues and twos flashing and wailing, and the rest of it, but it was more blue-arsed fly (in his words) than focus.

Even so, they'd eventually get organised. Whichever way Angela looked at it, the conclusions were the same. She was in deep trouble. And she was going on the run.

Chapter 14

Sterling was tempted to cross the square, go down Diksmuidestraat and pop in to see Martin de Groot at his bicycle shop a few hundred metres down. If Martin wasn't busy, he'd take Sterling into his pristine back office and they'd catch up, chew the fat and listen to dated English language rock music on the radio. During the conversation, they'd inevitably discuss the merits and disadvantages of mudguards on bicycles – except that as far as de Groot was concerned there were no disadvantages.

Instead, Sterling started off back to the station. With luck, he'd be able to catch up with the cycle shop owner when the case was over. If he didn't want to be diverted by seeing Christina, it seemed unfair to her to see someone else. He'd established from Agnes Van de Velde, reporting from her daughter, that Guy, following his usual monthly pattern, had not returned home last night.

The train ride back to Kortrijk was quickly getting familiar. Deer continued to graze in the abandoned army compound. The countryside beyond was still studded with walled Commonwealth cemeteries of greensward carpets and geometrically immaculate white gravestones. The train again flitted past all the small, interchangeable towns of red brick and Flemish gables.

In Kortrijk, he did a quick patrol around St Martin's Church close to both entrances to the beguinage, expecting nothing and getting it. He gravitated to the Grote Markt through the connecting lane. It was six o'clock. A pre-prandial Hommelbier on a café terrace looking over the square would suit him very well. There was something about Kortrijk. He'd noticed it when he and Angela had first arrived yesterday evening – not enough to talk about it with her – more an intuition than anything tangible, and it was the same now. Edginess. Excitement. He trawled back through all his experience on the job, trying to find clues, reminders.

It came to him. Sometimes he'd been drafted in to help with football matches up at Gillingham. Before kick-off, the town had the same atmosphere. A sense of build-up. A hint of violence. The notion that things might run out of control, suddenly and viciously. He'd never been comfortable with it, but some of the lads from the London fringes, young officers who'd been fans at Charlton and Millwall and further in – they'd loved it.

He looked around the square. The cafés were full of people of all ages, but youngsters milled around the belfry. Sterling paid little attention to fashion, but it struck him that young Kortrijk people – the ones he was seeing – were not following the fashions of their British and Western European counterparts. He saw little denim and no jeans, but peasant blouses and simple, loose-fitting trousers, shirts and skirts in muted colours. Something else struck him. Usually, right hands contained mobiles and iPhones, and leads trailed from them to earbuds. In these clusters and small groups, he saw none of the digital wizardry of modernity. It was as if old Kortrijk – the medieval beguinage and church – had spilt out into the twenty-first century. He thought of Morris Dancers and the street fairs of the various Kentish coastal towns he and his restless father had flitted between as he'd grown up.

The beer tasted good – one thing, he reflected, that the Belgians did well. But it wasn't over-enthusiasm to get it down that caused him almost to choke as he took in the panorama. It was the Big Man who appeared as if from nowhere in the far bottom corner of the square. If it had been almost anyone else, Sterling would not have recognised him because of the distance, but the man's bulk and posture were unmistakable. Instinctively, Sterling slipped down in his chair, although there was little chance of the Big Man even seeing and knowing him, let alone picking him out from the throng on the crowded terrace. The giant was with someone else, too far away to identify, but in Sterling's memory banks there was the vaguest sense of familiarity. All he could think of was that it didn't seem to be Guy Verstraete. The two men were strolling about in animated conversation in a small zone in front of a building obscured by a network of scaffolding enclosed in vast sheets of plastic. Occasionally, the duo stopped. One would nod with his chin at something and the exchange would continue. Then, like actors exiting from a stage, the two men disappeared in the direction from which they'd originally come.

Sterling finished his beer and set off diagonally across the square. Around the corner, there was no sign of them, and they could have gone down any of the dense side streets. Sterling turned to the back of the building. The scaffolding and the sheeting only covered the façade in the square. Here, a crane stood eyeless guard over a construction site partitioned off from the pavement by chipboard panels plastered with utopian pictures of what the redevelopment would look like when finished. Sterling stood on the corner, hands in pockets. This must be another piece of the jigsaw puzzle. He was getting a whole table-top full of them now. But that didn't mean he was getting any closer to fitting them together.

*

He was asleep in bed after an evening of complete blandness before anything else happened. But he'd woken up, and his copper's gut told him that something potentially very interesting was happening in the vicinity. He padded over to the window and looked out over Schouwburgplein. To his right he could see into – what was it? – Doorniksestraat, and a fire engine, emergency lights flashing, followed closely by a police car, turned down into the pedestrianized Lange Steenstraat. He looked at his watch – 3.20 in the morning. Further communication from his gut propelled him into his trousers, shirt, summer hoodie and shoes, and in less than two minutes he'd roused the night porter and was walking out into the still-warm darkness. Central Kortrijk had an eerie quality from a combination of muted orange street lights and the toned-down displays of the shops. Sterling padded along in the direction of the blue lights and joined the gawpers, insomniac dog-walkers, early morning postal staff and shadier characters emerging from the shadows.

A pair of young female police officers, in dark navy uniform and glengarry caps, were setting up barriers hauled from the back of their squad car. Obviously on the graveyard shift, they were shouting something that might have been translated as "keep back" or "get back" at the swelling crowd. In front of them, a fire engine was stationed at a haphazard angle to a storefront from which flames roared and black smoke billowed into the air. Shattered glass crunched underfoot.

The little audience watched as fire-fighters swarmed to their work, hoses unrolling and bodies scurrying purposefully about. A jet of water stuttered and then surged, and two men struggled momentarily as they wrestled to direct it at the flames. There was an immediate effect, as the flames abated and the smoke intensified. A crash resounded as a heat-mangled bit of metal broke off from the wall and clattered onto the pavement, sparks flaring. In the same moment, a small figure emerged into view on the far side of the barriers, wavy, flaming red hair unmistakable even in the shadows. Instantly Sterling knew the target – the optician's shop from which Guy and Big Man had been unceremoniously ejected the day before. On the pavement lay the grotesquely contorted remains of the pair of spectacles once rakishly affixed above the shop.

Sterling edged round the barrier towards the woman, debating whether he'd have any luck if he tried to engage her. Dried tears left two streaks down her pale face, but in her eyes Sterling saw the anger of yesterday. He was about to take the plunge when the woman spotted someone else in the crowd, a man of medium height, fortyish, with thick hair of indeterminate colour in the light of the blaze, wringing his hands. An uncanny trick of angle reminded Sterling of Guy Verstraete – his handsome much older brother or even father. He watched as the woman plunged through a small knot of bystanders and pulled the man aside. Sterling sidled back out of the light towards the spot he thought they'd retreated to. Soon he was eavesdropping on a furious broadside from the woman – helplessly in fact – because the tirade was in rapid-fire Dutch. Her forefinger, with a long, manicured, red-painted nail, jabbed into the man's chest. His hands were together, as if praying.

There was another crash from the stricken building in its swift, direct transition from going concern to dereliction, further shouting from the police officers as the little crowd surged forward to get a better view and scrambling of renewed energy from the fire-fighters. When Sterling turned back into the shadows, the woman and the man had vanished. His policeman's antennae picked up something else. Another car had pulled up next to the patrol car, engine noise masked by the shop-blaze. Two men emerged and gently pressed shut the doors. Not crowd control. Investigation. Criminal investigation. Some arsonists loved to return to the scene, look at the flames, feel the heat on their faces, smell the smoke and the burning, and revel in the damage, the disarray, the scampering and the scrabbling, all their handiwork. One of the detectives raised a small hand-held video camera and fiddled with the controls. It would get better images than night-time CCTV. The other produced a notebook.

Sterling knew it was time to make himself scarce. He flipped up his hood and eased away into the blackness. He'd go around St Martin's Church into the Grote Markt, pick up Doorniksestraat and slip back into the hotel. He'd live to fight another day.

Chapter 15

'**M**ike?'

'Yep.' The publican of the Cinque Ports Arms, Sandley, and ex-spy, was famed for his economy of words.

'Thank goodness. It's Angela.'

'Angela. I thought you were in Belgium with Frank.'

'I was. Something came up in Kortrijk, and Frank and I agreed that I should come back to England to check where it led to. I did, and now I'm in a pickle.'

'OK, well, where are you calling from?'

'Oxford. North Oxford. A phone in Summertown.'

'Give me a sitrep, and then we'll have a clear idea what to do next.'

When Angela had finished her story, and had received reassurance, she was relieved. Mike was one of the most capable people she knew, matched only by his wife, Becky. It wouldn't really have mattered who'd come to the phone so long as it was one of them. Things were already improving.

'Here's what to do. I know Summertown, and it's probably got even more fancy shops in it than when I was there a decade ago. Find a clothes shop, buy a scarf and wrap it over your head – not like a hijab, Angela, just so that it looks western-style fashionable. Abandon your stuff at the bed and breakfast. From what you've said, the owner is reasonable enough, and you can collect it when the dust has settled. Catch a bus northward. Don't go back to the town centre. Keep your head down under the scarf and avoid the on-board cameras. There should be frequent buses to Kidlington. See if you can get a bus from Kidlington to Bicester. Don't use your phone. You were sensible to use the phone box. You've got my mobile number. Use that to contact me via another phone box in a couple of hours. Find an independent pub or café – somewhere that's less likely to have cameras. Get a paper and don't go anywhere with a radio on. I'll come up in the van, starting now.'

'Thanks, Mike.' The instructions had been bordering on the loquacious. Angela couldn't remember that having happened before. 'Can you somehow get an update to Frank to put him in the picture?'

'I'll get Becky to try. We both know that Frank isn't the best communicator. One last thing, Angela…'

She sensed what was coming and wasn't wrong.

'… lose the aura.'

'I'll do my best.'

Mike was right about shops in Summertown. Angela found a headscarf to match the rest of her outfit virtually straight away and spent an arm and a leg buying it. Bearing in mind Mike's instruction, she wore it loosely around her head and shoulders rather than granny-style knotted under the chin and tapering to a point between the shoulder blades, vanity trumping dowdiness.

Three hours later – three hours of buses, suburban walks, and lunch with gin and tonic in a shady corner of a Bicester pub garden away from cameras and people, Mike picked her up and installed her in the specially engineered seat in the back of his van. Three hours after that, she was in another quiet corner, this time in the Cinque Ports Arms, safe for the moment and pondering her options. The bonus was that, using Mike's phone at a service station on the way down, she'd managed to speak to Sterling and update him on her adventures, and receive an update on his. Even hard-to-impress Frank Sterling was surprised at all that had happened and everything she'd packed in.

'You've been busy, Ange,' he'd said. 'Done well. I reckon I'm going to need you back over here before the balloon goes up, which has got to be soon, what with the Kortrijk Chest nicked, the firebombing and a battle anniversary coming up. Talk to Mike and Becky. They'll know a way that doesn't involve, shall we say, the usual channels. One of them coming over with you might be handy too, the way things are going.'

Her spirits, battered by the stresses and discomforts of the day, lifted, and she appreciated the compliment. But admitting to feelings and being pleased by praise somehow didn't seem to be de rigueur on this assignment.

'Wilco,' she said, as laconically as she could muster.

Chapter 16

Albertin strolled into the hotel at 8.15am, as arranged, joining Sterling in the restaurant area. Aurélien nodded conspiratorially from the desk and waved him through. Sterling had constructed a bacon butty, a nutritional world away from the healthy, high fibre, vegetarian breakfast Angela was enjoying in Oxford.

'Do you want anything to eat, Yves? Aurélien seems to have taken a shine to our little team, so I don't imagine he'll mind.'

'I've had breakfast, thank you, but a cup of diesel will be good.'

'Diesel?' said Sterling. He frowned.

Albertin shuffled in his seat – hardly noticeably. 'Sorry, even now I get the strangest words mixed up, and I've been a bit out of practice up till recently. Not diesel. Tea. A cup of tea.'

'Right,' said Sterling. He got up and went to the machine. Were 'diesel' and 'tea' words you could easily mix up if you were a foreigner? He shrugged to himself. Whatever.

The stout, cheerful young woman who managed the breakfast buffet bustled round as the two men conferred. The hotel seemed to be one of those places that were soulless and anonymous until customers stayed a day or two, and when they were known, staff started treating them like family.

Albertin sipped his tea as Sterling started the demolition of his butty. 'How did you get on in Ypres yesterday, Frank?'

'Fine. I didn't see Christina, but I saw Agnes and Willem in the hotel. Agnes translated for me.'

'Agnes, eh? What's that expression you English use? You've got your feet under the table there. More than I and my family ever managed.'

'Well, I didn't have a son who...' *I'm rising to the bait*, reflected Sterling. *There are undercurrents in Christina's family, but they're nothing to do with me.* He tried again. 'Agnes wants a result, just like the rest of you. She's bankrolling this and getting on with me is going to help her get what she wants. And I'm on first name terms with everyone else. Anyway, Willem's on board. He's going to sound out some of his active nationalist friends and see if he can find out about the meeting on Sunday.'

'Forgive me,' said Albertin the emollient. 'I can be a bit too sensitive. Remember, I haven't had as much opportunity as Willem to know my granddaughter. What's the plan today, Frank?'

'We'll hear from Angela in Oxford at some stage, probably around lunchtime. That might mean we go in a certain direction here. Guy didn't go back to Ypres last night, so he'll be around here if he didn't go to England. Willem will probably have something for us in due course. There were a couple of other things that happened which we can follow up. Have you found out who the Big Man is? You said you'd seen him occasionally in Comines.'

'Not yet. How do you say it? – I'm still making enquiries.'

Sterling nodded. 'Well, after you and Angela had gone yesterday, I saw him.'

'Really? Where?'

'Here in Kortrijk, obviously. In the main square, right at the far end. If it had been anyone else, I wouldn't have recognised them. He's a big bloke, and you can't really miss him, whatever the distance. He was walking about with another bloke.'

Albertin leaned forward, blinking. 'Yes?'

'Yeah. I'd never seen him before, I don't think. Too far away.'

Albertin leaned back. 'Not, perhaps, the man you saw in the beguinage?'

'It's possible, but it would be a coincidence. There was something else too, which I'll show you in a few minutes. A firebombing.'

'A what?'

'At about three in the morning, someone torched the optician's shop that Guy was kicked out of yesterday. It was a smouldering wreck last night. It will be a damp smouldering wreck this morning.'

'Shocking.'

'It would be difficult to add two and two up and get anything other than four. What I think we'll do before anything else is see if there's any further protection-style activity, if that's what it is, going on this morning. After that, there are two people I'd like to talk to this afternoon if we can track them down. One is the optician and the other is a bloke she was having a conversation with outside her blazing business in the early hours. They disappeared out of it before I got my opportunity.

The optician, if we can find her, will lead us to the mystery man. We'll have to tread carefully. The police were videoing the scene last night, and they'll already have spoken to the optician. I don't want us to be on their radar before we have to be.

'You go down the main drag, Yves, and I'll hang around the church in sight of both the exits of the beguinage. About halfway down, you'll see the burnt-out optician's. Phones at the ready. It might not come to anything, but we'll give it a whirl.'

As it turned out, the corner of St Martin's Church did give a view, between the trees, of the small passageway entrance to the beguinage, but not the main one that had Begynhof St Elisabeth inscribed over the archway. Instead, Sterling installed himself a little further down on the right angle at the Café Rouge, one sight line down the lane and the other past the restaurant at ninety degrees. He settled to wait in a slight recess in front of the white roller shutter of a garage and tried to give the impression that he was waiting for a rendezvous.

The town was in the process of coming to life. A young girl strode past, face painted and powdered for a day at a beauty counter, grinding her cigarette out on the cobbles. Cyclists rattled past, and a removal van appeared further up towards the church from whose cab two men in blue overalls sprang and started bustling, the driver much older than his mate. Twenty-five minutes passed, slowly. Soon the café would be opening, and Sterling would no longer be able to lurk without being noticed. A chair outside the café would only cover observation of the passageway. It didn't look as if Guy and the Big Man, if they were around and based in the beguinage, were making an early start, or indeed any start at all.

Boredom, and hankering for the jag of a market square cup of coffee, fosters errors. Sterling all but missed the short, nondescript figure who stole like a thief from the passageway. It wasn't Guy, and it certainly wasn't Guy's giant companion from yesterday, but Sterling decided straight away that he was a person of interest, and therefore worth following. Sterling slipped out from the recess, fumbled for his phone and as he started off after the figure disappearing around the far end of St Martin's Church he pressed speed dial for Albertin. 'Yves, I'm on the move. It's not Guy or the Big Man, but Pieter Van Leuven, the man Angela and I spoke with yesterday in the exhibition house in the beguinage. It looks as though he's coming your way. If I'm right, he'll come out in Grote Kring, about fifty metres further down from the burnt-out opticians. I'm assuming no one of note, like Guy, has come your way beforehand.'

'No. See you shortly,' replied Albertin.

*

Sterling had been right. Van Leuven was about thirty metres ahead when he entered Grote Kring, an insignificant man in drab grey and brown, his bald head covered by a battered hat that didn't belong to the current century or any other as far as Sterling could imagine. Angela might have a theory, or even Willem, but all that would have to wait. Van Leuven walked at a steady pace, but with a limp in his left leg. The shops and bars at the less fashionable end of the high street held no interest to him. His attention was entirely and doggedly focused on something beyond. Soon, after a forlorn pharmacy with its expanding and contracting green cross electronically flashing, a jumble of roadworks separated the pedestrian area from a busy main road.

Sterling and Albertin, who had joined the surveillance further back, looked quizzically at each other as the workmen hailed Van Leuven with smiles and thumbs up. Van Leuven bobbed his head and grimaced as if embarrassed by the fuss. He crossed the main road, shaking his head and clearly tut-tutting as the arterial road sliced through what had clearly been the old and established part of the town, and then continued westward flanked by busy traffic. A hundred metres down, he turned right and immediately disappeared. Sterling and Albertin upped their pace, and in a few short moments reached what looked like a classic nineteenth-century faux-medieval greystone archway. It was flanked by small decorative towers with mean arrow-slit apertures on each side and crenellations across the top.

Albertin pointed to the shield and inscription between crenellations and arch.

'Behold,' he said, a faint, sardonic smile across his handsome features, 'the Black Lion of Flanders and Groeningeveld 1302. This is where the Flemish nationalists worship. Near this spot is where their ancestors beat the French knights.'

Sterling looked through the arch and down the handsome, wide pathway, flanked by tall elm trees. Van Leuven's small figure limped onwards. 'What's he going to do down there?'

'Who knows?' said Albertin.

They set off again, keeping at a decent distance and ready to veer off the path and onto the grass, like the dog-walkers, and mothers with their pushchairs and small children. Sterling wasn't sure if Van Leuven would recognise him but was taking no chances. One hundred metres beyond the arch, Van Leuven stopped in front of a grey metallic sculpture redolent of two pairs of bandy-legged compasses melded together. It could have been Sterling's imagination, but he fancied that he saw his quarry imperceptibly genuflect and dip his head. Van Leuven stood still for perhaps thirty seconds before moving on to a grander monument a little further on. The sprawling base depicted figures of soldiers and horses and weapons fashioned in high relief on grey stone. The edifice was topped by a dramatic, cloaked, golden woman in flowing robes holding a spear aloft in her left hand, her right grasping the mane of a roaring lion.

Van Leuven circled the monument slowly, taking in every feature. With the Walloon Albertin restless and sceptical by his side, Sterling tried to concentrate. If Van Leuven's demeanour meant anything, it was as if he was drawing strength from the symbols in the little park, steeling himself, seeking justification.

Having limped around his circuit, Van Leuven started back the way he came. In anticipation, Albertin and Sterling had eased away to the park's boundary hedge to the right, and they fell in behind Van Leuven as he picked up his pace.

'Well, that was a waste of time,' muttered Albertin. Symbols of Flemish nationalism seemed to be making him irritable.

'You think?' said Sterling. 'In my experience as a plod, there's plenty that is boring in this kind of activity, but not very much that doesn't add up to something in the longer term. We're building up a picture. Some things are relevant. Some things aren't.'

Albertin looked at his shoes. Then he glanced across at Sterling. 'Sorry, Frank. Again. It's strange sometimes, living in a country like Belgium. Most of the time you don't notice two cultures. You're in your own community. Then something comes up.'

'Alright,' said Sterling. Albertin was a funny one. You couldn't always predict which way he was going to go. Angela thought he was wonderful. His leftist politics aligned exactly with hers. He was urbane and cosmopolitan – at least compared to old Opa Willem. But somehow you knew where you were with Willem. He was gruff and surly – that was the image he presented, anyway – but straightforward, whereas Albertin was more complex, and provoked more complex feelings.

Sterling had no time for this. He speeded up, his spurt for a moment leaving Albertin in his wake and hurrying to catch up.

Van Leuven was approaching the Groeningeveld Arch. It would be frustrating to lose him on the other side.

Chapter 17

Van Leuven didn't go back the way he'd come, and that made things easier. Instead, he crossed the busy road at the arch and carried on into another park opposite the Groeningeveld. Sterling and Albertin followed him down the path and through a circular metal lattice-work structure into which the thin branches of small trees or large shrubs had been espaliered to create a cool, leafy arbour. Encased in the middle within was a raised dais that could have been a bandstand. At the other end, they watched him cross at a junction and continue straight down a quiet, one-lane central street perhaps parallel to the high street, past a café on the left and a hotel called The Square on the right, its whitewashed stone stretching down into Groeningestraat.

Fifty metres down, Van Leuven disappeared to the left, and the two pursuers upped their pace. Sterling began to feel disoriented, and Albertin didn't know Kortrijk very well either. They reached the gap between an office block and a building that was clearly modern but built in an older, medieval style, with arched, semi-oval windows and rounded roof. At this point, Sterling felt himself relax. The gap, blocked off from motor traffic by bollards and lined by saplings, would lead back towards the beguinage, if his geography was accurate, or to some other obvious destination.

His usually reliable instinct was correct. The gap widened and passed through an elegant brick wall into an attractive, grassy open space, relatively unaffected by the dry summer, with a small sign introducing them to Begijnhofpark. To their right was the front of the old-style building with an ultra-modern, brilliant-white annexe tacked on at right angles. There was no limping figure in the near distance, so Sterling knew Van Leuven had for now gone no further, and Albertin's hand on his arm confirmed that the other man was thinking the same thing. The Flanders Lion fluttered limply from a flagpole, and others that Sterling didn't recognise, from other flagpoles. The two men had found themselves almost at the entrance of the 1302 Kortrijk Museum.

Of one mind, they retreated behind the wall.

Albertin raised his eyebrows.

'Van Leuven has gone into the museum,' said Sterling. 'He probably knows it like the back of his hand, so he's not gone to see something, he's gone to see someone. He's met me fleetingly, but he'd probably not remember. We can't take a chance. He's not met you yet, so go into the museum as a tourist and see what he does. I'll wait at this bench.'

Albertin nodded and ambled off. Sterling settled down to wait. Through the foliage of the tree overhanging the bench, dappled sunlight warmed his upturned face. He closed his eyes and let his thoughts drift, taking advantage of the lull to get his energy back, energy depleted by his interrupted night's sleep. A scent of recently mown grass drifted over from the sward lapping up to the small courtyard of the museum and the wall in front of him. A blackbird twittered nearby, and there was a faint hum of insects foraging in the greenery.

How long had he been in Kortrijk? He and Angela had arrived on Wednesday and now it was Friday – only one clear day, and yet it seemed like weeks. His phone began its quiet buzzing. Normally, he hardly bothered to turn it on – nothing was that urgent except to a caller – but it was different on a case.

'Angela. How are you getting on?' He straightened up on the bench and focused, catching the vibe immediately. He listened on, keeping comments and questions short, and then gave his own update. Even he knew when to give encouragement, and there was still plenty Angela could do in Kortrijk.

'Wilco,' she said as they ended the call. One word, speaking volumes.

The fates were not letting Sterling catch up on his disrupted sleep. A few minutes later, Albertin appeared back at the bench and stood over him. 'He spoke to the museum manager. I can't really think of the words for him. Nervous, not very happy.'

'Timid? Edgy?' said Sterling.

'Yes, both. Not that pleased to see Van Leuven, though they clearly know each other well enough. He came around from the counter and took him into a side room. Van Leuven's just walking across the grass towards a car park, and if my calculations are right, that's the way back to the beguinage. We could still follow him if we go now...'

'No,' said Sterling, making a quick decision. 'He's finished his morning's business, I'd imagine. If he goes back into the beguinage, we won't really be able to follow. Let's go and see this bloke in the museum. Before we do, sit down. I've spoken to Angela. I might as well update you straight away...'

The museum entrance, through electric glass sliding doors, was in the whitewashed modern section. Hire bikes were lined up in the glass wall-window next to the doors, and behind them toilets, cloakrooms and lockers. At the junction of old and new inside, a map of Medieval Flanders was etched in black relief on the stone floor, with a large, slowly revolving representation of a pencil suspended obliquely above it, the point sticking into Kortrijk. Revolving atop the pencil was a large cube, tilted because of the angle of the pencil, and depicting idyllic Flandrian scenes – windmills, cyclists on car-free lanes, and young women in traditional clothing, smiling with preposterous joy.

A thin, angular woman sat behind the counter by a cash till, beehive of greying hair, matching grey eyes, mean mouth over a stabbing chin. Further behind her was surely the man Albertin had referred to at the bench, the museum curator. *Interesting.* It was the same man who had been talking to the optician in front of the burning shop in the small hours. Sterling went over to the map, the pencil and the cube. He needed a moment. He glanced at Albertin and beckoned him over with a tilt of the head.

'Yves, what's the name of your intelligence service here in Belgium?'

'Sûreté de l'Etat.'

'Our one, the one that looks after abroad, is MI6. You're promoted to Sûreté de l'Etat. I'm MI6. We're working together, and you're translating. Let's go.'

'Wait a minute, Frank. I don't understand...'

The case was reaching a pivotal point. 'We've done enough shadow-boxing. Enough pussy-footing about. It's time for a more direct approach.' He made off to the welcome counter, a frowning Albertin in his wake.

'Good morning,' said Sterling. 'We need to speak to your colleague over there.' He pointed. Albertin translated.

The woman's mean mouth widened into a smile, transforming her severe face. She turned her head and called out a few Flemish words, repeating and projecting them more loudly. The man's head was bent low into a document on his desk, and every aspect of him indicated distraction – the thumb and forefinger rubbing his earlobe, a leg quivering as his foot tapped. He looked up and started. The woman said something else, and the man reluctantly rose and approached.

'Somewhere private,' said Sterling.

Albertin translated and translated the response. 'What's it about?'

'Something private. And important.' Sterling glanced at the woman and back to her colleague. He waited. Waiting was very effective for intensifying nervousness. Out of the corner of his eye, through the generous glass frontage, he could see a crocodile of young children, hand-holding two-by-two, flanked by teachers, with leader at the front and young rookie marshalling the rear. The fluorescent yellow tabards were dazzling in the midday sunlight. Shortly, chattering chaos would overwhelm silent tranquillity.

The man rose from his desk, even more good-looking than Sterling remembered him from the dimness of the night before, gave a let's-get-this-over-with shrug and lifted the hinged counter, directing Sterling and Albertin towards a small meeting room just before the entrance to the museum proper. It was ideal for Sterling's purposes. Bare room, high window, plastic chairs and a small table with a grey rectangular top – as fitting for a police interview room as for a museum. If Angela had been there she would have said there was a room in the Ashmolean just like it – an architect's afterthought. Sterling was assertive in setting it up – not for a leisurely exchange of views but for an interrogation, seating Albertin and himself on one side of the table, and the museum man, Jan Planckaert according to a surreptitious earlier glance at his name tag, on the other. The proximity of three bodies in the small room induced a sense of pressure. A high-pitched wave of noise seemed to roll up to and get muffled by the closed door. The children had arrived.

'Mr Planckaert,' said Sterling, 'I assume you're the manager here. I am David Smith, from MI6, the British security service, and this is René Henry, from your own Sûreté de l'Etat.' He'd struggled for a French-sounding name for Albertin, and just in time remembered an ex-Arsenal footballer. He felt Albertin quiver next to him, as when laughter is being suppressed. He glanced sideways, deadpan, trying to avoid infection, clasped his hands on the table, and waited for the translation. When he heard 'Staatsveiligheid', he knew Albertin had finished.

Planckaert launched into his reply and Albertin translated. 'He's not the manager. He's the curator. He's asking what this is about.' He paused. 'And he wants to see our... credentials. Some means of identification.'

Sterling smiled and leaned forward. 'You've been watching too many films. That's not how we do things in the security services, Mr Planckaert. That's why we're the security services. We need some information from you.' He stopped. Albertin translated. The room was air-conditioned, but beads of perspiration pricked up on the curator's low forehead as he spoke.

'He's asking what he could possibly know that we need to know.'

'Guy Verstraerte. Tell us about Guy Verstraerte.'

The curator looked down, the briefest of tells, and then spoke. Albertin translated. 'He doesn't know any Guy Verstraete.' Albertin was getting into his role. The urge to laugh was gone and he delivered his translations flatly and with an air of professionalism. Planckaert's anxiety was dissipating. Sterling knew from last night, confirmed by the curator's encounter with Van Leuven this morning, that he was a weak link. But even a weak link wouldn't break without the right pressure. Sterling's time on the job had taught him that, often. He changed tack.

'Let me tell you what we know, Mr Planckaert. Then you'll realise what serious trouble you're in, and why you should tell us what *you* know. If we don't sort things out here, you can kiss this cosy little job goodbye.

'Verstraete has come recently to the attention of the security services here and in England. We think he is either intimidating business people here in Kortrijk or collecting subscriptions. He is strongly connected to or part of a fringe new nationalist organisation. Earlier today, in England, a gang raided a museum in Oxford and stole the Kortrijk Chest and we can establish a link between Verstraete and that incident. We have seen Verstraete with Pieter Van Leuven and we have seen Pieter Van Leuven in conference with you not half an hour ago. Even worse for you...,' – Sterling waited as Albertin wrestled with the translation – '... you were observed at three in the morning at the firebombing of an optician's shop in the high street, and in a big argument with the optician herself. As I said, you're in serious trouble.'

The curator wrung his hands. Sterling was familiar with the dilemma. Damned if you do and damned if you don't. In trouble with the law or in trouble with your criminal associates. Then Planckaert straightened his back and pulled his hands apart, looking Sterling straight in the eye. When he spoke, his voice had developed a firmness that hadn't been there before.

'He doesn't have a clue what you're talking about,' said Albertin. 'We have no reason to arrest or detain him. He's going back to work.' Planckaert stood up stiffly and formally, as if expecting a challenge, and then, when it didn't materialise, opened the door and gestured with a sweep of his hand for his interrogators to leave.

'Tell him it doesn't end here.'

Planckaert left his interrogators in front of the map, the revolving pencil and the cube, and strode off into the depths of the museum. Sterling and Albertin went outside. The children and their teachers had gone – probably also into the museum.

Nobody noticed the assistant behind the counter, taking in the scene between Albertin and Sterling and her agitated colleague, and the fractious parting. Nobody noticed her pick up the phone.

Chapter 18

'This is not about Guy anymore, is it, Frank?'

Albertin and Sterling were walking through the small park towards the centre of the town, continuing from the direction they'd come after their detour into the museum. Sterling was curious to find out where they would come out. His eyes cast around while he considered Albertin's question.

'Yes, it is,' he said eventually, eyes settling back on his companion. 'But not just about him. And if we sort out the bigger thing, we'll find out everything Christina needs to know.'

'OK,' said Albertin, 'but really, what was the point of that?' He cocked his head back towards the museum. 'We've just moved ourselves into the open.'

'Exactly. It's time for them – whoever they are – to come to us. The battle anniversary is coming up and time is getting short.'

'Do you really know what you're doing?' Albertin blurted out.

Sterling stopped, unruffled, and considered. His way of operating didn't suit everyone. 'Kind of. There have been... similar situations in the past. It's worked OK then.'

Albertin shook his head and walked off a metre to two and then came back. 'It's dangerous. A firebombing. The Kortrijk Chest stolen in broad daylight...'

Sterling shrugged. 'Christina wants to know what Guy is up to. We're finding out. Of course, if you want to bail out...'

'No,' said Albertin. 'I suppose I can look after myself, and I imagine you can. Anyway, you need me.'

The grassy area gave way to a small car park, and then the two men were back in the square which contained the passageway entrance to the beguinage, with Café Rouge further along and St Martin's Church opposite.

'We've come in a kind of circle,' said Sterling. 'I'm thirsty. Let's cut through to the Grote Markt and have a drink.'

'Then what?'

'Dunno,' said Sterling. 'That's why I need a drink.' He ignored Albertin's muttering, just as he ignored Angela's occasional dissent. It might be private investigation at its most haphazard and ramshackle, but more often than not it got results.

*

In the museum, when the strangers had left – *surely, they couldn't really be intelligence agents* – Jan Planckaert reappeared and nodded at Marta on the welcome desk. 'I'm going up to see how the children and their teachers are getting on in the galleries.'

Marta nodded back and smiled an acknowledgement. She'd been with him in the museum for two years, but he'd never got used to how the smile transformed her face.

He needed to think. He cursed the time he'd ever set eyes on Pieter Van Leuven back in school in Bruges.

They'd set off down different thirty-year paths, but now they were back together, in Kortrijk of all places, and things were in turmoil just as he had been coming to terms with his quiet life and low-trajectory career. Pieter had been his usual charming, flattering, persuasive self. His proposition had been so attractive.

'I'm in Kortrijk for a reason, Jan. Over the last ten years I've made real progress. I've founded a new movement, the Liebaarts, which will achieve our lifelong dream – an independent County of Flanders, liberated from the French, Dutch, Spanish, and Walloon yoke. You can imagine how thrilled I was to learn that you are in charge of the 1302 Museum. Destiny. Destiny linked us together again. I don't just need your academic skills and knowledge. You were always good with money too. I want you as my historical adviser and treasurer.'

Pieter knew what other levers to pull. He said nothing about it directly, but soon after they had left school he had encouraged a young, clever but unfocused Planckaert to apply to the University of Ghent, acquire his degree in medieval history and then move on to his museum and curator qualifications, which they'd done together in Brussels. Planckaert's sense of obligation had dwindled over years and distance but was now strong again. His nationalist beliefs hadn't changed. If anything, they'd intensified, immersed in the theme of Flemish glory in the museum. So the chance to join a new nationalist organisation had been a strong incentive. His children were grown up and gone. His wife, Griet, was busy with her shop. He mused again on his dull life, and how he had been sinking into late-career torpor. Nothing could have improved the timing and thrust of Van Leuven's approach.

Eight months ago, it had been exhilarating. The meetings. The fervour. The energy. The activity, at times frantic. New blood, impatient with the snail-like pace to independence of the mainstream nationalist parties, had made him feel young again. He'd enjoyed the old-school approach to meetings and communication. That the next generation was embracing its Flemishness comforted him. His life had a renewed direction and purpose. Pieter, when he was surrounded by his followers, was at the peak of his charm and charisma, and he made Planckaert feel important through their long association. The museum curator felt a sense of belonging he hadn't experienced for decades, ignoring the inkling of something ominous stirring under the surface.

It hadn't taken long for things to grow darker, for the undercurrents to overwhelm the naïveté, including his own. Older, hard-eyed, grizzled nationalists had appeared on the fringes, uninterested in general meetings but huddled in their own cabals. Planckaert wasn't always a fool. He could recognise entryism when he saw the signs, and Pieter's role, pulling the strings. When Planckaert had questioned the source of the regular amounts of money that he faithfully paid on a weekly basis into a Liebaarts account at the local ING bank, and Pieter's, and others', cash withdrawals for mysterious 'miscellaneous purchases', he'd been told to keep quiet.

'Just keep the accounts, Jan,' Pieter had growled. 'Leave the strategy and all the rest of it to me.'

Now events were spiralling out of control, and the situation could only deteriorate up to and beyond the 1302 anniversary.

Things had not only grown darker. They had become wilder and more madcap. But that wasn't even the worst of it. That wasn't why Planckaert had got cold feet and decided that he wanted out. It had been the firebombing in the middle of the night that had dominated his thoughts. The violent criminality would have been unsettling in itself but to attack his wife's optician's. How could Van Leuven have sanctioned that? He had never got on with Griet, nor she with him, but for Van Leuven to override his long friendship with Jan, and sanction something so vindictive and destructive against his wife, was unforgivable.

Planckaert remembered his professional duties reluctantly. The school group and the teachers would be waiting. He plodded the back way up to the auditorium. Schools were the museum's bread and butter, but he was less able than ever to cope with the children's racket, and even the demands of the teachers, for whom the museum was a break from lesson preparation and routine, with himself a convenient substitute teacher. He arranged his face into a smile, trying to hold it together so it didn't become a rictus. In the noisy auditorium after the film, he managed half an hour of questions and answers, most of it plumbing the depths of banality, 'How did knights in armour go to the toilet?' setting the standard, asked by a tall plump child in a bright red baseball cap. He sighed with relief as the young mob finally disappeared around the corner of the museum and back, presumably, to their coach.

Alone in the merciful silence. his thoughts drifted again. Those men had been unsettling. The younger one with his policeman's hard stare. The older one with that faint sardonic look, as if there was nothing in the world he could take seriously. Intelligence officials – laughable

– but they were up to something. Their interest had been the tipping point.

Now, having made an uncharacteristically crisp decision, how was he going to extricate himself from the Liebaarts and Van Leuven's baleful influence? At the burning shop, he'd persuaded Griet that it was too dangerous for the moment for everyone – her, the children, himself – to go to the police. 'When it's all over,' he'd said, 'and it will be soon, I'll make sure things are right. I might be able to get you something in addition to the insurance pay-out.' He'd tell Pieter after the meeting on Sunday night that he was leaving, hand over the books, swear that he'd keep quiet about everything. They'd been friends for a long time. Pieter might not understand, single-minded as he was, but he'd accept the situation. Anyway, there was too much else happening, and Pieter was too near to realising his life's ambition on Tuesday to fuss about a resigning treasurer.

Griet had given her husband an ultimatum six months ago – *Choose Pieter Van Leuven or me* – and Planckaert was still astonished at his insanity in having chosen Van Leuven. He'd swapped stability and comfort for a wild fantasy. He realised how much he loved his fiery, honest and plucky wife. He'd give up the flat on the river at Handboodstraat and they'd start again. It wasn't long before he'd qualify for his pension. He could return to his old life, but with a new appreciation of its worth. Griet was quick to anger but quick to forgive. The children, busy with their own lives and young families – Juliaen up in Knokke and Sandrin in Poperinge – didn't even know of their parents' difficulties. When he'd told Griet what he was going to do, she'd come round... 'I hope so, anyway,' he muttered to himself.

He went back to his desk, ignoring Marta's sideways glance. *What a bloody mess.*

*

'I guess you'd call these various strands "lines of enquiry",' said Sterling. He took another pull of Hommelbier. It was the kind of earthy, strong Belgian brew he could easily develop a taste for. 'The Chest, the subscriptions, Guy, the firebombing, the beguinage, the bloke at the museum. I don't reckon there's much more we can actively do for the moment. Angela's got into a bit of a mess, but we've got friends at home who'll get her back over here. Hopefully, we'll hear from Willem about the meeting on Sunday.'

'So we just hang around, drinking beer and looking out at all the people in the square?'

'I do, at least till I've finished this.' Sterling picked up his glass and made a little toast. 'There's something you can do that I'd struggle with. The manager or owner of the firebombed opticians – the one I told you about – it would be good if you could discreetly track her down so we can speak to her. Obviously we don't want the police to know or be involved at this stage.'

Albertin nodded. 'Obviously,' he said. 'What's the name of the opticians?' He got out his phone. 'I'll start with this.'

'I don't remember. Actually, I don't think I ever knew. The sign had long melted by the time I got there.'

Albertin stared down at his phone, pressing the touchscreen with a kind of awkward deliberation and furrowing his brow, even less accomplished with technology than the Luddite Sterling. After a few minutes, he sighed. 'I'll have to go down Lange Steenstraat and find out. I can take it from there. Will you come?'

'I don't think I will, Yves. Two of us sniffing around will raise more suspicion than one.' Sterling shared his burgeoning experience as a PI. 'The way to do it is to go into a neighbouring shop. Pretend you've come for an eye test, seen the burnt-out shell and want to know what to do next. Someone's probably got a mobile number, and the optician's probably busy trying to sort things out.'

'OK,' said Albertin. His face brightened as he saw a way of getting what was needed.

'After that, let's call it a day. I don't think much else is going to happen for now. Oh yes, and you've got that other little research job – finding out who the Big Man is. You've got enough to keep you going. We'll meet at the hotel tomorrow morning – say 9.30 – and you can tell me what you've found out.'

Sterling was careful not to say what he'd be doing as Albertin and the others all did his bidding, which in the first instance was to go back to the hotel and have a bit of shut-eye, since last night's excitement had been catching up with him. He watched Albertin walk up the square and turn into the lane that led to St Martin's Church and the small entrance of the beguinage. He wasn't sorry to see him go. The teamwork aspect of the current job had its advantages but was also challenging, especially when Angela and Albertin presented doubts and questions. The 'Do-as-I-say-and-not-as-I-do' mantra was losing its effectiveness. He left euros on the table for the waitress and set off in the opposite direction from the Walloon, across the square to Doorniksestraat. The two opas had been set their tasks and would get back to him. Angela would be back sometime tomorrow with her report. As for him, he'd poked the hornet's nest. From now on, things would be getting livelier.

Chapter 19

Sterling had been thinking about momentum. When he was in the job, some investigators liked the idea of maintaining it, almost superstitiously. If you had momentum, there would always be progress. If one line of enquiry was stalled, others had to be promising and active. Without momentum, morale seeped away and things slowed down or even stopped. Sterling wasn't against the idea, but doing nothing could work too, provided that there had been stimulation beforehand. So, with the opas busy, Angela absent, and a little intimidation applied when the opportunity arose, he wasn't fussed that things were quiet.

When he woke up later in his room, he realised that he'd napped longer than planned. So, sleepless and alert at about half-past ten in the evening, he decided on a night-time promenade around the town. At reception, Aurélien was nowhere to be seen. A young woman, intricately made up and her dark hair in a bun, had replaced him, and the detached formality was back. She and Sterling exchanged cool nods as the electric doors swished open and Sterling stepped out into the balmy street.

He was drawn to the Grote Markt. It was Saturday night after all, and that's where the town would be liveliest. In the square, knots of people, mostly young, stood or ambled slowly about. A Frisbee shimmered in a triangular pattern through the air, the three spinners showing off their fancy flicks and catches. There were shouts and laughter, and other Saturday night sounds less easy to identify. Litter riffled and shifted on the cobbles and asphalt. Sterling was again struck by the old-fashioned clothing of many youngsters – jerkins and peasant blouses.

He gravitated towards the far corner where he had seen the Big Man and his mystery sidekick looking at the building façade encased in scaffolding and plastic sheeting. The crane still stood silent guard over the construction site behind, accessible from the side street. There was no one around now.

Sterling turned and walked diagonally back, past the belfry and into the lane to St Martin's Church. Perhaps there was something going on at the beguinage, but when he arrived, the gates were shut and the enclave dark and silent. Candles flickered on the outside tables of Café Rouge. One last couple leaned together, foreheads touching, hands clasped, as waiting staff cleared dishes and glasses, and hovered about, waiting to stack chairs.

Sterling moved on, around the church and into Lange Steenstraat and the shopping area. It was quieter, but people still emerged here and there from bars, or strolled along in both directions. He found himself looking at the wrecked remains of the opticians, yellow and black warning tape fluttering listlessly under the streetlights.

He thought he might go down to the Golden Spurs sculpture in Groeningeveld Park. Or maybe down towards the river. Bars were bound to still be open on a warm summer Saturday evening. A nightcap would help him sleep.

At Grote Kring, he knew something was wrong as soon as a man in a black leather jacket and blue jeans appeared at the corner of the square from the direction of the beguinage. Sterling veered away to the right. Other men, similarly dressed, emerged from that corner. Sterling turned around.

'They're in fucking uniform,' he muttered, as the party merged into one. He cursed himself for his inattention. If you stir things up, you need to keep your wits about you.

There were two reasons Sterling could handle himself in a ruck.

One was because of his peripatetic childhood around the Kent coastal towns. Every new school meant a fight, usually with a larger boy, and he heeded his father's advice: 'Be mean, be unpredictable, go high, go low, punch, elbow, bite, kick, don't stop. Win or lose that one time, and no other kid will want to scrap with you. Then you'll get left alone.' A mother might have put a different, gentler view, perhaps invoking the protection of teachers, but his mother had never been around.

The second was Sterling's stints as a plod on the beat in some of the same coastal towns. In Margate and Folkestone, eruptions during drunken Saturday nights on the seafront were commonplace, and he'd been adept at dealing with trouble by more conventional methods, though assisted then by truncheons and spray.

Now he was cornered, unarmed and alone, as his ambushers approached. He might do a bit of damage, but he was in for a beating, or worse.

A voice, oddly disembodied and high-pitched, drifted over from Lange Steenstraat. Sterling thought he recognised it, but not the context.

'Mr Sterling,' it said, strongly accented, 'Frank, is everything OK?'

One of the men approaching Sterling from behind turned and hissed something. It wasn't English, but there was no doubt about its meaning. The owner of the voice was being told to fuck off. Sterling turned as well, and saw Aurélien with another young man, equally slender. There was shock on both their faces and in the street lights, white-eyed fear. Aurélien put his hands up, supplicating and surrendering. 'OK. OK,' he said, words and gestures recognisable anywhere in the world. He edged backwards, drawing his boyfriend back with his hand on his forearm.

Shit, thought Sterling. *Still, what could I expect? Hotel hospitality doesn't extend to assisting guests in street fights.* The best he could hope for was that Aurélien would call the police. Even so, the damage would be done in under two minutes, and there were plenty of ways his attackers could disappear.

He turned to face the alpha male, who, unlike the others, sported not a short leather jacket but a full-length leather coat, Gestapo circa 1942, totally over-dressed in the warm air. Sterling took in his pock-marked cheeks and greasy hair. "Be unpredictable", his father was saying. Sterling barrelled into action, darting forward and cannoning into the leather coat. He smelt his childhood barber shops – razor strops and brillian-tine – and then he was pummelling and kicking and kneeing and elbowing and trying to bite, his target straining to do the same. Sterling felt rough hands on his forearms and round his neck, pulling him from the man beneath him on the ground. Leather Coat rose to his feet and dusted himself down, a dead-eyed leer on his moon-crater face. He nodded to an accomplice punching his fist into his palm, like a pitcher throwing the ball into his mitt, and Sterling, pinned upright by two others, awaited his punishment. Would he do better to relax or tense up to mitigate the pain? He couldn't remember.

The first blow went to his stomach. He gasped and tried to bend over, but his attackers held him upright. A terrible scream pierced the still air. Everyone in the square, which amounted to Sterling and his assailants, paused, as if the director on a film set had bellowed 'Cut'. Then from around the corner came Aurélien and his boyfriend, faces drawn into berserker snarls, bicycles held aloft across their bodies. They charged Leather Coat and Punching Man, powering them to the ground and then pinning them.

Sterling recovered quickly – he had no choice – wrestling away from his two startled captors. He saw the scared eyes of the younger one and attacked the other. The small square filled with Aurélien's and his boyfriend's shouts and howls, the grunts and suppressed screams of the cycle-pinioned men and Sterling's scuffles with the attackers who were still standing. A moment later, the scared one broke away and bolted off towards the church and beguinage. Leather Coat and Punching Man wrestled and writhed in vain to get out from under the bikes pressed down on them. Sterling was in full and vicious street-fight mode, and quickly felled his opponent.

Sterling approached Leather Coat. 'Who sent you?' The man turned his face away and spat blood, muttering in Dutch. Sterling slapped him palm and backhand. 'Come on. Who?'

The man muttered on. 'No English,' he said, a sardonic grin on his ravaged face. Sterling felt Aurélien's slender fingers on his sleeve. He smelt the metallic tang of fresh blood. There was a faint and growing sound of a police siren.

'Frank. Mr Sterling.' Aurélien was flummoxed about the degree of formality or otherwise he could use with a hotel guest. 'If you don't want to answer police questions, we have to go.'

Sterling allowed himself to be pulled to his feet. His stomach felt tender, and a wave of nausea welled up from his throat.

'Back to the hotel?' said Aurélien.

'Yes,' said Sterling. 'Thanks. But not that way' – motioning towards the church and beguinage – 'can we go in the other direction?'

Aurélien and his boyfriend supported Sterling as he limped away, but as they turned left into an alley next to a shopping mall that Sterling hadn't noticed before, he gently cast off his arms from around their shoulders and made his own way. The young men were giggling. Nervous energy made them dart and jitter along the pavement. It wasn't every day you rescued an Englishman from thugs in Kortrijk town centre. As they reached the end of the alley, jitter turned almost into swagger. Sterling noticed they'd turned into Vlasmarkt, and at the end of that, the familiar territory of Dorniksestraat and the hotel came into focus.

'What can I get you, Frank?' said Aurélien. The victim and rescue duo had moved to the back of the ground floor area, away from and out of sight of the plate glass frontage.

'Coffee,' said Sterling. 'Black. Strong, with a little jug of milk.'

'Straight away,' said the receptionist.

While they waited, Sterling and Aurélien's boyfriend, introduced as Denys, smiled and nodded to each other in the breakfast booth.

The coffee, when it arrived, had a generous tot of brandy in it. 'I thought you would need it,' explained Aurélien. 'It's...' – he searched for the right expression – '... on the house.'

'Cheers,' said Sterling. Aurélien was useful to know, and not just because he seemed to play fast and loose with the hotel's facilities. 'I owe you blokes a big "thank you". It was getting very nasty back there.'

Aurélien translated for Denys, and Sterling recognised a kind of heavily-accented French. They seemed to be Walloons in a Flemish town. Denys nodded and smiled. He sat up straight and waggled his shoulders, preening in a parodying kind of way. Sterling looked down and swirled his coffee to hide a smile. A couple of boys coming out on top in a man's world.

'Frank, how do you come to be in a fight in this town? You have only been here two days. And where is Miss... Ms Wilson?'

'Long story, Aurélien, which I can't share now, but I can tell you that Angela will be back sometime tomorrow.'

'Is it something to do with what is happening over the past week?'

Sterling perked up. 'What is happening?'

Aurélien started speaking rapidly to Denys, who replied excitedly. 'We are French-speaking Belgians. I am here because the hotel chain that employs me sent me here for a few months. It has been short of people. Denys is staying for a few days. When we go out into Kortrijk, we notice all the young Flemish people in their strange old-fashioned clothes. And no phones! There is a lot of drinking and excitement. Sometimes, they shout names at people who are not Flemish. It is not very nice in the town sometimes.'

There were just the dregs to swirl. Sterling rubbed his stomach gently. There'd be a bruise, and there'd be some discomfort, but he was pretty sure he'd got away without any more serious damage.

A strange atmosphere around the town. Excited, xenophobic Flemish kids shunning modern fashion, technology and all the other paraphernalia of the twenty-first century.

And his own adventure. He'd poked the hornet's nest and had been too dozy to be ready for the consequences. From now on, he'd have to be more careful. He might not get so lucky next time.

Chapter 20

Albertin eased into the breakfast booth. The young breakfast supervisor was beginning to clear up and put away but seemed at ease with the fact that Sterling had converted some of the space into a meeting venue. The smell of coffee, smoked ham and cheese drifted over. A young couple in Kortrijk for the weekend lingered over their drinks, breakfast debris scattered over their table. Sterling's breakfast fare at home was monotonously the same every day – cornflakes and two slices of toast – but the range on offer in the hotel had quickly palled. So much choice, but in the end not much he enjoyed.

Albertin had the air of someone who'd found a large denomination banknote in a deserted alley. 'You asked me to do two things, Frank. What do you want first?'

Sterling shrugged.

'OK, then, I'll start with the Big Man. I know some people in Comines who are well connected, so I got quite a lot.' Albertin moved in his seat, as if trying to get a more comfortable position, and looked away. He fumbled for his reading glasses and took out a small notebook from a jacket pocket.

Sterling recognised the hinky movements and was getting used to their occasional appearance. It was a quirk of Albertin's, like a tic.

'His name is Leo Janssen, aged sixty-six. Career criminal. Recently moved to Comines from Poperinge. His wife is terminally ill and wanted to go back to be close to her family. Very devoted couple. He's done all kinds of blagging...'

Sterling looked at the crown of Albertin's head, since his face was turned down to the notebook. That was an interesting choice of word, and it was far from the only one Sterling had heard him use. Albertin carried on reading, oblivious to Sterling's reaction. 'So, armed robbery in the seventies and eighties. Some long spells in the nick in Ypres and elsewhere. He's got a used-car lot somewhere in Zulte-Waregem, and property that his oldest son helps him manage. Most of his known associates are fellow criminals. He's very anti-authority, like a lot of these kinds of criminals. Angry. Spent time in Brussels and Antwerp.

'You probably won't have heard about it in England, but in 1975 there was a huge jewellery heist in Antwerp for which he went down. Diamonds and stuff worth millions were stolen, and far from all of it recovered. It's said that he took the rap for an even more dedicated criminal associate – Jost Claes – who was jailed for life after a road rage murder on the Brussels beltway.

'Now they say he's washed up, a smash-and-grab dinosaur in an era of cyber-scamming. They say he's a man who wants one last big job.' Albertin looked up from his notes and over the top of his half-moon reading glasses. 'Maybe all this stuff with Guy.'

'Maybe,' said Sterling. 'Did your sources mention any nationalist sympathies he might have? Any connection with the New Flemish Alliance?'

Albertin shook his head. 'It didn't come up.'

'Right. We'll let all that sink in. What about the optician?'

'The way you suggested getting the information worked perfectly. The shop opposite had all her details. She's currently working from home trying to sort out all her customers, deal with the insurance, sort out builders – the whole thing. She's working with other opticians so that they can give her clients emergency appointments. The name is Griet Planckaert. Phone num…'

'Planckaert?' said Sterling.

'Yes. Why?'

'Didn't you notice? The museum manager's name was Planckaert, and he and this woman were having a row outside the burning remains of her shop in the middle of the night before last.'

'Right. Well, I've got her phone number and address – 6A, Gerstelaan, Kortrijk.'

Sterling looked at his watch. 10 o'clock. Sunday morning too. 'We'll go over and see her now. Walk up to the station and get a taxi.'

'Shouldn't we at least phone first?'

'No. I don't want to be fobbed off. Come on.'

*

The taxi glided south, under the railway line towards the south of the town, which unravelled in the way towns do. Tightly backed residential streets of Flemish brickwork, studded with bars, bakeries and corner shops, ceded to wide roads, business and light industry parks and car showrooms. The route went through Kortrijk's soft underbelly, as his father would have called it. The taxi crossed the bridge over a motorway, and then there was a kind of university quarter – green sports fields, car-parks, barriers, and blocks of glass and whitewashed brick. Behind the campus area, long flat lanes of manicured gardens, wide driveways and generously proportioned houses whispered discretion and money.

The taxi drew to a halt at 6A Gerstelaan, the only car in either direction on the road, all other vehicles parked exclusively in driveways.

'Ask the driver to wait a minute or two, Yves. We might draw a blank or have the door slammed in our faces.' The taxi driver – black, long-limbed, slender-fingered, silent – nodded and smiled. Sterling looked at the immaculately tended front garden and driveway, and the new fancy-bricked, big-windowed detached dwelling set behind them. It was mostly bungalow but had an upstairs area beneath an elegant gable. 'It must be worth it being an optician in Kortrijk,' said Sterling. 'Until Friday night, that is.'

He and Albertin walked up the drive, past the new Mercedes SUV and across to the solid, heavy-looking silvery-grey front door. It was generously proportioned in a modern European style, with a long, vertical glass side panel and accompanying tubular, stainless steel bar, also vertical. Sterling heard tinny chimes tinkle faintly through the house as he pressed the doorbell.

He was about to ring again when he sensed an eye at the peephole, and then the sound of locks tumbling made him withdraw his finger. As the door opened on its chain, he immediately recognised the woman at the firebombed opticians, pre-Raphaelite red hair not so wild, but attractive, oval face showing obvious signs of strain and fatigue, particularly around puffy eyes.

A short volley of Flemish poured out as she tipped up her chin and looked the two men up and down. Both stepped back, like respectful party-political doorstep canvassers, as Albertin fashioned and delivered his reply, introducing himself and Sterling with quiet courtesy. Sterling was picking up enough of the rhythms and cadences of Dutch, and Albertin's body language, to know that he was being introduced as an English private investigator.

'I'm very busy,' said Griet Planckaert in English. 'My shop had a fire. I'm still sorting out appointments for next week. You're not the police, right? Or from the insurance company?'

Sterling seized his cue. 'Neither, Mrs Planckaert. But it's important, and it won't take long. We do know about the fire. We're very sorry about it, and we think it's connected to our business.'

The woman shrugged. 'Well, I suppose I could do with a break.' The chain rattled and was freed, the sliver between door and jamb widened and she stepped aside to let the visitors in. Albertin turned and nodded to the taxi driver, who eased his car away.

The men stepped into a generously proportioned light space, more vestibule than hallway, brushing their feet and following the woman across expensive plain grey floor tiles and into a large sitting room with an expansive view of the quiet, bourgeois lane. Tiles gave way to strip flooring of light wood, almost certainly not common-and-garden pine. A large, angular, three-piece suite did not overwhelm the room and was supplemented and complemented by square and rectangular lights and lamps strategically placed to provide light in all essential parts of the room. A large, glass coffee table had been invaded by a mass of papers and documents that jarred with the precision and elegance of the rest of the room.

Griet Planckaert gestured her visitors to the large sofa and flopped down in one of the armchairs. She pushed her curly, lustrous hair back off her forehead, whereupon it sprang back to exactly where it had been before. 'So...' she said, after the introductions.

'Your English, what I have heard of it, is very good,' said Sterling. It was true and surely some well-intentioned and genuinely-felt praise could not hurt his cause.

'Thanks. I did some of my optician's training in London – City University. English is fine for this. I don't suppose you speak Dutch, and it will be quicker if we don't use your translator.' The woman nodded towards Albertin, speaking matter-of-factly and without rancour. 'Well,' she said, 'what's all this about?'

Sterling warmed to the woman. There was something about her – the directness, the confidence with two oddly-matched strangers, and her obvious resilience in the face of adversity. He felt confidence of his own that they could have an open, honest conversation, and, if he asked, that she would be discreet.

'Guy Verstraete. I've been asked by his fiancée to investigate him. You know him,' he stated.

'Yes, I know Guy.' The woman curled her legs under her and leaned her elbow on the chair arm. 'I kicked him out of my shop the day before it got burnt out. Silly boy. Too good-looking for his own good, but weak and easily led. Like my silly, handsome, weak husband. As you English say, I could pick them, and, in this case, I did. I never met Guy's girlfriend though. Where does she live? Not Kortrijk...'

'Ypres, like Guy, when he's there. Mr Albertin is one of the girlfriend's grandfathers and is helping me. The girl's name is Christina.'

Mrs Planckaert nodded her acknowledgement to Albertin. 'Yes, Ypres, I remember now. I don't mean to be unkind, Mr Albertin, but if Guy's going to join your family, some things are going to need straightening out.'

'We – I – originally thought that Guy might have got a girlfriend here,' said Sterling, 'which is why he apparently disappeared for a few days each month. You say you kicked him out of your shop. A colleague and I saw that. Also, the fire and commotion at your shop rousted me out of my hotel.' He plunged on. 'I went to the scene and noticed that you were... having a lively conversation with your husband.'

Griet Planckaert straightened up, torn between irritation and amusement. 'You know a lot about my business. I get that you saw me kick Guy out of the shop, but how did you know it was my husband at the fire?'

'We happened to go to Tourist Information at the 1302 Museum,' replied Sterling. 'He was there and I recognised him.' No need to bring the matter of following Van Leuven around Groeningeveld into it, or the spy stunt he and Albertin had pulled. 'You have the same name, and you're roughly the same age. You were talking outside the fire as if you knew each other very well.' He spread his palms out.

Mrs Planckaert gave a thin smile. 'Detective work,' she murmured.

Sterling smiled back. He liked her, and he could tell she was liking and trusting him.

'Why don't you ask Guy himself what he's up to? Why didn't whats-her-name, Christina, ask him?'

'Christina did, but he wouldn't give her straight answers. We've reached the stage where we know enough to do as you suggest, and we don't think there's another girl involved, but after you kicked him out of your shop, we haven't been able to catch up with him. From what we've found out, we think he's involved in something much more serious than a fling with a girl in Kortrijk. The fire, so soon after his visit, seems to prove it.'

Silence settled in the elegant, airy room, except for the tick of a clock somewhere out of sight, and the chirrup of a bird that penetrated the thick window. Albertin looked at the parquetry round the large fire-place, rapidly learning the discretion of the assistant detective. Griet Planckaert's steady gaze held Sterling's eyes. Then she blinked. 'It's time for my morning coffee. Will you join me? I'll tell you a story.'

Sterling leaned back and clasped his hands in his lap. 'Certainly,' he said.

Chapter 21

The coffee wasn't like the coffee in the cafés in the square, or in the breakfast room of the hotel in Dorniksestrasse. It was proper, fresh, delicious, and reinforced in Sterling's eyes the sense of acceptance that he and Albertin had engendered.

'A fling with a girl in Kortrijk,' said Griet Planckaert. 'If only... It's turning out to be much more serious than that. Let me give you some background before we get back to Guy and my shop. I was brought up in Bruges, as was my husband. We met when we were eighteen. "Love at first sight" I think is your expression. I come from a good family. My mother was a doctor, my father a dentist. Jan came from a good family too – teachers. It was a wonderful, heady, happy courtship. We loved each other, and our families approved.' Her eyes drifted off to a point in the back garden as the memory enveloped her. 'The relationship survived everything – our moves to different universities to pursue different career paths; the fact that I had get-up-and-go while Jan was... less energetic, more bookish; and... Pieter Van Leuven. You seem to know a lot already. Have you met Pieter Van Leuven on your travels around Kortrijk?'

'Briefly, at the beguinage in town,' said Sterling, 'with another frien... associate. It was uncomfortable. Our associate is black, has a degree in history, and she's clever…' He didn't mention how he and Albertin had followed Van Leuven to the Groeningeveld monument and how he'd led them to her husband.

Mrs Planckaert sipped her coffee. 'That makes perfect sense. Well, Pieter was the cross I had to bear for loving Jan. All through our time together, from the early days and marriage, through to having children and up to this very moment, Pieter has been ever-present, if not literally then somehow in spirit. He and Jan were friends at school, and nothing has loosened the hooks he had and still has in my husband. He was a sad, horrible, bigoted boy who turned into a sad, horrible, bigoted man, but Jan could never really see it. It was as though he had a blind spot where Pieter was concerned. "Pieter's not so bad. You don't really understand him. His strong beliefs and principles bend him in unexpected ways". A nasty little Flemish neo-fascist – that's what it boils down to, with a petty, provincial agenda – although he is a man transformed when he has a large audience.

'Everything was going well for Jan and me, in Antwerp where we started our married life together – he in the city museum, I as an optician in a local business, and then again at Ghent, where Jan managed the Gravensteen Museum and our children grew up.

'Kortrijk was our big opportunity. We had worked hard and saved up enough for me to buy my business. Jan's appointment to the 1302 Museum was a sideways move, but perfect in the circumstances. Our children were grown up and established in their own lives. But there was always Pieter Van Leuven, and he would always get in contact or appear. Worst of all was when I learnt that he'd got a job at the beguinage – an insult to me, and in a wider sense, of course, an insult to women.

'Pieter Van Leuven... and the effect he had on my stupid, dear, mindlessly right-wing husband. Every year there'd be a bloody meeting where Pieter and Jan and a stupid bunch of grown-up men and women would dress up in silly old clothes and stage some glorious triumph of Flemish people against whoever was the chosen enemy of that year. Not,' she observed wryly, 'that there were many Flemish triumphs from history to choose from.'

'Re-enactments,' murmured Sterling. His eyes too drifted off with a memory. When he was about nine and until eleven, his father had taken him to English Civil War events at Dover Castle, and even, one summer, up to Scarborough. They'd stayed in a budget hotel in York and got a local train to the seaside, walking from Scarborough station up the long hill to the keep. He remembered his father's shining eyes as the Royalists were ejected and the Parliamentarians triumphed, the acrid smell of gunpowder drifting in the sea air, picnic sandwiches and cola on the faded summer grass. Even as a child, he'd thought grown men and women in seventeenth-century costume stupid, and all the messing about with swords and muskets. It was his father who had been the idealist, the parliamentarian, the socialist, the republican.

'Re-enactments – I'll remember that,' she said, bringing Sterling out of his reverie. 'If you don't speak a language, you quickly get out of practice. Anyway, the *re-enactments* went on from year to year, and got bigger and bigger, but also, when I was around to see, nastier and nastier. Fringe elements from various corners of the country, and a large constituency of young people, of the neo-Nazi, extreme nationalist persuasion, began to be involved. There are a lot of them on the university campuses at the back of this house – VIVES and KUL. I came to realise clearly what I think I always somehow knew. With Van Leuven, it wasn't just a nostalgia for a Flanders of the past where our identity was fixed and we occupied a significant place in Europe and its economy. It was a dream of an independent country – a real 'County of Flanders' – with all the medieval borders and ruled by a real Count of Flanders like Guy of Dampierre. Who'd be the Count? Van Leuven of course, a sad little man until a movement and an audience sparked his charisma.'

'Like ISIS, al-Baghdadi and his caliphate in Dabiq,' interposed Albertin suddenly.

Sterling and Griet Planckaert looked at him, blank.

'Never mind. It's only probably a loose parallel, and it sounds as though the Flanders dream lacks an apocalyptic dimension. It would probably take too long to explain.'

You're a dark horse, Yves, thought Sterling once more.

'Jan became obsessed with it. My loving husband, dutiful but not really going anywhere much in career terms, got something from his close association with Van Leuven and his new organisation, the Liebaarts, as if he was compensating for the relative failure of his professional life.'

'Liebaarts,' interrupted Sterling. 'I haven't heard that one before, though we have been told about some of the other stuff – the Battle of the Golden Spurs and so on.'

'You've done some homework then, I think,' said Griet. She nodded her head approvingly. 'What I'm going to say now is mainly relevant to the time before the battle of 1302, so it probably fills another gap in your knowledge. *Liebaart* is an old *heraldisch* – heraldic – Flemish word that means "leopard" or "lion". In the thirteenth century, no zoological distinction was made between them. You can hear that Liebaart sounds like your word "leopard". Liebaarts were originally people from the Flemish nobility who supported the Counts of Flanders against French influence, but the term came to include commoners in cities who also wanted to be free of French occupation. You can see the link between the "Liebaarts" and the Counts of Flanders' black lion. Liebaarts were opposed by the *Leliaart* party – which got its name from the lilies on the French king's coat of arms. Leliaarts, obviously, were pro-French.

'Anyway, you can probably see why Van Leuven chose Liebaarts as the name of his movement or party. By the same process, among the twenty-first century Liebaarts, Leliaart is a term of insult, extending beyond being pro-French to being pro-European, liberal, and progressive.

'As far as my husband is concerned, Van Leuven has poisoned him, and a year or so ago I issued an ultimatum. It was Van Leuven, and his madcap ideas, or me.' The woman paused and gulped, seemingly partly upset at the memory, partly surprised at her frankness with strangers. 'I was shocked, but when I'd recovered a bit I realised that Jan really did believe that something big – bigger and more important than our marriage – was going to happen.

'I said "poisoned" and I meant it, and that's how we come to Guy Verstraete. My story and Jan's are context. Van Leuven has got his hooks into Guy, and now he's poisoned *him*.' She turned to Albertin. 'If I were you, forget what I said about straightening things out before he joins your family. I'd tell your granddaughter to get well clear and move on. Don't do what I did.'

'If all this is happening,' said Sterling, 'how come the police or the security services aren't involved?'

'The Liebaarts have been growing, but quietly. It's all low-tech. No mobiles or computers. Virtually medieval. It's probably been seen as a joke – the *re-enactments* and all the rest of it. It must seem that it's an organisation going nowhere. I expect the security services concentrate on the N-VA – the New Flemish Alliance.'

'OK,' said Sterling. 'So, back to Guy.'

Griet Planckaert put down her coffee cup and sighed. 'Guy Verstraete. In so many ways like a younger version of my husband – handsome, charming, weak, easily led. He went from being a bright-eyed idealist, a bit naïve, to something more... hard core. Fanatical, in his quiet way. An optician like me, so through that and the N-VA we came to know him. He clearly comes from a Flemish nationalist family, and when he went on one of the Liebaarts's re-enactment weekends, he was hooked and left the N-VA behind. I got the impression that increasingly he kept his life in compartments – the family and the girl in Ypres, the Liebaarts and nationalist politics in Kortrijk. Now I remember, the girl is busy with the family hotel business, and doesn't pay much attention to politics. A no-nonsense, practical type.'

Sterling and Albertin nodded in unison. That was Christina.

'Van Leuven took to Guy. I know this because Jan was jealous. It was as if Pieter had adopted Guy as his son and even as his successor. He groomed him and gave him responsibility, and he wanted him for longer and longer stretches of time in Kortrijk. Among other things, he put him in charge of what they called fund-raising – collecting "subscriptions" from local businesses, including mine. The thing is,' – Griet smiled ruefully at the memory – 'nobody told him that, having separated from Jan, I wasn't paying subscriptions anymore, that I wanted nothing to do with the Liebaarts, that my interest in nationalist politics was over. I really lost my temper, and Guy was shocked.'

'While we're on the subject of that little incident, do you know the big man who was with Guy?'

Griet shrugged dismissively. 'I'd never seen him before. If he's a Liebaart, he's new, or a member from another region. There's been a massive expansion recently, as if Van Leuven's building up to something. Smaller nationalist groups have merged with it or are cooperating.' Her clear green eyes, previously bearing on Sterling and Albertin with a strong, frank gaze, flickered away.

'Your opting out, the refusal to pay subs, must have been sudden.' Sterling felt a tug of mischief. 'What with Jan's involvement, and your knowledge of the politics and the Liebaarts's development, weren't you a kind of fellow traveller?'

'I'm not sure what you mean,' said Griet, but the deep flush that spread from her chest and collarbone, up her neck and into her face made a different statement. 'When Jan and I were together, I was inevitably part of it sometimes. We were in the N-VA, though not very active, and that's where we first met Guy. I am proud of my Flemish roots. I can trace my ancestors back to weavers' guilds in Bruges and Ghent from the early medieval period. But Van Leuven's poison... and I've left that far behind. I believe in diversity and an open society.'

'Just interested, in passing really,' said Sterling. He put up his hands in a gesture of conciliation. De Groot, his friend the bike shop owner, had been the same – from nationalist to internationalist through professional cycling teams that opened his bigoted eyes, as he lived and raced with riders from every country in the world.

It was funny how a tranche of Flemish people was so aware and proud of their origins. As far as he knew, which only stretched back to late Victorian times, his own ancestors on his father's side were farming stock around Chatteris – the menfolk smallholders and labourers, the women housemaids – and on his mother's side, mystery.

'Anyway, what it boils down to is that Guy was collecting subs, you refused to pay and turfed him out on his ear, and then later, we can assume, someone from the Liebaarts came back and torched the shop.'

'To punish me,' said Griet, 'and to warn other people. That's what Jan said when you saw us on bonfire night. He was apologetic. I think he was finally seeing what he'd got himself into. He said he'd help me sort it out. He said he was finished with Van Leuven and the Liebaarts – though knowing him he'll be finding it hard to come to a decision.'

'What have you told the police?'

'Nothing much yet. We are waiting for the fire report. I'm checking the insurance. I'm not sure if it includes paying out for firebombing. That's why I was cautious when you first knocked on the door.'

Sterling looked at Albertin and then back to the optician. He put his cup and saucer on the glass-topped table opposite the papers strewn about. 'As I said, we're sorry about your business. We hope it gets sorted out satisfactorily. When our case with Guy is over, or even if it isn't, we'll be glad to help if we can.' Albertin, having been invited to commiserate, nodded in agreement.

'Thank you,' said Griet. 'I hope your granddaughter has a satisfactory outcome, Mr Albertin.' She turned back to Sterling. 'What's next for you?'

'Well, as I said at the beginning, Guy has disappeared and we need to find him. What you say chimes with everything else we know. Something big is brewing, probably some re-enactment on the 1302 anniversary the day after tomorrow. We're trying to find out details, and that's where Guy will probably resurface. We've reached the stage where we need to have a conversation with him and sort everything out, for better or for worse.'

Griet Planckaert gathered the cups, saucers and spoons to go with the cafetière, milk jug and sugar bowl on her tray. 'For better or for worse,' she repeated.

Chapter 22

On the unibus back to town, Albertin was humming softly, and Sterling was trying to identify the tune.

It came to him. *'House of the Rising Sun.'*

'What?' said Albertin.

'The song you're humming.'

'I hardly realised I was. Yes, before your time, and almost before mine. It must have been what Mrs Planckaert said – she was a little... melodramatic.'

Sterling made the link. '"Don't do what I did." A man advises a mother to tell her children not to follow the path he's trodden and warns of the sorrow and hardship that will come if they do.'

'Right. I make those odd associations, even more so now I'm older. I think she's right. I think Christina can do much better than Guy Verstraete, not that my opinion will make much difference.'

'Maybe,' said Sterling. They were pulling in to the bus stop at the railway station.

In the breakfast area of the hotel, not ten minutes later, Sterling and Albertin came upon a party atmosphere in what had become the team's *ad hoc* meeting and office space, with Aurélien and Angela clearly exchanging stories about their separate adventures. A third person had her back to the approaching detective and his sidekick. Sterling recognised the plaited blonde hair and slim, compact shape of Becky Strange.

'Ladies, Aurélien,' said Sterling as he and Albertin joined the group. Angela kissed the opa's cheek and Albertin kissed Becky's hand. A startled look flitted momentarily across her face. In her world, such gestures were rare and sometimes questionable.

'We thought you'd need reinforcements, Frank,' said Angela, 'so Becky came back with me. I have to say that a crossing by powerboat in the early hours, and pick-up by van from a deserted beach, was the least comfortable way I've crossed the Channel.'

'Tailored to your needs. In your circumstances, beggars can't be choosers,' murmured Becky.

The next hour of updates and theorising was chaotic. Controlling meetings was not among Sterling's attributes. He knew better than ever why in most cases he worked alone. But there were benefits too, not least the insights that others supplied.

Angela had the floor. 'Something's been nagging me for a while, and now it's got clearer. There's a desperate, reckless quality to everything that's happening,' she was saying. 'Collecting subscriptions so openly. Firebombing a shop in the high street. Stealing the Kortrijk Chest in broad daylight. Trying to beat up Frank. All those kids milling around the market square. It's as if Van Leuven and these Liebaarts are building up to something, and they don't care what happens beforehand. It's got to be to do with the battle anniversary on Monday.'

Sterling's phone vibrated. It was a message from Agnes. 'News,' he said. 'Opa Willem has managed to find out from his contacts details of the meeting tonight. He's going to attend with one of them – 8 o'clock at the beguinage.' He put his phone on the table. 'I agree with Ange. Something's going to happen on Monday, and it isn't going to end well. We'll have a clearer idea about what when Opa Willem comes out of that meeting. I'm pretty sure what we need to do next. I'll arrange for Willem to come back to the hotel when he's finished. I think we can all stand down until then – except for you, Becky, if you don't mind. You're just about the only one now that Liebaart people won't recognise around the town. They probably even know that this hotel is our headquarters. I wonder if you can circulate near the beguinage to see if anything's going on. Ange can show you on a map how everything's set out.'

'Glad to have something to do,' said Becky. 'I feel that I've come late to all the excitement.'

'I'm sure we can fix up something for you. In fact, the best is probably yet to come.'

*

Opa Willem stood on the Ypres platform with his acquaintance of forty years, Denys Wouters. It was half-past six on Saturday evening and they were waiting for the train to Kortrijk. "Acquaintance" is the right description, Willem Van de Velde was thinking. They'd done some things together all those years ago, mainly street brawl stuff against various leftist groups, Flemish nationalist graffiti in the underpasses and on the tene-ment walls, and marching – trivial activities when he looked back.

But they weren't friends. The hotel, together with Agnes and Christina, had saved Van de Velde from the kind of life that had enveloped Wouters, who laboured on the roads and railways, slinging out traffic cones from the backs of lorries in the early hours, spending weekend evenings on a stool in the bar around the corner from his sad little flat, and all the while bitterness festering in his heart. The navvy spat onto the railway line, wiping a dribble of spittle from his stubbly, broken-veined chin with a tatty sleeve. He'd never made anything of himself, and he knew it. The annual excursions to the van Raemdonck memorial with nationalist fellow travellers, and the raucous, beer-fuelled fellowship that came with them, masked his failure.

'Thought you'd deserted the cause, Willem,' Wouters said. His hands were nonchalantly in his pockets, and a scuffed brown shoe kicked at a pebble that had found its way onto the platform, but his rheumy eyes looked shrewdly across at his better-dressed companion. 'It was a surprise to see you in t'Ganzeke looking for some action.'

Van de Velde said nothing for a few moments. A confusing melange of feelings nagged at him. He could effortlessly rehearse all the opinions that Wouters and his ilk spouted. After all, he was or had been, of this ilk, he thought moodily. He could recite the slogans in his head. Flanders for the Flemish. Protection and promotion of the language. An end to immigration. Repatriation of foreigners. Repatriation of their dead too, as the Germans had done, generally speaking. An end to Muslim infiltration. No place for Shariah. An independent County of Flanders. Flemish jobs for Flemish people.

He still had his sympathies too. The world – their world – was changing rapidly and he hardly recognised it anymore. His town, his hotel – most of the year filled with foreigners – the British, the Canadians, the Indians, the Australians, New Zealanders and all the others – commemorating the sacrifices of their ancestors and forgetting the sacrifices of his. The *Dodengang* was the Flemish Passendale (oh yes, and the Walloon one too, he supposed). Now young Flemings were speaking English rather than their own language, dominated by the cultural pap of England and the US. Forgetting their own history.

But he'd changed as well, because of Agnes, Christina – above all Christina – and the hotel. His eyes drifted over the platform and across the tracks to the ticket hall. Ethnic diversity started right here. Ypres wasn't just overrun with battlefield tourists. Flanders had its fair share of migrants from its colonial past in the Belgian Congo, and more recent ones from the current great migrations – young, energetic individuals and families. He recognised the incomers' contributions and benefited all the time. He ate in Chinese, Turkish and North African restaurants in the town. Dark-skinned young men emptied his rubbish bins, and Asian women prepared his prescriptions in the pharmacies. Flanders was no different from anywhere else – unique in itself but never immune from change. Christina showed him that with a mixture of love and exasperation with his old-fashioned ways. He felt a pang of unease as he reflected on his surliness with the English investigator and his team. The intelligent young black woman deserved politer treatment. He hated admitting that he might learn from Albertin's way of going about things.

On the train hugging Belgium's southern border, he let Wouters chunter on, stoking the fulminations with sympathetic comments, like the agent provocateur he knew he was becoming. Wouters's red, boozy face and eyes took on a wild, enthusiastic sheen, but when Van de Velde pressed him about where in Kortrijk they were heading from the station, he tapped his finger against his nose, delighting in the secrecy, and nothing could make him say more than 'wait and see. It's going to be amazing, Willem. We'll never look back. The Flemish will remember us for centuries.'

Wouters backslapped his way from the station into the centre of Kortrijk, milking recognition from small knots of young people spilling out of the bars that lined Burgemeester Raynaertstraat. He revelled in the greetings – "*Hallo, Jan*", "*Veel succes*" – a big important show-off nationalist, and Van de Velde wondered sourly what they'd think if they knew as much as he did about the straw man beside him. It seemed obvious that they'd head up towards the Groeningeveld and the monument. Instead, they moved towards the Grote Markt and then down the small lane to the beguinage, which Van de Velde, despite his recent visit to the town, hadn't been close to for years. Just inside the archway entrance, a couple of bulky, hatchet-faced hard men in ill-fitting dark suits, like bouncers outside pubs and clubs, which perhaps they were when they weren't moonlighting at the beguinage, greeted Wouters familiarly and gave Van de Velde the once-over.

'It's OK, lads,' winked Wouters. 'He's with me. Seen the light. Back in the fold.' And then, with a tilt of a bullet head, they were in, Van de Velde astonished at the casualness of it all. 'It looks casual, mate,' said Wouters, 'because, firstly, I'm one of the trusted ones, so what I say, and who I invite to these things, goes. Secondly, what we're going to do is unstoppable, so at this stage it doesn't really matter who comes. Thirdly – well, it's hardly worth mentioning, but I will – we've got our own little security operation, us Liebaarts. Some say it's more Keystone Cops than Sturm Abteilung, but they apparently check what needs to be checked, enforce what needs to be enforced and do whatever else needs to be done, together with a small string of what you might call informers. You won't see that crew at any meeting. Oh yes, and fourthly' – he waved his hand vaguely around him – 'we're in a fortress here, interestingly enough. Getting in and out isn't so easy.'

The two men tramped further into the beguinage, Van de Velde inwardly surprised for once by how shrewdly Wouters spoke. It was a quarter to eight, and men, exclusively men, singly, in pairs or in small groups, moved magnetically towards Saint Anna Hall, where Sterling and Angela had met Pieter Van Leuven a few days before. In the gloaming, Van de Velde became aware of bats, black shadows flickering and darting in the cooling air, out at feeding time.

At the hall entrance, individuals and groups coalesced into a large crowd of middle-aged men, with a fair smattering of bald and grey-white heads, pot bellies and sour faces. They waited patiently to get in through the bottleneck, and once inside, Wouters and Van de Velde, like those before them and those after, ignored the exhibition Van Leuven had set up on the ground floor and clumped up some stairs next to a lift and into a spacious, modern and well-lit meeting room on the first floor. Wouters was familiar with the surroundings and had obviously been before. He made towards the seat he normally seemed to occupy and motioned Van de Velde to sit next to him, three rows from the front. There was a hubbub of greetings and small talk, and an atmosphere pregnant with anticipation.

Van de Velde knew something about UNESCO world heritage sites. You couldn't be a hotelier in Ypres without such knowledge, what with all the liaison with the tourist office, Ypres's own reconstructed Cloth Hall, and Commonwealth cemeteries everywhere you looked. He stared down at the parquet floor and half-smiled to himself. The beguinage, in existence since the Middle Ages, was obviously one of Kortrijk's own UNESCO sites. He wondered what the supervisory board, local, national or international, or however else it was organised, would think of its centrepiece commandeered for the dubious activity he assumed he was about to observe and participate in. The irony of an aggressive all-male gathering in a place traditionally reserved exclusively for women wasn't lost on him.

All the chairs were filled now, and men lined the room's walls on either side and at the back. There was a close, fuggy smell of male bodies, not all acquainted with regular washing. Wouters was in animated conversation with a small, wiry man on his other side, and the hubbub grew louder and more excited as the assembly struggled to hear and be heard. Van de Velde did a quick calculation – number of chairs in each row, number of rows, number of standers on either side – and judged that the crowd was about sixty-five strong. If Guy was in the room, Van de Velde hadn't seen him, but he'd prepared a cover story just in case – which would involve equal amounts of feigned surprise and pleasure that the young man who was to be his grandson-in-law (as it were) was also a political fellow traveller. '*Vlaams Blok, Vlaams Belang, N-VA* – none of them going anywhere,' he'd say. 'Time for something different. Direct action. The Liebaarts are a new path for patriotic Flemings.' He hoped that would work. He still had very little idea what was going to happen.

Just as a restive mood seemed to permeate the tube-train mass, a side door opened, and a small man Van de Velde didn't recognise strode up the steps of the dais at the front of the room and grasped the sides of a lectern with each hand. Four other men emerged with him and lined the wall behind him. Van de Velde ducked behind the large, wide man in front of him as he recognised Guy Verstraete as the most prominent of them. A loud round of applause erupted around the room, supplemented by a smattering of whoops and cheers. Pieter Van Leuven raised his hands and bowed his head, pride and deprecation jostling in his features and body language. Eventually, the noise died down and he began to speak.

Van de Velde was familiar with the message. He'd heard a cruder variant from Wouters half an hour ago on the train from Ypres. He knew too of his own tendency to agree or be swayed by the contribution, in any debate or conversation, of the last person to speak. But this was something very different. The seemingly insignificant little man at the lectern, his chin barely above the top edge, his glasses glinting under the ceiling spotlights and sweat beading on his high forehead, soon had his audience mesmerised as he rehearsed 700 years of oppression, betrayal, martyrdom and erasure from history of a noble and plucky Flemish nation. He railed against the oppressors and betrayers – the French, the Spanish, the Dutch and the Walloons. He lamented the battering of Flanders as the battleground in the struggles of other nations and empires – the Germans and the British. The litany of wrong and bitterness flowed on in a twenty-minute harangue.

Then, having worked up the anger and indignation of his audience, Van Leuven changed tack. His voice dropped, and the audience, leaning forward in their chairs, strained to hear. 'We understand what's happened', he whispered, 'but future generations will judge us for what we do about it. Are you ready?' he said more strongly. 'Are you ready?' he roared. 'This will help you!' With a flourish, he gestured with a sweep of his arm to the side door, and from it emerged two men bearing a large chest on poles in the manner of a sedan chair. The chest was set down on a raised plinth on the dais. 'Behold, the Kortrijk Chest, stolen from us and now restored.' Already stirred by the little man's rabble-rousing, the assembly erupted in cheers, whoops, clapping and now a chant that Van de Velde hadn't heard for thirty years. 'Vlaanderen de leeuw' – Flanders the lion – rang out in the upper room as everyone rose to their feet, Opa Willem among them. 'Vlaanderen de leeuw, Vlaanderen de leeuw,' over and over again, clenched fists and raised arms working in time to the cry.

Van Leuven let the excitement die down until the racket became a mere babel. Wouters's face was redder than ever, and even with the windows flung open on each side, the atmosphere had become stuffy with the sweat and heat of sixty-odd men. 'The Chest comes with us on Monday, whatever happens. We have Guy Verstraete and his team to thank for bringing it back from England to its proper home.

'Step forward, Guy,' Van Leuven said with a gesture, 'our own Guy of Dampierre,' and the young man edged up to the front of the dais and bowed his head almost sheepishly.

Amid the renewed applause, banging on chairs and stamping, Willem smiled secretly. He could not imagine anyone less like the colourful late thirteenth century Count of Flanders than Christina's optician-fiancé, troublesome as he was.

Then Van Leuven and his lieutenants left the stage and disappeared back into the side room, and with the morale-boosting, sinew-stiffening part of the evening apparently over, a functionary with a reedy voice took the gathering prosaically through a final briefing. It was no surprise to Van de Velde, given his experience of meetings over the years, and not just political ones. From high drama to nuts and bolts was the norm and not the exception. This time, however, once the business element ended, the chairs were folded up and stacked away, and barrels of beer and a buffet appeared on trestle tables at the far end. A raucous, back-slapping drinking session, with songs and chants, rounded off the evening. *Don't mind if I do*, thought Van de Velde as he grabbed a glass and acquired a litre of proper Flemish beer from a Watou brewery – not the tasteless golden muck that was lately appearing everywhere. His spying duties had produced a thirst.

Guy hadn't disappeared with Van Leuven. He was doing some networking with the comrades, pressing flesh, keeping morale up and milking the accolades. Van de Velde had originally thought it best to avoid letting Guy know that he was at the meeting. But now he wondered if any harm could come of it. Guy knew about his nationalist background and beliefs, and they'd had discussions about them, often lamenting Christina's lack of interest and sharing a cheerful disappointment. When he reported back to Sterling and his team, surely something about the person who was the whole focus of the investigation would be useful.

'Opa Willem,' said Guy, as he suddenly spotted Christina's grandfather from a couple of metres away, between the grey heads of two grizzled Liebaarts captains. 'I didn't expect to see you here. I thought you were still N-VA.'

'Well, we haven't caught up for a few months, Guy. I've lately got impatient with those old farts – well, not so old maybe, but certainly farts. I bumped into Denys Wouters a few days ago' – he nodded over to where Wouters was loudly holding court, his fist wrapped around a stein of beer, his free arm waving vigorously – 'and we got talking about you Liebaarts, so he invited me over. Agnes and Christina are looking after the hotel. Actually, Guy, Christina's mentioned she hasn't seen much of you lately.' Van de Velde's expression was innocent, but he thought his comment would trigger a useful reaction.

Guy Verstraete's handsome brow furrowed. 'Yes, your darling granddaughter. I've been so busy lately. I know I've neglected her, but as you've heard, we're on the verge of something so big things won't ever be the same again.'

'Yes, I've gathered. I'll be there on Monday.'

They chatted for a few minutes, and then Van de Velde began to realise how he could increase the pressure – playing the Christina trump card. 'Are you coming back to Ypres tonight, Guy?'

Guy looked down at the floor. 'No, I'm here in the beguinage for the duration now.'

'Christina says you've given up your mobile. Your family can't locate you – she's tried them. What if she wants to get in touch? It doesn't seem fair she can't contact her fiancé.'

'After Monday...'

Van de Velde cocked his head.

Guy looked around the room. There was a din of drinking, shouting and back-slapping. 'I'm in number eleven with a couple of others.'

'Thank you, Guy. At least Christina will know that you're safe.'

'I must go, Opa.' Guy smiled wryly. 'The morale of the troops must be attended to.'

Wouters was now at the far end of the room. The last time Van de Velde had seen him, the navvy's gaze was glassy and he was engrossed with a more recent set of comrades. When the drift homewards began, it wouldn't be difficult for Van de Velde to detach himself from Wouters and the other nationalist brethren and slip into Sterling's hotel, as agreed, to share what he'd found out. The range of conflicting emotions continued to nag at him, eased by the alcohol hitting his bloodstream. He was still proud to be Flemish but shamefaced about the xenophobic, vicious, insular messages of the Liebaarts. And now, in addition, he was troubled by his activities as a double agent while suddenly realising something else – that he was enjoying the sense of danger and excitement.

The celebration broke up and he stumbled out of the hall, into the beguinage and through the arch into the street, drifting along with all the other revellers. He consoled himself that his motives were decent. Family above ideology. Family above nation. *'Het is allemaal voor Christina,'* he murmured softly on the way to the hotel.

Chapter 23

'Pieter,' said Jan Planckaert, 'I need a word with you.' The executive meeting was just breaking up in the small room off the larger one. Members of the group were shuffling papers into briefcases and having murmured side conversations. The Kortrijk Chest was stowed in a corner, relegated from the high point of the evening so that it simply looked like a nondescript black crate with a block of carving on the front panel, as likely to be found in the corner of a junkyard as anywhere grand like the Ashmolean. The poles, threaded and rolled into the linen stretcher on which the Chest had been carried, rested vertically against the wall. From the meeting room, there was still a rumble of singing and toasting even through the well-insulated door.

'Go on then,' said Van Leuven.

Planckaert looked around him. Guy Verstraete was back in the small room, flicking the bar over the handle of his old briefcase, receiving another round of congratulations from two of his colleagues for the raid that retrieved the Chest. Others were heading for the door. It was as if a sober group of accountants had just been through their spreadsheets and finished their deliberations, as trustees of an alms-houses charity. Nothing so sinister and desperate as a nationalist movement plotting for secession and a new dawn.

'In private, if you don't mind.'

Van Leuven shrugged. 'My office downstairs then.' He and Planckaert said their farewells to the others and made their way to the emergency stairs. Van Leuven unlocked the door and ushered his old friend in. Seated at his desk, he leaned back and put his tiny feet up on the surface as Planckaert perched himself on the visitor's chair opposite.

'A successful evening,' said Van Leuven, 'to cap the most successful period for Flemish independence in modern times. Heh heh. Guy has done wonderfully well to get the Chest. On Monday we'll be on the brink of an event that will change history. And we're leading it. Thirty years of graft. Heh heh. Thirty years of chipping away and never losing hope. We can be proud, Jan. We've come a long way together.'

Planckaert mumbled and fidgeted. Usually, he struggled with crisp decision-making. Now, he hadn't changed his mind, but the manner of the telling was challenging him. He raised his eyes from his hands, clasped and writhing in his lap, and looked directly into Van Leuven's glittering eyes.

'Good news,' he said. 'I'm happy for you. Happy for the Liebaarts Party. God knows, you've worked hard enough for it, and for long enough. I hope everything goes well on Monday.' He swallowed. People who knew Van Leuven but were not connected to the nationalist movement looked on him as a sad, inadequate little man. Planckaert knew better. 'But I'm not going to be part of it. I'm out, Pieter. I'm leaving.'

Van Leuven slid his short legs off the top of the desk. The truth was that the pose had been more for show than comfort. His heels had barely reached the surface edge. In his surprise, his feet clumped down on the floor and his body rocked forward. 'Are you insane? After everything you've done for us? After everything the Liebaarts have done for you? When we are so close to fundamental change in our nation? When we are about to change the direction of history?' Surprise and anger made an odd contortion of his features. The smug giggle disappeared.

Now that Planckaert had taken the plunge, his nervousness began to melt away. His back stiffened. He put his hands on his knees. He wondered more than fleetingly who, between the two of them, was the insane one. 'I wish the project every success, of course I do. I'll be a proud citizen of the independent County of Flanders. I'll make every legitimate contribution I can make.' He hoped that Van Leuven would notice the slight inflexion on 'legitimate'. 'But I can't be a part of Monday. I realised, especially after Griet lost her shop in the fire the other night, how much I love and miss her. You can't give up over twenty years of marriage so casually. And,' he paused, 'that – the fire – was wrong. She didn't deserve it. I need to support her in sorting it out.'

Van Leuven's eyes narrowed. '*We've* been together for decades, Jan. Working together in this noble cause. It's more important than family, more important than career, more important than a dull bourgeois existence slipping into old age. Do you want to be remembered by history, or do you want to go back to being a nobody?'

Then he changed tack. 'It's not just Griet and the shop, is it? There was an Englishman here in the beguinage, with a black, a woman. Sniffing around. And I heard that an Englishman, maybe the same one, turned up to see you at the museum with a Walloon...'

He let the statement hang in the air. Planckaert probably knew that one of the women in the museum was an informant.

'I haven't seen a black woman,' replied Planckaert, as if telling that truth compensated for not admitting the rest of it. 'But who I've seen or not seen doesn't make any difference.'

For twenty more minutes, Van Leuven used all his charm and powers of persuasion to get Planckaert back on board, and for twenty minutes Planckaert became more stubborn in his position. He was going back to Griet. He was resigning as treasurer and executive committee member from the Liebaarts, effective immediately.

Eventually, Van Leuven conceded. 'The business with Griet's shop – the firebombing – was wrong. I made a mistake. The boys got out of hand. Of course, I can understand your point of view. I know Griet and I have never seen eye to eye. I know she doesn't like me and resents our association, but when this latest phase is over, I'll do my best to make it right.' He put his elbows on the desk, steepled his fingers and smiled ruefully. 'But I can see that even that is not going to change your mind. Well, we can let bygones be bygones, and we can still be friends. Go back to your family and be ready to serve again when the County of Flanders is **legitimately** re-established.'

Planckaert nodded and grimaced. He knew that Van Leuven was combining mockery and absolution. But he was also relieved. The two men stood up, almost clashing heads, which raised another small shared moment of amusement. 'Naturally you can rely on me to say nothing of Liebaarts activities, not now and not in the future.'

'Jan, I trust you completely. You know that. And I wish you well.' The ex-comrades clasped all four hands firmly and then performed an awkward upper body hug across the desk. Van Leuven stood in his office doorway and watched Planckaert walk off between the glass cabinets and digital displays of the Beguinage Experience, ease through the automatic doors and disappear into the still-warm starlit night.

He turned back into his office and sat at his desk. A scowl settled over his pale, puffy, little face, eyebrows almost touching as a deep furrow appeared at the bridge of his nose. His fists, placed on the desktop, showed white knuckles. Time was too short for a coded message. He picked up the receiver of the phone to his right, punched in some well-remembered numbers and waited for the connection. 'Hans,' he said, 'another job for you. Serious and urgent.' He ran through some details. 'And Hans,' he said finally. 'Don't mess this one up.'

Chapter 24

When Opa Willem, as arranged, slipped into the hotel and moved swiftly to the eating and meeting area, out of sight of the large glass-fronted hotel entrance, greetings were muted. He lacked the easy charm and openness of Opa Yves. His gruffness and his politics invoked unease. He'd been persuaded to be a spy on his own political comrades and fellow travellers, and that spread the unease to his daughter. Only the pragmatist Sterling was relatively unaffected. The man was helping his granddaughter. Nobody had forced him into anything. People had to take responsibility for their own actions.

A chair awaited the old man. His daughter rose and gave him a light kiss on the cheek, and he nodded to Sterling, Angela and Albertin. He bowed gravely as Sterling introduced him to Becky. Aurélien appeared with a coffee pot. The group let him settle and take a few sips.

'So… Willem,' said Sterling.

Willem cleared his throat and started, Agnes watching and listening closely. She and her father had done it before – speak and interpret, speak and interpret – and they quickly got back into their rhythm, Willem careful not to go too fast and say too much in one segment, Agnes more and more skilled in faithfully conveying meaning. Willem left nothing out, from the journey over from Ypres with Wouters and their conversation, to everything that happened in the beguinage. At one point, Willem looked directly at Albertin and held him in his gaze. 'In the meeting on the top floor of St Anna's Hall,' interpreted Agnes, 'it was all the usual... rubbish.' She stopped. A surprised look flitted over her face. The others looked at both of them. Had there been a mistake? Had they missed something? Or had they seen something – a tiny glint in Willem's eye for a fleeting second, the glimmer of a smile at the corners of his mouth? Up till now, there had been nothing but scowls. Albertin laughed, and Willem's face widened unmistakeably now into a smile.

Then it was back to business.

'Yes, the usual rubbish,' said Agnes, 'much as my father says he is still attracted to aspects of it. An independent County of Flanders is good, and a return to some of the good old days. But a lot of it is poisonous nonsense.

'The leader is called Pieter Van Leuven, whom my father had vaguely heard of, someone forever on the far fringes of the nationalist movement. After his speech there were practical details, but Father had the impression that many of those details had been arranged before this last meeting so there was no need to return to them. Certainly, there will be a gathering of Liebaarts at the Groeningeveld monument from all over Flanders on the anniversary of the Battle of Kortrijk on Monday. The Kortrijk Chest will be there. Willem confirms that it was stolen from the museum in Oxford by Guy and his team, and Van Leuven congratulated them on their... "heroic expedition". A minimum of 20,000 people is expected at the march. Tomorrow is for all the regional captains to organise their groups.'

The team fell silent for a few moments, digesting the information from the father-and-daughter act, and material from elsewhere that had corroborated it. It had been complicated ensuring that everyone was brought up to date with all the different strands, with Sterling at the centre of the nexus. He was glad that Becky had arrived. She had known the least, but her questions were the most coherent and logical, and her summaries supplied everyone with the whole picture.

'Well, Willem's managed to confirm a lot of what we vaguely knew already,' said Sterling. 'Agnes, can you ask him if he saw someone who looked a bit like Guy but twenty years older? Jan Planckaert, curator at the 1302 Museum. Handsome. Dark hair.' He waited for interpretation and response.

'Maybe someone in the… executive group,' reported Agnes. 'He was at the back, if it was him. He looked unhappy, as if he wanted to be somewhere else.'

'What about a man there with a heavily pock-marked face and greasy hair, possibly in a black leather trench coat.' Sterling backed up his words with gestures, drumming each cheek lightly with the fingers of both hands, and then rubbing them on his skull.

'About a dozen,' said Agnes, mirroring a second smile from her father. 'It's what you expect from such a meeting – but no one stood out.'

'And a big, white-haired, shambling man, the one who went with Guy collecting subscriptions in the high street? There may have been one or two large men there as well, but this one has got a real presence.' Sterling looked at Albertin. 'Yves has found out about him. He comes from Comines – sorry, Komen – and his name is Leo Janssen – a career criminal…'

Agnes turned to her father, spoke and waited. 'Nobody like that stands out, but he can't be sure. Almost certainly not,' she concluded.

There were further questions and answers, the further relaying of information by Willem and his daughter, and a build-up of the most complete picture of Guy and Liebaarts that Sterling and his team had had so far. Midnight was approaching. At the front of the hotel, Aurélien, now a willing and eager team member, was locking the doors and dimming the lights. Empty coffee cups and plates spattered with croissant crumbs littered the table.

Eventually, Sterling called for order. Leading wasn't natural to him, but he was adapting. 'This is what we'll do,' he said. 'The case is still about Guy, whatever else is going on. We need to get him out of this situation before he gets himself into any more trouble, which there's bound to be on Monday. It's obviously too late this Saturday night, and he'll be hard to catch up with tomorrow in the daytime, but there should be an opportunity to "extract" him on Sunday evening...'

'How, Frank?' said Angela. 'Becky went over to the beguinage today after we'd arrived, and it's just as Willem's mate Wouters said – it's a fortress. I don't think even Becky's got the skills to storm the walls, get into number eleven and get Guy out...'

'I was coming to that, Ange, before you interrupted.'

'Sorry.'

'We don't go into the beguinage to get him. We draw him out and then we nab him. How do we do that? We use their code to send a message. Irresistible. We'll work on that tomorrow morning. I think we go on the march on Monday. We owe it to Christina, and Willem and

Agnes, to get the fullest picture possible of what Guy's been involved in.' He stopped speaking. He'd thought of something. For a moment, he couldn't look at his best friend. 'Some of us. Ange… obviously…'

'Don't worry about it, Frank,' said Angela briskly. 'It's hardly your fault that rabid racism and white supremacism still prevail in so many places, including Flanders. I'm sure there'll be something for me to do. Keep tabs on Guy, maybe.'

Opa Willem looked over to Angela and said something. His face had reddened. 'Father is sorry too,' said his daughter. 'And ashamed.' She added something else of her own. 'He's seeing sense. Finally.'

'Thank you,' said Angela.

'So, I'll be marching,' said Sterling. 'Willem and Yves too, maybe Becky, maybe Christina if she's interested. Whoever's not looking after the hotel.' Sterling noticed a slight movement next to him. 'OK, Yves?

'Should be fine,' said Albertin. He was shuffling, as if the chair had just become too hard.

'We'll sort all the details out tomorrow. Keep phones switched on and at the ready. Willem, thank you for what you've done tonight. We know why you did it, and I know that you and Agnes will update Christina, but it can't have been easy.'

'And still no police, Frank,' said Angela, 'not even about the Kortrijk Chest.'

'You're always keen on the plods, Ange. I reckon they'll be involved at some point, but why complicate things for ourselves? And let's face it, the Chest is too precious to the people who've got it now. It's not going to come to any harm. On the contrary.'

When the meeting was over, upstairs in Angela's room, where Aurélien had arranged a divan bed for Becky, they were discussing Sterling and the meeting. 'How does he do it, Becks? As per usual, we're all dancing to his tune, including the hotel receptionist.'

Becky, in inclination and training, was more a doer than a thinker, but she considered it. 'His job is about trouble. Where trouble is, Frank turns up. We get involved, and Aurélien, and even Frank's principals, the Van de Veldes, because we want some excitement. One thing leads to another. The plans seem sound. They should work out OK as far as they go.' She arranged her bedding. 'The trouble is, it's what isn't in the plans that messes it up.'

Much later, when it was all over, Angela remembered her friend's prescience.

Chapter 25

The weather on Sunday 10th July, the day before the anniversary of the Battle of Kortrijk, was almost exactly the same as the days that had recently preceded it. The sky was cloudless and blue, the blue deepening as the day progressed, and the temperature creeping up into the mid-twenties under an unrelenting sun. On the town's streets, an atmosphere was also building, a mixture of odd and tense as the cafés, squares and bars filled up. Aurélien and his colleagues were busy too, booking in a line of people stretching up to the glass front doors and then curving back towards the inside. But there was no sense of a football crowd limbering up raucously and menacingly before kick-off. The restlessness was palpable, but people went about their business in a muted and disciplined way.

Willem and Agnes had gone back to Ypres the night before, and Albertin presumably back to Komen, though when he walked out into the darkness he didn't say. Sterling reflected that since the case had begun, he had seen little of Christina. It seemed that her family was acting on her behalf, and almost as if she had lost interest in any outcome.

After the usual, predictable breakfast, Sterling and his two remaining companions took a stroll around the town, restless themselves, and cautious. Certain people in the Liebaarts knew they were in the town because of Van Leuven and Planckaert, and the brawl in the Grote Kring had represented a warning. Although he was vigilant, Sterling also had a vague sense that they were, or had become, small fry, and therefore not worth troubling with.

In the wander northwards, into new territory beyond the Grote Markt and the retail quarter of the town, he had a feeling he'd become familiar with during his lengthening second career as a PI – that brilliant plans hatched the night before, often developed and embellished by a few pints and chasers, don't look so plausible in the daylight. As Becky and Angela moved ahead, chatting quietly, he also remembered what Albertin had said outside the 1302 Museum – that it wasn't about Guy Verstraete anymore. It was true, but now something else began to nag at him, and he struggled to give it shape. He thought it through and concluded that he was almost getting bored – bored with the case, bored with Kortrijk, bored with Belgium. What was it all about? A madcap nationalist faction organising a demonstration, its activities funded by a mixture of willing donations and extortion, its legitimacy underpinned by an old box with a bit of carving on the side.

He had plenty of time. He could simply go over to Ypres and give Christina his report face to face. Agnes and Willem knew almost everything, but he'd do Christina a full independent summary and save them all some money. He pictured himself sitting opposite her at a table in *Au Miroir* café across the square from the hotel. Cups of coffee would be on the table in front of them. Christina would be sitting erect with her hands clasped. He wouldn't have to sugar-coat anything.

At that stage, and in those circumstances, it would just be business.

Right, Christina, you probably know most of it from your mother and Opa Willem, but this is my formal, oral report. I'll give you a written version with my invoice... I've investigated your fiancé Guy Verstraete for you, as requested. I can report that he hasn't got another girl in Kortrijk who he half-abandoned you for. He's left the N-VA and appears to be an executive member of a group called the Liebaarts Party. He's spent his absences in Kortrijk helping to build up the organisation led by a self-described "beghard" called Pieter Van Leuven, the curator of the "Medieval Experience" in the Kortrijk beguinage.

I don't believe that Guy has been to his job for months. We didn't really need to check because we saw him doing other things. Angela and I followed him when he was apparently collecting subscriptions. When an optician threw him out of her shop, it was burnt down the same evening. We can't tie Guy directly to that, but your opa Willem did witness Van Leuven publicly congratulating Guy for leading a team to England to steal the Kortrijk Chest, which, as you may know, is a powerful symbol of Flemish nationalism. Again, you'll probably be aware of this from your grandfather, but the Chest is going to be paraded at the Battle of Kortrijk commemoration march tomorrow, which Guy is almost certainly going to be on.

I can't gloss over anything, Christina. Guy is in big trouble, and I strongly think he could be in worse trouble tomorrow. On the current list of crimes, we can put extortion, theft and assault, both here and in England, and that's probably just for starters.

As I said at the beginning, I've done what you've asked. I'm not willing to take any more instructions from you and your mother. It would waste your money and my time. I don't usually give my clients personal advice, but as it's you and I know you so well, I'm going to make an exception. Finish the relationship with him. As we say in English, dump him. Give him the old heave-ho. I can't say it more plainly than that. He's lost his way big-time. Don't let him drag you down with him.

On the bridge over a river Sterling hadn't seen before, Angela and Becky were resting their elbows on the railing. Angela turned back to him and called out, but her words were carried away on the breeze. Two medieval twin towers with grey slate coolie-hat roofs, guarded the town 500 metres downstream, only cars and bicycles shattering the historical illusion. Sterling could see an old woman in a café next to the bridge, a clutter of bright red beer cans on the table before her. She looked directly his way with unseeing eyes. A bicycle rattled over the bridge, its ancient rider in an antiquated dark suit and shoes, billowing trouser legs tamed at the bottom by fluorescent cycle clips.

Sterling knew he wouldn't be scuttling off this afternoon to the station and catching a train to Ypres. There were still too many loose ends and unanswered questions – too much information that staved off the boredom and kept intriguing him. What was really going to happen at the Groeningeveld monument? What had happened to Janssen – the Big Man – who seemed to have gone to ground? Angela's situation nagged at him. She didn't seem overly concerned, possibly because of Becky's reassuring presence, but she was a fugitive, and the English police would be wanting to 'speak to her urgently' or 'help them with their enquiries'. Vaguer issues also troubled him. The subject of his ruminations called again. She was pointing to the café and tipping her thumb and fingers to her mouth. He put his thumb up. He was gasping for a coffee.

'I don't know if this is going to work.' He and the women were sitting in the same café as the old woman with the beer cans. A lively Asian woman took their orders with an efficient smile and discreetly removed the cans from the nearby table while slipping on a full, opened replacement.

'There's no point in trying to use the lion and goe-dendag logos because it'll be obvious that the paper's photocopied', said Angela. 'The same with using code. It looks as though only Van Leuven bothers with that. It can't be a message from Van Leuven to Guy. He could just walk over from the hall to number eleven.'

'So the message comes from outside the beguinage,' said Sterling. 'We take advantage of the fact that Liebaarts don't seem to use much in the way of telephone and internet communication. It's from Opa Willem and it says that something's happened to Christina. Guy needs to come out and get the full picture.'

'It's a stretch,' said Angela.

Becky tilted her head, weighing things up. 'I think it's got a reasonable chance. I've known more far-fetched things to work. From what I've heard, things are going to be chaotic for Van Leuven and his gang this evening, but fluid as well. If Guy gets the message it might be quite easy for him to get out for a few minutes.'

'Well,' said Sterling, 'If it works it works. If it doesn't, we'll have done our best. Guy's got involved in a lot of naughty things already – never mind what might come up tomorrow. Christina is fed up with him. Whichever way you look at it, he's going to hell in a handcart.'

Chapter 26

At nine fifteen on the evening of Sunday 10th July, when the light had bled completely out of the cloudless evening sky, Becky Strange materialised at the tall wooden main gates built into the archway of the beguinage. She rapped boldly, and then again when she received no reply. She heard scrapes and creaks from within and then a reluctant, hostile slab of pasty face appeared in the crack of an opened gate.

'This is urgent,' she said in a sentence of Dutch prepared in a phone tutorial with Agnes Van de Velde. She thrust forward a sealed letter. 'For Guy Verstraete, and no one else. From his fiancée.'

The eyes in the face dipped down to look at the letter and then up to Becky's face. 'No further communications in or out. Orders.'

Becky Strange held eye contact, guessing the refusal. 'It's an emergency. The consequences if you fail to act will come back to haunt you.' She held out her hand so that the letter went into the gap. 'I'll wait. Otherwise, I'll have to take it up with your superiors.'

The stand-off lasted seven or eight silent seconds, and she'd reached the limits of the language. But gatekeepers are gatekeepers for a reason. They aren't strategists. They follow orders. Mention of superiors, and unpleasant consequences for non-cooperation, had the required effect. The face scowled. A hand appeared and plucked the letter away. The door slammed shut and the bolts squeaked again. Becky Strange retreated to a shop doorway opposite, merging completely into shadow. From the town, light flickered against the side of St Martin's Church and a popular tune tinkled from a nearby café. A bicycle rattled and juddered over the cobbles, the front lamp giving a jerky illumination of the lane ahead.

*

A mile away, Jan Planckaert in his second-floor apartment heard the flap of the letterbox as he was washing up from his supper. He dried his hands on the tea towel and went from kitchen to hallway mat, picking up an envelope with an old-fashioned wax seal, imprinted with a signet ring. Jan Planckaert sighed. He'd had a difficult day, indecisive in the way that always plagued him. He didn't regret having broken with Van Leuven, but his resolve had failed him on the other half of the plan, seeking reconciliation with Griet. He'd meant to telephone but had spent the day procrastinating. Van Leuven, continuing to play his silly coded communication games, just added to his unease, and Liebaart rituals now seemed both tedious and childish. Still... he took the letter to the kitchen table and broke the seal. The letters on the page were in an unbroken block, but simply applying the monoalphabetic cipher and then separating letters into identifiable words with vertical pen-strokes was a small effort that took barely five minutes.

Meet me at your museum at 10 pm tonight. I have thought again about the way we have treated Griet.

I am determined to make it right. She should not suffer for our mistakes. PL.

Planckaert looked at his watch. 9.35. *Why doesn't Pieter just come around here? All this stupid cloak and dagger.* He sighed again. Well, a short late evening walk wouldn't hurt him, and if it meant that a fat envelope of hard cash was coming Griet's way, with him bringing it, he might get back into her good books. Telling her he'd resigned from the Liebaarts would do him no harm either. He found some matches from the kitchen drawer and a bowl from the cupboard and went through the rigmarole, dinned into all Liebaarts executive members, of burning message and cipher sheet. He didn't have to, not now, but habit impelled him. Leaving the flaky ashes in the bowl, he found his keys and slipped out of the flat and down the stairs.

*

At 9.45, a figure emerged from the entrance of the beguinage and looked around in the darkness. Becky Strange stepped out of the doorway. 'Follow me,' she said.

Guy Verstraete replied rapidly in Dutch. If she'd had to guess, Becky would have said that he was asking who she was, where Christina was and what was going on.

'I'm taking you to Christina,' Becky continued in English. 'Come on.'

'No. Not another step until you tell me what's going on.' Verstraete also switched to English, which was surprisingly good.

'Suit yourself, but I warn you, she's in a dangerous state.' Becky moved into the lane towards the Grote

Markt. This was the crucial point. It depended on the young man's concern for his fiancée outweighing the nationalist destiny to come. In a way, he'd already neglected Christina, so the odds were against him leaving the environs of the beguinage now.

But the way Becky turned on her heel and strode off towards the Grote Markt was magnetic. Guy was buoyed by the triumph of his heist at Oxford – conventional bourgeois stick-in-the-mud optician become invincible relic-robber and budding patriotic hero. He was curious rather than anxious about Christina, whom he knew was easily capable of looking after herself. So he set off to follow at a brisk pace.

Without turning around except for an initial check, Becky moved quickly, down the short lane into the Grote Markt, across the south side into Dorniksestraat and then into Burgemeester Reynaertstraat. Opposite the rectangular glass box that contained lift and stairs down to the underground car park, vaguely outlined in a dirty yellow light, was the combined service and fire exit door to the hotel. Becky rapped sharply on it – two bangs, a pause, and then a third – and almost immediately the door – squeezed between a Foot Locker shoe shop and a costume hire outlet – opened outwards, the person inside clearly waiting for the signal.

Becky hung back at this, another potential stumbling block, but Guy, still apparently propelled by his confidence and curiosity, did not hesitate as he passed into a blackness more intense than on the street. In a trice, he and Becky were gone, and in the short corridor, hands pulled the door shut and clicked the panic bar firmly back into place.

*

At five to ten, Jan Planckaert was just passing the Square Hotel. He knew the owner, a plump, jolly man of rabid right-wing views with whom he'd sometimes sit on bar stools lamenting the state of the world in general and Flanders in particular. He'd call in on the way home for a nightcap. Through the window of the hotel bar, he saw a group of company people knocking back the drinks before a hard week of meetings and sales, the men large and confident, the women younger and sleek in their business suits. Although the town was busy in the run-up to the anniversary march, the east end of Groeningestraat was away from the centre and therefore quiet. Planckaert saw no one as he turned left onto the tree-lined path that led through the ancient wall and around in a rightward curve to the entrance of his museum.

He looked at his watch and moved away from the light to the shadows of the museum entrance. It was 10 pm exactly as another figure emerged from a dark corner.

'Pieter,' said Planckaert, 'you gave me a fright... Oh, it's you.'

The pock-faced man strode forward swiftly, not saying a word. His right arm, held behind his back, suddenly moved to the front, something glinting dully out of his hand. Startled and off-balance, Planckaert didn't stand a chance as the thin, super-sharp knife-blade eased through his thin summer shirt and under his ribcage, piercing his heart. It was a single wound – there was no need for frenzy. Did the thrust go through left atrium or right atrium, left ventricle or right ventricle? Did it rupture tricuspid valve or mitral valve? Most likely the damage was overlapping and widespread. It didn't matter. The details would be the pathologist's business. For Planckaert the end was quick, quiet – because his assailant had a hand over his mouth as the knife went in – and moderately painful for the final thirty seconds of consciousness. Forty-five years of existence, consisting of many good things among the dubious, were snuffed out in just under two minutes.

The murderer had no time or imagination to reflect on that. He'd had the foresight to bring a towel to wipe the knife and inhibit the spread of too much blood. When he'd eased Planckaert, almost gently, to the ground, propping his back against the glass of the museum, he tossed a small, bright metal object onto Planckaert's chest and pinned a sliver of paper to his shirt collar. Then he marched rapidly off westwards across the park towards the beguinage.

In the Square Hotel, the owner sat at the bar with a double Scotch, wondering if he'd see his pal Planckaert tonight to talk over what was happening for the battle celebration.

No, he wouldn't. Not then. Not ever again.

*

Fortunately for Guy Verstraete, as his former colleague and friend was bleeding to death outside his own work-place, the optician's alibi was being established by his abductors, or rather, as he had come voluntarily, his persuaders. Becky and Sterling had him in the lift and they were taking him up to Sterling's room, the means chosen perfect for avoiding all the nationalists in the lobby, at the bar, and in fact swarming over the hotel. It would have been odds-on that someone would have recognised Verstraete. As it was, he was hurried along the third-floor corridor, into the bedroom and out of sight, his body language now indicating resignation as much as curiosity, the invincible aura much diminished.

He stood uncertainly but calmly in the centre of the room as Sterling surveyed him from the room's only chair at the desk, and Angela stood leaning against a curtain that rested next to the window.

Now that he was meeting the subject of Christina's desire properly for the first time, Sterling experienced curiosity of his own. He thought he was well acquainted with this young man. But what did he actually know? Christina had talked at length about him. So had Griet Planckaert. Even Opa Willem and Agnes had made their contributions. He was an optician – a highly skilled and well qualified professional – and a Flemish nationalist, operating at a high level in a rogue organisation. He'd shown himself to be a determined and resourceful man of action as well as an apparently ordinary citizen. Sterling and Albertin had followed him and formed another impression. But now that they were meeting directly for the first time an additional perspective would be emerging.

'At last, Guy,' he said familiarly and in English, the only language he knew, 'we meet face to face.' He pointed to the kettle. 'Cup of tea?'

Chapter 27

'Who the hell are you? And for the second time, where is Christina?' the young man replied in English. Sterling noticed a sulky downturn in his handsome mouth, as if the optician was used to getting his own way. It undermined the anger.

'Never mind about Christina for the moment, and never mind who we are. Just assume that we've got Christina's best interests at heart, which means, in a way, that we care about you.'

'I don't understand. This is stupid. I'm not wasting my time talking to you. I've got more important things to do.' As he spoke, Verstraete turned abruptly and made for the door, but Becky was blocking his way.

'I wouldn't try anything, mate. Becky is much more dangerous than she looks. Sit down on the bed over there and have that cup of tea. I've got things to tell you.'

Verstraete weighed things up and then sat on the bed, folding his arms. Angela, without a word, busied herself with the kettle, having got extra mugs, tea bags and milk from her room next door. Over the next twenty minutes, Sterling outlined to Verstraete everything he and the others had witnessed over the last few days.

'So you see the pickle you're in, Guy.'

'Pickle?'

'Mess, difficulty.'

Verstraete shrugged. 'Who cares?' he said. 'After tomorrow, everything changes. Do you think anyone in the Liebaarts is worried about our funding methods? And I'll be a hero in Flanders for getting back the Kortrijk Chest – our rightful property. Anyway, as you English say, you don't make omelettes without breaking eggs. You know, you're interfering with something so much more important than the engagement of an optician and a hotel worker. Anyway, Christina is my business, and I am hers. It's for us to work things out, which is what we'll do without you, and without the Liebaarts. Keep your noses out and let me get back to my duty.'

Sterling leaned forward in his chair. He could see Angela by the curtain, impressed by what she'd heard. Becky's expression was more neutral – the whys and wherefores meant little to her compared to the tasks at hand. But Verstraete's sulkiness had gone, replaced by zeal and belief in his cause to go with the anger, and Sterling too felt a faint stirring of admiration, the kind he had occasionally experienced when his idealistic father was in full flow about the possibilities of socialism.

It didn't last long. He was much more in the pragmatic camp, like Becky. The absence of ideological genes must have come from his mother's side. 'Exactly what we hoped you'd say – about you and Christina. Never mind the rest of it. We're going to tell Christina to come over here right now. It's time the two of you had an honest conversation.'

'So, she really is behind this – not her mother, not Opa Willem.' Verstraete stated it rather than asked the question. Now trust had been broken on both sides. Still, what he and Christina did about it was up to them.

Sterling went into the corridor with his phone. It was approaching midnight.

*

The dog-walker from Sint-Niklaasstraat had known at 10.30 that sleep wasn't going to come. His insomnia was a curse, but one that he'd come to terms with, and his two Dachshunds, brother and sister Mitzy and Albie, always loved a walk, whatever the time of day or night. He got out their leads, and the trio slipped out into the warm night, heading for a circuit around the Begijnhofpark. The dogs' legs were too small for chasing rabbits, or the occasional fox that came into the town for easy pickings, but trying was part of the fun. There was a short detour across the Houtmarkt, in the man's opinion the best and most imaginative piece of urban renewal he'd ever witnessed – a small pedestrian and cycling nirvana on the surface, and a hardly noticeable car park below. As usual, he savoured its grace and beauty, and then turned through the arch with the dogs, going left away from the museum, whose new annexe shimmered in the moonlight.

The dogs sniffed and snuffled their way around the perimeter anticlockwise, going right up to the ancient wall that divided the park from the environs of St Martin's Church. The dog-walker wondered about the tricky project he was grappling with at work, and whether his client would leave him alone on Monday or continue the meddling she'd initiated before the weekend. There was talk of a march or demonstration at the Groeninge Monument on Monday. There were plenty of oddly dressed young kids and others in the town during the day. He remembered vaguely that it was the anniversary of the Battle of Kortrijk. He didn't pay much attention. His business took all his time and energy.

On the way back, as the little evening party went closer to the museum, the atmosphere changed. Albie, always the most inquisitive, put his nose up and stayed stock still for a moment, and then moved quickly off, followed immediately after by Mitzy. It happened occasionally. The walker took little heed. A rabbit, a rodent. His amusing, affectionate, hopeless little mutts didn't stand a chance.

After the scent, the yapping – small, rapid, urgent yaps that suggested something amiss. The walker, forty metres back, quickened his pace. He wasn't worried, exactly – Kortrijk was a safe and law-abiding town, after all, and it was a Sunday evening – but something might not be right. He rounded the edge of the annexe and saw his dogs licking something next to a crumpled heap mostly obscured in the shadow. As he approached, the picture came into sharp focus. He'd found a body, and the dogs' late-night snack was blood. He shooed the dogs roughly and angrily away and went closer. A combination of long-ago first aid training and a regular diet of cop shows featuring crime scenes tainted by, well, dog-walkers, confused him. Tentatively, he found the body's neck and felt for a pulse. Satisfied that the man was dead, he avoided the pool of blood and retreated to what he assumed would be a non-polluting distance, herding the dogs close to him. Hands atremble, he fumbled in his pocket for his phone and punched in the well-remembered number.

*

Deliveries to the 1302 Museum came in through the back, which abutted Groeningestraat. Access by cars and vans to the front entrance was all but impossible because of the small size of the arch that led into Begijnhofpark. That's why there was only the faintest trace of flashing blue light from the ambulance and two police squad cars in Groeningestraat as a forensics team went about its business around the corpse of Jan Planckaert, within a cordoned-off area that extended from the front of the museum to the path. The detective in charge – temporarily at least – had transferred from Oudenaarde to Kortrijk following his recent promotion to inspector. He hovered near the team leader in her white coverall suit as the flash of a powerful camera lit the scene like lightning. The suit crackled as she held up a bloodied ID card and a driving licence. This investigator was helpful, quick and bold in her initial judgements. Her older colleague, fortunately on holiday, was cautious and squirrelled away information to boost his own importance, a habit that frequently led to clashes.

'His name's Jan Planckaert. An address in Gerstelaan. 6A. I think it might be down near the university quarter. I wonder what he's doing up here. You'll need to wait for the pathologist, but cause of death is almost certainly a single knife wound into the heart from under the rib cage, which makes it murder. He hasn't been dead long, given body temperature and so on – maybe an hour or so. It could not be self-inflicted, and any notion that it could be an accident is also outlandish. Not much pain – or rather, pain, probably, but not for very long. It was professionally done, in my opinion. We haven't found the weapon.

'Robbery is not a motive. His wallet and cash are still here, and his phone, which might be useful to you but is password protected, so you'll need a technician and the phone company. I'd be surprised if the attacker didn't have a certain amount of blood on his, or her, clothes. So far, we've found no fingerprints, hairs or footprints. There are no defensive wounds on the victim's hands or arms. I think he knew his attacker. The venue suggests a rendezvous. Interestingly, we found a couple of things on the body that obviously weren't the victim's. If we're careful, I can show you. They edged closer to the corpse, and the team leader pointed. 'See there, on his chest. Gold-coloured. It might even *be* gold. I'm waiting for the photographer to finish, and then I'll have a closer look.'

'A spur, perhaps,' said the detective. His niece rode horses. She didn't use spurs, he was sure, but the livery stables she went to had a display of old equine equipment.

'Perhaps,' said the woman. 'And this.' She had a metal pointer and indicated the slip of paper pinned to the lapel.

'Leliaart,' read the detective. 'What does that mean?'

The woman shrugged. 'That's your department, I think. It's a word with an old-fashioned ring to it. That's as far as we've got. Remember, as always, that my conclusions are tentative until you have my final report.'

'Thanks, Lisbeth.' The detective moved away from the crime scene towards the dog-walker, who was speaking to another detective he hadn't yet met. He nodded to both men. His colleague, newly promoted from the uniformed branch, looked briefly at his notes. 'Mr Smid here was walking his dogs, and they found the body at...' – he squinted at his own writing – '11.30.'

'Did you see anyone, Mr Smid, anywhere in the park or at the front of the museum?'

'Not a soul, officer. Sometimes there is a drunk or a homeless person, even a fox, but tonight it was as quiet and empty as a graveyard. As usual, I couldn't sleep, which is why I was out.'

The inspector was thinking that graveyards could be quiet but were far from empty. He shivered at the thought and then focused back on the dog-walker. 'OK, thank you. Presumably my colleague has your details in case we need to ask you any more questions.' It wasn't unknown for murderers to report their crimes to throw the police off the scent, but this fussily-dressed little man seemed a very unlikely candidate. No doubt at some stage someone would have to look into possible connections between victim and finder – if and when better lines of investigation came to nothing.

Forensics might come up with something more, but until they did there was only one real lead, which would be combined with the duty many police officers would far prefer to avoid. He motioned to the detective constable to finish what he was doing and follow him to his car behind the emergency service vehicles in Groeningestraat. Having not met his colleague before, because of the current bedlam in Kortrijk, he completed formal introductions. 'I've got an address for the victim,' he said. 'That's where we're going next. On the way, I want you to find as many details as you can about Jan Planckaert, Gerstelaan, 6A.'

The young detective constable was keen and competent, his small face and sharp nose illuminated by the ghostly light of his phone as he used his thumbs expertly on the small screen's keyboard. The inspector, still only in his late thirties, felt older.

'Here we are. Jan Planckaert, curator of the 1302 Museum for about three years.'

'That was quick,' said the inspector.

His DC didn't seem to take it as a compliment. He probably considered the task he'd been set as triflingly easy. 'We had his name,' he commented. 'He was slumped outside the museum. It seemed obvious to go first to the museum's website and find the staff roster. He's pretty involved in the goings-on in the town. I've got photos of the museum's re-launch, with the mayor and councillors and so on. Other meetings. This looks as though it's his wife.'

He offered the phone. The inspector took a quick sideways glance and then returned his attention to the road. 'Give her a ring and warn her that we're on our way.'

Who knows how things might have changed if the two men had been on duty a couple of nights before when the firebombing of the optician's had happened, what connections they would have made, and what they might have prevented? But there had been no general briefing. One was newly transferred, and the other had just come back on duty after a holiday. The street lights in Gerstelaan had gone off as the unmarked police car pulled into it, and they craned to see house numbers. The buildings themselves seemed to brood under the moonlit sky.

'This one,' said the DC, and the car pulled up outside Griet Planckaert's place. She appeared at the door soon after he had rung the bell. Even though the security chain was on, the detectives could see her slender frame wrapped in a mauve dressing gown that set off her striking red hair. 'What's this about?' she said on the doorstep as she took in and examined the policemen's badges under the hallway light, around which a moth fluttered.

'May we come in?' said the inspector. 'It's too... delicate for the doorstep.'

The chain rattled and the two policemen were ushered to the same seats occupied by Sterling and Albertin earlier in the day. This time, however, at 1.30am, no coffee was forthcoming. Griet Planckaert perched on the end of her chair and drew her gown more tightly around her.

The inspector cracked his finger joints, unaware that he was doing it. It wasn't helping that he could sense the tenseness in the young man next to him. He'd done this a few times but no policeman would tell you that you'd get used to it. He squirmed in his chair, staring at the small vase in the middle of the coffee table that had replaced the sprawl of papers there earlier. He started his spiel – because that's what it was really – and gained a certain poise as he got further into it.

'Mrs Planckaert, I'm very sorry to have to tell you that we found a body outside the entrance to the 1302 Museum in the centre of Kortrijk tonight. We will need you to confirm this, but an ID card and driver's licence found on the body, and visual confirmation from photographs we've gained access to, indicate almost 100% that it's your husband, Jan.' Finally, the inspector managed to stop addressing the vase with its sad little arrangement of small blue campanulas and look up into Griet Planckaert's face. 'We're very sorry for your loss.' Next to him, he could sense the DC nodding.

The woman sat absolutely still, as if nothing at all had been said. Her face transposed into a faintly glazed look, and her eyes stared at the inspector without really seeing him. Then they came back into focus, and he could see the effort she was making to compose herself, her hands so clenched together that her knuckles almost glowed white against her already pale hands.

'How…?' she rasped.

'I'm sorry… but we think he was murdered – a single stab wound to the heart.'

'He didn't live here,' Griet said in an abrupt non-se-quitur. 'We had been separated for a few months. He had a flat near the museum. We said then that we'd talk about getting back together after we'd had time to think about it. There had been hints, but we hadn't got around to it.' Her eyes brimmed and she sniffed before recovering again. 'Now it's too late.'

'May we ask a few questions? It would help us in these early stages of investigation. We could come back, but then we'd have lost some precious time.'

'Ask,' said Griet.

'Well, can you tell us why you separated? You must have been married for some time…'

Griet shrugged. 'Marriages. You only know what goes on in your own. The happiest-looking can be mis-erable, and the difficult ones successful. Jan and I were indeed married a long time – almost twenty-five years – but maybe things had got stale. Maybe we started wanting different things. Our children are grown up and gone.' Her gaze left the inspector's face and went down to the right.

'So, no link between the separation and… the inci-dent tonight.'

'You mean, did I…?' she stopped and took a breath. The inspector and his clever, well-attuned young colleague stayed silent. 'Did I get a knife and stick it in my husband outside his place of work earlier this evening?' She laughed without humour. 'Well, I haven't got an alibi. Go and see if the bed looks slept in or is still warm. Maybe pop the hood on my car and see if the engine's warm. Check my phone for calls and messages. Search the bloody house, why don't you? See if a knife is missing from the rack in the kitchen.'

'We really can do this another time, but we must look at everything.'

'OK, well, no – no link between the separation and Jan's... Not that I know of anyway. Your colleague can check the house if you want. I've got nothing to hide.'

'Unofficially then, Mrs Planckaert, while we continue our conversation. Thank you.'

The DC got up and moved to the door. 'Don't make a mess,' said Griet.

Somewhere a clock chimed. 'Did your husband have any enemies, Mrs Planckaert?'

'He was a museum curator, for goodness' sake. How could he have enemies?'

'Anyone can have enemies.'

Griet said nothing.

After a few more minutes, the DC returned and thanked the optician gravely, and the inspector took out his phone. We found these on the bod... on Mr Planckaert.' He leant over and showed the photo of the gold-coloured spur, or spur facsimile, and the piece of paper pinned to the lapel. 'There's a word on the paper. You might not be able to read it. "Leliaart".'

Griet stared down at the phone. Her unruly hair flopped forward and covered her face, but she made no effort to push or hold it back. A few seconds passed

– enough for a thorough examination – and to mask and then adjust the expression on her face.

'No, inspector, I simply have no idea.' She folded her arms below her chest. 'I doubt if Jan got involved in anything while we were apart, but I suppose you can't rule out the possibility. Look, I need to phone my children and tell them what's happened. I need to... do whatever it is you do when your husband's been... murdered.'

'Of course. Of course.' The inspector held up his hands. 'But you understand that we'll probably have to return. If you think of anything else, here's my card. Can we leave you by yourself, or should I arrange a family liaison officer? Maybe a patrol car to come by every now and again?'

'Thank you but no, inspector. I'll phone my daughter. She'll be able to come over from Poperinge.'

The ride back to Kortrijk police station was smooth and quiet. The suburbs were still. The inspector had come to rate his new young colleague highly, even after such a short acquaintance. 'Did you find anything?'

'No unwashed-up, bloodied knife in the rack.' (The faintest hint of a smile flitted across the DC's features – another positive point noted by his older colleague). 'A lot of folders in a large cardboard box – clients' details and a blank insurance claim application – I didn't really have time to examine it any further. The key was in the back door so I slipped out and felt the engine of the SUV, as she suggested. Completely cold – not used since this morning I shouldn't imagine. Bed in the main bedroom slept in by one person.'

'Do you think she's involved – a contract hit of some kind?'

'No. They had separated but her upset was genuine. I think she still loved him. But I got the impression she was holding back – just little indications here and there. She knew what that golden object was, and she may well have recognised the word on the lapel.'

The DC was sharp.

'Good. How long have you been a detective?' said the inspector.

His colleague stared out at the road ahead, not one to milk praise. 'A few months.'

'You haven't wasted any time, and you've summed up my thoughts exactly. Check the life assurance situation, will you? See if there's a policy and if there is, who it favours. We need to keep an eye on Griet Planckaert.'

Chapter 28

Griet sat for long minutes in her chair. Both detectives seemed competent and astute, but it struck her as strange that they didn't seem to know about the firebombing of her shop and therefore hadn't made a connection between that and poor Jan's murder. It wouldn't be long before they did, though, and then they'd be back, or the ones dealing with the firebombing would be.

She got up, went to the drinks cabinet and poured a handsome slug of cognac, swilling it distractedly in the balloon glass as she returned to her chair. She wasn't sure if she was all right by herself, but she wasn't ready to phone Sandrin yet. The effect from the swig of brandy spread quickly through her body and helped her start weeping. Soon, racking sobs were convulsing her, and she encouraged and welcomed them as tears flowed copiously down her cheeks. She had felt despair when she learnt the fate of her shop – all that time and effort invested in building up the business destroyed in minutes – but after that shock, she'd known that she had the energy and determination to retrieve the situation.

Losing poor, dear Jan was utterly different. There had been signs, especially outside her blazing shop, that he was hoping to come back to her, and she thought she'd be receptive. After all, there hadn't been much wrong with the marriage without Van Leuven's poisonous contribution. But now it was too late. Everything was too late. She knew what she could expect in the next few days after this shock and numbness. There would be grief, a growing sense of loss, and guilt that her impulsive nature had caused the separation in the first place. (*"Van Leuven or me" – how could I have been so crass?*). Mixed up with all that would be fear for the future, and more immediately the dread of having to break the news to the children.

She allowed the drink to numb the pain. The sobs subsided and the tears dried, her face sticky as she blinked and her cheeks wrinkled. There was time enough for all the sorrow. What was more important right now was to focus on the rage she felt, and what she had always known was part of her – the capacity for revenge. The policemen hadn't realised it, but they'd virtually told her who'd killed Jan, directly or more likely through one of his thugs. The Golden Spurs. Leliaart – that contemptuous word, twisted by Van Leuven and his friends so that in the twenty-first century it was an insult. The arrogance of the man. He'd regret ever crossing Griet Planckaert. He'd get what he deserved, and she'd be supplying it.

She rummaged in her handbag for a card and punched a number into her phone. Surprisingly, given that it was 1.30 am, Frank Sterling picked up almost straight away. Christina had arrived, and she was closeted with her fiancé in Angela and Becky's room while the English trio retreated next door to Sterling's.

'Sterling.'

Griet took a breath and composed herself. It seemed strange that she liked and trusted someone she'd only met once. 'Mr Sterling, Griet Planckaert. I'm sorry to be calling so late.'

'That's OK, Mrs Planckaert. As it happens, I'm still up. It's been a... busy evening so far, and I'm not sure it's over yet.'

'I hope I won't make it more complicated. I've got some information for you, and at the same time I need some from you.'

Sterling glanced at the two women and raised his eyebrows. 'Go on then.'

Griet wondered if she could say what she planned without breaking down. 'I'm sorry to say – desolated in fact – that my dear Jan has been found dead tonight, outside his museum, a couple of hours ago.' She sipped her cognac. It was as if someone else was speaking.

Sterling stayed still and quiet. He liked and admired this woman. She'd be in a state of shock, so a sympathetic reception was essential.

'Are you still there, Mr Sterling?'

'Yes. I'm very, very sorry. I know you were separated, but the marriage wasn't over, was it?'

'No, well, it's too late now. He'd been stabbed, so it was murder. It was Van Leuven, through one of his thugs.'

'How do you know, Griet?' Sterling smoothly crossed the boundary from formality to friendship.

'A golden spur had been left on his body, and the word "Leliaart" pinned to his lapel. The police have not long left here, and they showed me photographs.'

'"Leliaart"? You told me about Leliaarts earlier – French supporters, back in the thirteenth century.'

'And, if you remember, for Flemish nationalists a term of abuse in the twenty-first. To call Jan a Leliaart, after all his commitment to Flemish culture and independence, is one of the worst possible insults. I expect the police will find all this out eventually but by then it will be too late. Jan is dead, and I've got to get on with life. But Van Leuven isn't going to get away with it.'

'You haven't told the police this yet?'

'Funny coming from you, Frank. I could tell straight away when we met earlier that you don't have much time for them.'

'Even so... aren't they best placed to get justice for Jan?'

'Frank, I haven't got time for this. I've told you what's happened. What I need you to tell me is what's happening tomorrow. Where is Van Leuven going to be?... Are you still there?'

'Yes, I'm here.' Sterling looked away from Angela and Becky. 'He'll be at the Groeninge Monument at eleven am tomorrow, amazingly enough with the genuine Kortrijk Chest that seems to have been stolen from England. Along with about 20,000 Flemish nationalists, according to my source.'

'That's all I need to know. Thank you. And finally, Frank, a warning. I gather that girl of Guy Verstraete's, the one you're working for, is a decent person. I don't want to upset her. If you've got any chance at all, keep that young idiot Verstraete out of things. It's stupid people like him who've helped to stoke Van Leuven's delusions of grandeur. If the boy's around, he'll be in danger. Goodnight, Frank.'

'Wait a moment, Griet, what are you planning? You need to be caref...' The dial tone hummed in Sterling's ear.

Angela and Becky looked at him expectantly, and he relayed the conversation. 'Another complication for tomorrow,' said Angela.

'I'm sorry for the optician,' said Becky. 'Her life has been turned upside down twice in a matter of days. If I were in her position, and a criminal arsonist had burnt the pub down with Mike in it, I might be considering the same thing – not bothering with the police and sorting out the punishment on my own. Let's face it, that's what she's got in mind. But if we're going to get involved in this demo or whatever it is tomorrow, what's happened could work to our advantage.'

'I was thinking that,' said Sterling. 'It didn't look too promising when we put Christina in with Mr Fanatic just now. It looked as though it was shaping up for the mother of all rows. Christina's just not the sobbing and pleading type, and Guy is too involved with the Liebaarts. But he might come to his senses if we talk about murder. If he doesn't, what do we do with him to keep him out of the way tomorrow? Come on. We need to work something out with those two.'

When they went next door, the atmosphere was full of tension. Christina's usually pale, freckled face was pink – whether with rage or upset. Sterling again noticed Guy Verstraete's sulkiness – not just in his downturned mouth and surly eyes but in his whole demeanour, a young man too used to getting his own way. Christina had turned the only chair away from the desk under the wall-mounted television, leaning back, one arm spread across the desk, legs crossed at the ankles. Verstraete was on the bed next to the bolster, hands clasped and staring towards the window. Anyone who might have expected a tearful and loving reunion twenty minutes ago, when Christina had arrived from Ypres, would have been woefully disappointed.

'Sorry to interrupt,' said Sterling. He resisted adding "you lovebirds". Why make a dire situation worse? 'We've just had some pretty awful news that might affect your... discussions.' He turned directly to Guy. 'Your mat..., your associate, Jan Planckaert – he was murdered tonight outside the museum. There's apparently strong evidence linking it to the Liebaarts, and as you're high up in the movement, and as you seem to oversee the executive arm, as it were, you're highly likely to be a person of interest to the local police. Never mind all the rest of it. Whatever happens over the next few days, you're going to be in the frame for that.'

Sterling kept quiet about the solidness of the young activist's alibi – that he had been enticed to the hotel with a whole range of witnesses at exactly the time the murder had taken place. He let his comments sink in. There was a shift in Verstraete's manner. He seemed shaken and upset, and his hands twisted together on his lap. His gaze shifted from the curtains and towards Sterling. 'Jan was a friend. I'd never have harmed him. Something's not right here.' His clouded expression cleared. 'This is a trick.'

''Fraid not, old son. There's more. My source indicates that you might be in danger as well.'

'Your source?' Verstraete sneered. 'You don't know anything.'

'Whatever. But we can't go back and forth all night to sort this out. You've got a choice now. You drive back to Ypres tonight with Christina, and between you work something out, or we find another way to keep you from getting into further trouble and danger.' Sterling looked at Becky, arms folded, sole of one foot planted on the door and with her back to it, and then at

Verstraete. 'Don't think we don't have the expertise to do that, and, if we do, it will be uncomfortable and boring.' Becky's expression was neutral, and she was a small and slight woman, but it was apparent that Sterling believed she was capable of anything he asked. 'Of course, we don't have to be involved ourselves. We could just call the police, give them a tip-off, and let them pick you up.'

'It's not a choice I'm getting here.'

'Well,' said Christina, getting abruptly to her feet. 'I'm not wasting any more time. You can come with me, or I'll leave you with Frank and his friends.' Her words hovered in the air with the heavy whiff of an ultimatum.

Verstraete got to his feet. He'd also made a quick decision. 'Alright.' He switched to Dutch and his face broke into a glorious, transforming smile, obliterating the sulkiness instantly, to which Christina responded with a smile and some Dutch sentences of her own. This was more like the man she loved, and the love seemed plausible.

Sense at long bloody last. 'You give your word you'll go back with Christina, Guy? Becky, will you see them down to the car park?'

Becky pushed her back off the door and opened it, standing aside for the Belgian couple.

'Alright, Becks?' said Sterling, when she'd returned.

'Well, they drove off together, so probably. I expect we'll hear from Christina if anything happens. Keeping him quiet somewhere in the hotel, probably in one of our rooms, might have been tricky and not just boring for him but for me as well, since I expect I'd have been his keeper. So it's risky but saves me from hassle.

'He's still in a mountain of trouble,' said Angela, 'and I doubt it's going to go away. Any change of plan for tomorrow, Frank?'

'Not much. I don't think Christina will be back because she'll have her hands full. I haven't heard from Yves, but he said he was coming over. Willem will be there. I think it would be best if Becky joined you on the fringes. You'll need to be careful, Ange. Let's remind ourselves – there'll be some nasty, hard-core types around, racists and the like. It isn't going to be any kind of touchy-feely, liberal-lefty love-fest.'

'So delicately expressed,' murmured Angela.

'You know me,' said Sterling. 'Not only that, since Griet Planckaert is on the warpath, that's something else to look out for.' He yawned. 'Bloody hell. 2.30. The shenanigans start at 10 o'clock tomorrow. I need some kip. See you women at breakfast.'

Chapter 29

'You'll be interested in this, Ange,' said Sterling the next morning, taking long pulls at the cup of coffee he'd procured from the coffee jug. 'Straight into the veins. Much needed. Anyway, I had a dream. Vivid.'

Around the table, the noise level was rising, with the restaurant area seemingly packed to the gunwales with Flemish people getting ready to assemble at the Groeninge Monument and tucking into good breakfasts to fortify themselves for the adventure ahead. There seemed to be a force field around the little English group, whether because of the language barrier or because of its ethnic diversity.

Becky, seated next to Sterling, gave nothing away and concentrated on her croissant, but Angela became alert. Dream analysis enthused her. She'd been known to talk, only half-jokingly, about the ego "bobbing along" in the vast ocean of the unconscious. 'Go on, then.'

Sterling took another sip of coffee and a mouthful of muesli. Though he'd given his face a good wash, he still rubbed his gritty eyes. He knew dream descriptions always hooked Angela in, but paused to tantalise.

'All right. Here it is. I'm in a waiting room, maybe connected to a station or something, though it doesn't seem obvious. Nowhere I recognise. It's very airy and light, with big windows and doors. The colours are neutral and, in a way, glassy – not even pastel hues. Kind of nothing.

'I'm sitting by myself on one of the benches in the middle. The benches make up a square of four, with a mucky bit inside where the cleaner can't reach. People seem to have tossed a bit of rubbish in there – a lolly wrapper, an empty box of Maltesers.

'People come into the waiting room, men and women I don't particularly recognise. The first is a tall woman with sad brown eyes, who speaks softly and gently and leaves reluctantly. A man in a dark grey suit follows – surly and brusque, saying a couple of words and moving quickly off, and another one in a long, expensive great-coat like a football manager. Then another, all charm and smiles, with grey hair and sparkling eyes. This one sits next to me but he too still eventually leaves.

'A rodent of some kind scuttles around on the floor, foraging for food and probing in corners – seeming to be impatient and hurried, and not resting a second. It squeaks and its whiskers are very prominent. I get up and walk around myself. I'm feeling anxious, unsettled and mercurial, but I don't leave the building. A black cat comes from nowhere and settles quietly on my lap and stays there. It has a calming effect on me, and from being agitated and restless I become patient and thought-ful. The rodent has disappeared.

'The waiting room, previously colourless, is infused with a pinkish evening sunlight. Now the cat has disap-peared. I get up and leave the building.'

Sterling looked sheepishly down into his bowl of muesli. It was only since his close friendship with Angela that he'd started to cast away the macho side of his personality, or more accurately temper it with acknowledgement and even acceptance of world views that were not utterly pragmatic, empirical and mirror images of his own. Angela was persuasive on a range of fronts, and her interest in and knowledge of dream psychology had begun to pique Sterling's interest.

'There's a lot to explore in that,' she said. 'Loads of images. Just off the top of my head, the waiting room, the benches and how they're organised, the rubbish behind them. That brown-eyed woman, who might represent some aspect of your inner wisdom. She's worth keeping an eye on. The clothes are interesting, and the colours, and those animals – the rodent and the cat. That ending, when you leave the building – there's a lot in that. But whoa... It's your dream, Frank, your connection between consciousness and the unconscious.'

Finally, Becky put down her croissant. 'Listen, have we got time for this? It sounds like mumbo-jumbo to me, and' – she twisted her wrist and looked ostentatiously at her watch – 'we're in action in just over two hours.'

'You're right, Becky.' Sterling turned to Angela. 'There'll be plenty of time to analyse it later.'

A curious expression formed on Angela's face – curious, because Sterling hadn't seen it before – a mixture of sly and amused. 'If you don't analyse it now it could be gone forever, Frank. First and foremost, it's about your inner awareness' – she ignored Becky's exasperated head-shake – 'but it might have an external relevance. It might help with this whole case. When something's important, there's always time.' She leaned back and folded her arms. The expression now was surely a smirk.

Obscurely, Sterling thought of an angler in waders, and bait. Angela knew that something in the whole affair was bothering him – a sense that he was missing something. Maybe she was right, and the dream would provide a connection. 'So, remind me, what do I need to do?'

Becky rolled her eyes, not even bothering to disguise it. She clomped off for a refill of coffee. Angela watched her go, leaned forward and spoke urgently. 'Four things. Firstly, note down all the images. I've started it off. Secondly, connect the images to what's going on in your inner life – events, emotions and so on. Thirdly, see what this is telling you. Lastly, and importantly, do something with the information, even if it's just writing it down.'

'And you're wanting me to do this why?' said Sterling. 'To help with the case, or so I learn more about myself? Allegedly.'

'I think the second thing is more important to be honest, Frank. You're my friend. I want the best for you. But you've said yourself that you're missing something in this case. Maybe the dream analysis will help you find it. You've got time, and it will do far more good than harm.' She glanced over to the buffet area where Becky was queuing for the coffee. 'I love Becky like a sister. She and Mike have helped both of us out so much over the past couple of years. They are the very best at what they do. But the fact that they're the most practical, pragmatic people I know makes them inflexible. Use every arrow in your quiver is what I say, and rule nothing out. I don't care if people think dream work is mumbo-jumbo. They're the ones missing out, not you and me. You've shown your flexibility and openness of mind by going along with me.'

Becky returned. The thing about her, and part of the reason Sterling was also so fond of and grateful to her and Mike, stemmed from the fact that when they were on Sterling's business, they simply did as he asked. They didn't ask questions, except for clarification, and they didn't raise objections. Becky's view of dream analysis was a rare revelation and a temporary exception. When she sat down again at the table, there were no recriminations and no tension. She'd probably absented herself for a few moments to allow equilibrium to be restored, and for Angela and Sterling to sort things out between themselves. It had worked perfectly. Breakfast wound down, both on the English table and around them. Aurélien was helping his colleague on buffet duty and smiled over as he cleared away the breakfast debris.

'OK,' said Sterling. 'We have got a bit of time so I'm going to go to my room. No point in being sneaky, Becks. I'm going to do a bit of dream work. See you both in forty minutes.'

Upstairs, he sat at the desk and cleared the jumble of breakfast and Wi-Fi literature away into a drawer, along with the remote for the TV up on the wall. Through the net curtains, he could see people milling around on Schouwburgplein – more than usual, surely, on a Monday morning – among them three boys and three girls having a lively game of "tig". One part of him wondered what on earth he was doing, just as everything outside was going to erupt. But another part knew that when he started putting pen to paper, writing out the dream and then starting to relate images to what was going on in his life, then he'd develop momentum and become engrossed. That's what he'd found on previous occasions. Even within the description of the dream, emotions and feelings were emerging – in one section agitation and anxiety, and in another, calm and thoughtfulness.

This time, instead of the wheel and spokes approach Angela had once shown him, he used columns.

Image	Association
Building/waiting room	Life, possibilities, openness, opportunity; not a prison, airy, light, empty, going nowhere, neutral, glassy, no weight.
Benches	Shape of four, making a square; rubbish in the middle, stuff that doesn't matter but can't be reached.
Woman with sad brown eyes	Mother figure; actual mother?; inner wisdom?; me not listening to her messages so she goes; desertion (unwillingly because sad); brown, soft, kind, gentle.
Charming man and others	Familiar – one of the opas; Jose Mourinho overcoat circa 2002, smart; but he goes too; all the people go; letting me down, betraying.
Rodent	Fussy, impatient, rushed, up and down, thoughtless, unfocused.
Black cat	Calm; thoughtful, thinking things through *properly*; picking up clues.
Colours – brown, grey, neutral, pinkish	Not harsh, not strong, soft, thoughtful. Pinkish – revealing, peacefully accepting.

Departure   Release, breaking the mould;
finding a solution; overcoming
betrayal; moving on; balance,
calmness, flash of understanding.

Sterling rubbed his temples. He could feel the dull beginning of a headache. It would be good to get outside into the air after this, but he could probably depend on Aurélien to produce some aspirin if it really took hold. In the square, the tig-players had gone or at least had merged into the steadily growing crowd.

The tricky bit, he always found, was the interpretation. When he'd been through the stages, he could ask Angela, but he didn't know when he'd get the opportunity over the coming day.

He mulled over various ideas. He had to remember – the dream was probably about him and his inner life and not what was going on in the world, but he had to be ready with external interpretations if there was an energy surge connected with them. The building represented opportunity. It wasn't a prison, even if he was the only one who remained in it. It was light, open and airy. He wrestled with the idea of the woman with sad brown eyes. He'd never seen his mother, not properly, so the woman was a symbol within himself. The idea that she was his inner wisdom, according to the gospel of Angela Wilson, was plausible. She left sadly because he wasn't listening to her. All the other leavers pointed him to his recurrent dreams of betrayal and desertion – but who was doing it? Was he betraying others, or were they betraying him? Even if all the figures were representations of his inner personalities, one at least – Jose Mourinho man – seemed to have further significance.

The rodent suggested that the message of his unconscious was telling him he was being too hasty and impatient – as all his appraisal interviewers had said when
he'd been on the job, he thought ruefully – but the black
cat indicated that he was also capable of calm and sensible thinking.

After the long, edgy and uneasy section, the dream
had ended optimistically, with a sense that he was breaking the mould, finding release, identifying a solution.
Perhaps he was overcoming episodes of betrayal and
desertion and moving on to acceptance. Sitting quietly at
his desk, he felt a surge of positive energy generated by
his analysis. He could almost see the glorious, liberating
pink glow as he left his dream-building at the end.

He looked at his watch – 9.45 – he'd been working
for over three-quarters of an hour. There was still plenty
of time. He was glad he'd made the effort and Angela
would be pleased, but he didn't think his unconscious
was helping him solve his case. The dream was about
inner stuff. The trouble was, something was still nagging
at him, and he still hadn't got to the bottom of it.

Chapter 30

At 10 o'clock the foyer was packed. There was a long queue to check out. Aurélien and his colleagues, summoned no doubt from near and far, toiled away patiently at their computer screens.

Sterling was relieved to see a mixture of attire in the swarm of nationalists. There was a large retro element, with gear that reminded him of his Sealed Knot adventures with his father – all coarse wool of strange design in muted browns and greens, and crude leather sandals, with awkwardly shaped bags and knapsacks, also predominantly of leather. But there were others who hadn't really bothered, dressed in a modern, casual, camping style of familiar brands, with swanky, aluminium-framed rucksacks of the most up-to-date waterproof fabric. It was clear that everyone was leaving the hotel and unlikely in the short term to return. The point was that Sterling, and whoever turned up to join him, did not look jarringly out of place.

'Any joy, Frank?' said Angela.

He'd just rejoined her and Becky in the breakfast area, now utterly devastated by the horde of hungry, short-of-time breakfasters. He felt sheepish, despite Becky choosing to pay no attention to the conversation. Something caught her eye in the melee near the permanently swooshing glass doors at the front and she moved away with a laconic 'Back in a moment'.

'Depends,' said Sterling. 'The betrayal theme, as usual, and how I deal with it – optimistically this time, apparently. A lot about impatience and fussiness, represented by the rodent, and calmness represented by the black cat. I don't think there's much about what's happening externally – to do with the case – to be honest. I'm missing something, but the analysis hasn't helped.'

'Still, self-knowledge, Frank. Connecting with your rich unconscious. Becoming more whole.'

'Hmph. Mumbo-jumbo. I don't think I'd have had a bash at analysis if I hadn't thought it might give a bit of practical help. Where are the opas? We haven't heard from Yves for a while. Willem can be a miserable git, but he's turning out more reliable.'

'Talk of the devil. Here he is now with Becky.'

'And a text from Albertin.' Sterling showed the others his screen. "Apologies, Frank. Something has come up. I can't join you today after all." 'Can't be helped, I suppose. But it's inconvenient. How are we going to communicate with Willem now?'

As the throng heaved around the small group, Sterling conducted a brief team meeting. 'As agreed, Willem and I will go to the gathering. Ange, you and Becky stay close by – or as close as you can manage.' Sterling mimed to Willem, pointing at the two of them and indicating a march by waggling his index and middle fingers. Willem nodded and grimaced. A slight deviation in the straight line of his mouth hinted at a smile. 'Phones at the ready but remember that Willem and I will have to be careful using ours because there won't be other phones in the crowd.'

As Sterling spoke, a change of atmosphere cascaded through the lobby and ground floor, like a suddenly unstopped bottleneck. From a disordered, jumbled mass, a kind of column developed that surged into the street, stopping traffic and creating a thick human wedge in Lange Steenstraat. People from other directions – the railway station, the Grote Markt – swelled the group.

'Take care, Frank,' said Angela, as she and Becky allowed a gap to open between themselves and the crowd. 'To be honest, you're welcome to it.'

Sterling stopped. It didn't matter that he and Willem were falling behind. 'All right, Ange?'

'You didn't really notice, did you, back there? My presence wasn't popular with that lot.' Angela pointed with her chin down the pedestrianized area. 'You didn't see the looks. I was the only person of colour in that whole hotel. It's lonely sometimes, Frank.'

'Actually, I did notice, but we choose our battles, don't we? Fuck 'em. We'll sort it all out.' He gave Angela a quick hug. 'Whatever it is,' he murmured in her ear.

Willem stood on the other side of the road, nodding. He caught Angela's eye and gave her a thumbs up. Then he and Sterling marched briskly off to catch up with the crowd, fortunate that some unseen obstacle ahead had temporarily slowed its progress. Communication between them was going to be difficult without Albertin, or Agnes, or even Christina, but for the moment Sterling wasn't too fussed, and Willem did not seem to be either. Sterling was thinking again that there was more to Willem than met the eye. He was not the grumpy, one-dimensional, unreconstructed Flemish nationalist of their first meeting. There was a sensitivity about him, and not just in relation to his granddaughter. He'd demonstrated that with Angela. Though they did not speak, there was an easy familiarity between the two men as they mingled with the crowd.

Down Lange Steenstraat, shoppers gawped and exchanged glances. Occasionally, from the shops Guy Verstraete and the Big Man, Leo Janssen, had collected subscriptions from, owners or managers came to their doors and applauded. The split between those "in the know" about the event and those who didn't was stark. As Willem and Sterling reached the Grote Kring, a Chihuahua started a frenzied yapping as it strained on its lead, front legs airborne, the owner maintaining control with amused and indulgent ease. Willem turned to Sterling and rolled his eyes. Janssen, Sterling was thinking – no one has seen or heard from him for a while. He wondered if the Big Man was implicated in Jan Planckaert's murder, or if he'd be up at their destination.

At this juncture, the marching nationalists were quiet, sober and focused. It would have been a Sunday stroll but for their numbers and density, which was increasing all the time. Soon Willem and Sterling, towards the end of the column, passed the burnt-out shell of Griet Planckaert's shop, standing out like a reproach on the prosperous thoroughfare, and a few minutes later they emerged at the other end of Lange Steenstraat away from the shops and into the residential district. Inevitably, the weight of pedestrian numbers halted the traffic, and the mass gravitated to and then through the entrance archway to the Groeningeveld, where Sterling and Albertin had followed Pieter Van Leuven days before. Then they were approaching the monuments. The sculpture of the two spurs resting together looked like the bandy-legged frame of a wigwam, points crossed at the top. Behind it, the golden statue of the Virgin of Flanders pointed to a defeated France, holding the mane of a lion above a stone relief of dead and dying French knights and horses, and victorious Flemish infantrymen with their goedendags.

As the column dissipated into a more amorphous mass on the sward, like fluid spreading out from a spilt bottle, a new raucous quality filled the warm, sunny, morning air. Sterling felt the surge of excitement himself as people saluted the monuments, and Willem's eyes shone as he too was carried along in the new atmosphere. Getting to the Groeningeveld was about discipline and avoiding exhibition – just a quiet and orderly demo on an ordinary Monday morning. The usual 1302 anniversary proceedings. If there was any kind of a police presence, it was discreet to the point of invisibility, in the form of observers from the blocks of flats overlooking the park, or infiltrators closer by. But Sterling doubted that there were either, with no notification to the police or interest from them. Van Leuven seemed to be running an unremarkable, low-tech organisation that was causing government no disquiet at all, because government was not aware that it existed.

The hubbub increased and there was even an occasional chant. On the fringes of the park, the usual Monday morning dribble of dog-walkers, dogs, parents and preschool children gravitated towards the exits, one or two people showing bemusement about the sudden turn of events.

Sterling dredged up his memories of the marches and demos he'd helped to police when he'd been on the job – generally tedious work with the occasional flare up, especially when he'd been deployed to London. March organisers tripled numbers attending for PR purposes, while the police went the other way. But he reckoned that the number here wasn't going to be far short of the 20,000 Willem had reported. Not bad for an obscure, and many would say unfashionable, political grouping.

Something caught Sterling's eye, a brief glitter in the sunshine. Then there were more glints, as people rummaged in pockets and bags and purses and drew forth badges and brooches and breastpins, fixing them to their blouses and shirts. Looking at the men and women closest to him and Willem, Sterling saw emerging an astonishing and varied array of beautiful, delicately wrought miniature spurs, exclusively fashioned in gold. Some were ornately filigreed and some of more solid, plain design, like the spurs sculpture nearby. In one or two cases, the little rowels actually spun in their intricately-crafted rowel boxes. Sterling assumed there had been a signal to get the emblems out, though the collective action seemed spontaneous. Willem handed him a badge and fixed his own to his jacket.

To the left of the larger monument, men and women in jeans and T-shirts were busy with a temporary podium, slotting a platform on to a trellised structure about three metres high. A set of silvery steps appeared from nowhere, unfolded smoothly and clipped to the platform. A young woman with a small, severe face and black hair in a ponytail tested the steps at the bottom and then systematically up to the top. Two burly young men wrestled speakers, microphone and mic holder up to the platform, fiddling with wires and other mysterious, less identifiable apparatus. The man in charge, obvious because of the barking of orders and imperious pointing and cajoling, prowled the platform seeking perfection, or at least satisfactory functionality. Sterling wasn't one for music festivals, but this had what he imagined was the same feel.

Soon the heady aroma of hot dogs and onions infiltrated the festive atmosphere, and Sterling could see a couple of hotdog and chippy vans setting up on the periphery, canopies held open by steel struts, and an ice-cream van not much further away. Either the operators had been quick thinking enough to spot the crowds and deduce that there was business to be done, or someone from the assembled multitude had tipped the wink to a brother, friend or business associate. The restless quest for profit never abated, whatever the situation. Although Sterling had taken care to fill up with a substantial breakfast, he started to feel hungry again.

Willem gestured at his watch. It was five past eleven. As if on cue, a small procession emerged into the park from the opposite direction to the archway entrance. Sterling immediately recognised Pieter Van Leuven, who, to a hostile-leaning eye like Sterling's, looked small and ridiculous in a merchant's finery circa Henry VIII, his little pot belly sticking out in front of him and his shoulders back as if to hold it up. Immediately behind him two young men carried what Sterling knew to be the Kortrijk Chest, wrapped and for the moment hidden in the flag of Flanders, the chest itself and the poles on the men's shoulders more than ever suggesting a sedan chair. The entourage was completed by a quartet of hatchet-faced bruisers, who, were it not for their own medieval garb, would not have looked in the slightest out of place as 'door attendants' outside a nightclub. One or two of them might have been in the party that had attacked Sterling at the Grote Kring. He didn't see the one with the pock-marked face and the Gestapo-style leather trench coat.

Oblivious to any notion of ridicule, the crowd roared and shook their fists, the discipline required to get to this point now redundant. Almost in an instant the Groeningeveld was awash with colour as flags and banners and pennants emerged, like the golden spurs earlier, from bags and backpacks. Politics, nationalism – in fact all the "isms" – left the individualistic Sterling cold, but even he was at least stirred by the spectacle that was developing. As the flags unfurled, Willem started a commentary, pointing and trying to explain in slow Dutch. 'Over there,' he seemed to be saying, *'Daar...'* *'De vlag van Ieper...* The flag of Ieper,' in halting English, pointing at a red cross with not one but two cross beams, the longest one underneath, against a white background. *'De vlag van Dendermonde, de vlag van Diksmuide, van Mesen, Oudenaarde, Waregem...'* Clearly, Willem was an authority on Flemish flags. His eyes were shining again. So many fellow travellers, or at least erstwhile fellow travellers, in one place.

Sterling could see the effectiveness of Van Leuven's work, creating cells and groups on a town to town basis throughout the Flemish region, and around each flag or standard, a distinct contingent had coalesced. He wondered if Willem would be recognised by the Ypres company below its flag forty metres away and whether it mattered.

Van Leuven clambered unsteadily up the steps to the podium, the antithesis of heroic history-changer. There were no rails, and he was forced to put one hand on the top steps to keep his balance. His entourage kept careful watch, ready for a stumble. The ascent negotiated, there he was at the microphone, a silly little man in a funny costume. Somehow, the sedan chair package wrapped in the Flemish flag was manoeuvred up behind him and left at his feet. Sterling shook his head.

But as soon as Van Leuven started to speak, he was quickly forced to revise his opinion. The voice was initially soft through the microphone, but rhythmic and fluent, and almost sing-song in its inflexions, repetitions and cadences. Sterling's Dutch had not improved at all since his arrival, and yet the words that flowed from the reedy voice were almost hypnotic. Willem was rapt, and so were the people around him. After a few minutes, with mini-crescendos at regular intervals, acclaimed by the crowd's roars, applause and foot-stamping, the voice grew louder and stronger, seeming to transcend its basic thinness.

At the final crescendo, Van Leuven gestured like a magician at the climax of a trick. '*Zie*,' he roared triumphantly, his hands sweeping over the ornately decorated chest at his feet, liberated with a flourish by an underling from the Flemish flag obscuring it, '*de kist van Kortrijk.*'

Willem turned to try and explain, but Sterling put a hand on his arm and gave a thumbs up with the other. 'I get that,' he shouted over the din.

Everything was making more sense, in an insane kind of way, from the theft of the chest to the firebombing of Griet's shop to her husband's murder and all the other drama between and beyond. But Sterling had always been anchored in the present. So true to form and his non-visionary nature he was thinking short-term: a battle anniversary in a suburban park; the flaunting of a stolen symbol; some tub-thumping; some flag-waving; then home for lunch. And that would be that.

Except it wasn't. Not by a long chalk.

Chapter 31

The short speech was over. Van Leuven left the microphone and tottered down the steps, cheers and chants and din ringing in his ecstatic ears. Sterling wasn't sure what to expect next, and Willem did not seem any better informed. The nearest group, according to Willem's earlier commentary about flags and banners, was from Dendermonde. A girl with poorly dyed blonde hair, dark roots showing from the parting in the middle of her scalp, and an angular, dissatisfied, disappointed face, detached herself.

She addressed Sterling with a tiny smile, half challenge, half curiosity. Willem interposed with a few words – likely saying that his friend was not Flemish and didn't speak Dutch.

'English?' she said directly to Sterling. 'Interested in what's going on here in Flanders on this historic day.'

'Yes,' said Sterling. 'A sort of fellow traveller.'

The girl nodded in a knowing way. There were calls from the Dendermonde group but she ignored them. 'Your friend here doesn't speak English.'

'No. My dealings are mainly with his granddaughter.'

A shout went up that immediately killed the conversation, and then there was jostling as the huge crowd surged and ebbed. Van Leuven, his thuggish entourage and the Kortrijk Chest on its poles struggled to get through the mass of people towards the Groeningeveld archway, march marshals and organisers trying to keep everyone back with staffs like sheep's crooks, not hitting but pressing the sticks horizontally to make a pathway.

The newly-formed trio fell in behind the Dendermonde group and milled around with everyone else while the marching column took shape. When order replaced confusion, Dendermonde and the three found themselves roughly in the middle of the huge column. Sterling could see the technicians dismantling the dais and sound equipment behind him. By a quirk, his eyes caught those of one of the "roadies", a unique connection amid the whirl of excitement and activity. The man, with a rapidly receding hairline and a straggly ponytail, looked cynically uninfluenced by the recent rhetoric, like someone in the set-up of a rock star who'd heard the shtick and repertoire many times too often. He raised his chin briefly and rolled his eyes, perhaps recognising a fellow pragmatist. *Someone has to do the everyday boring stuff* said his demeanour. Sterling nodded back and the moment passed, sightline obscured by bodies and banners.

The Dendermonde group shuffled off, and so did Sterling, Willem and the girl, who appeared to have adopted them. Small steps at first, avoiding but sometimes bumping into the bodies in front. The column moved laboriously towards the arch, Van Leuven and the Chest presumably in the lead. A rhythm developed. It wasn't unpleasant moving slowly along in the morning sunshine on a warm July day. The human mass had completely stopped the traffic on the main road outside the park, and then Sterling's section of the crowd was in the garden through which he and Albertin had followed Van Leuven days ago, and through the espaliered arbour and around the bandstand. Sterling for some reason was expecting the march to go down Groeningestraat and into the Begijnhofpark past the 1302 Museum and perhaps lead into the beguinage, but beyond the arbour and the smaller park the column veered to the right of Groeningestraat and passed the Square Hotel. The shuffling began again as the column bunched up, and the narrowness of the street made it difficult to see what was going on.

The Dendermonde group, of which Willem and Sterling seemed to have become honorary members, was animated. A moment later, Sterling understood why, and why at the same time a bottleneck had reduced the marchers to rows of only four abreast. To the right was a large, long block of flats, at least six floors up. At the bottom, the group came upon a line of garages. On the other side of the road, a line of small lorries was squeezed against a wall with railings set on top, behind which some trees were still blossoming in a wash of hazy redness. Standing in the lorry flatbeds and in the open garages, men obviously from a quartermaster contingent were rapidly handing out long staffs, with discs circling iron points at the end, to each marcher as they passed. Ragged cheers went up as people were armed.

A weapon was thrust into Sterling's hands, the smooth wood cool in his grasp. The young woman laughed, her teeth uneven, and sharply angled like her face. She shook her own. 'Goedendag,' she shouted above the hubbub. On the other side, Willem smiled and brandished his. Sterling hoped he wasn't going to go native. Sterling was excited himself though, and felt a nagging admiration for Van Leuven, Guy Verstraete and their Liebaart movement. The day, and everything leading up to it, was well organised. Not a police officer was in sight. It must have taken many months, perhaps longer, to requisition and secretly stock the garages with thousands of newly minted weapons. The funding had been sorted out, as Sterling, Albertin and Angela had witnessed what seemed a long time ago. Guy's expedition to Oxford to retrieve the Chest had succeeded. Even the crude, medieval communication system of monoalphabetic code, and the shunning of modern telecommunications and social media, had worked well. If there had been any police or secret service intelligence, it wasn't obvious, and there had been no action to nip things in the bud. Perhaps there was a longer term or more subtle play in the offing, but he doubted it on current evidence.

The marchers shuffled forward like a chain gang, the banners and pennants above it joined by an undulating hedgehog back of spikes glinting in the sunshine. Sterling noticed that he and his fellow marchers were going downwards, and after another couple of minutes his part of the column reached the river that the rest were already marching alongside. A hundred metres away Sterling could see one of the twin towers he, Angela, and Becky had last seen from the opposite direction, the other obscured briefly by foliage bordering the path.

The girl kept up her commentary. 'De Broeltoren,' she said. 'The Bridge Towers.'

There was another bottleneck caused by a twist of narrow bricked stairs up to the tower on the side of the main town and then Sterling and his companions were on the bridge itself. The girl pointed – 'Buda island' – and Sterling was realising why she had appointed herself companion, guide and translator to a foreigner. Her clear green eyes shone with pride and excitement.

History was being made. The Flemish people would show the world.

The scene on the bridge was chaotic. A tailback of traffic from the town was building up behind the nearest tower, while there was no traffic at all from Buda island. It was quickly apparent that a kind of checkpoint had been set up on the other side, with makeshift barriers and a large group of 'officials', some holding a cluster of goedendags pointing skywards and hovering menacingly behind it. The column was being waved through but no one else. A young male cyclist remonstrated angrily with the lead 'official', who spoke to some individuals behind him. The man was seized and frogmarched to the other side of the bridge, where he was dumped, and his bike grabbed and unceremoniously tossed into the river. The incident sparked an upsurge of additional strong-arm activity as motorists were dragged from their cars and pushed back from the island. Sterling tut-tutted, virtually as a reflex. *A fine way to get ordinary Flemings to flock to the cause.* He wondered as well what Buda residents would think of the invasion.

From the bedlam on the bridge, the column marched into relative tranquillity on the other side. Almost opposite was a combined hotel, bar and restaurant – Broel – which had been requisitioned by the Liebaarts. Hangers-on, messengers, aides-de-camp and other functionaries scurried in and out and dashed off in all directions. Sterling was gradually discerning that not all nationalists on this adventure were the same. The strategy group – those in charge and their acolytes – had already set up in the hotel. An administrative-commando corps was carrying out orders such as setting up the border post, and presumably border posts at all the other entry-points to the island, and then there was the cannon fodder, aka the poor bloody infantry, in which he and Willem found themselves.

Sterling half-expected that the marchers would stop and coalesce in the space around the hotel, but the column continued in a rightward direction parallel to the river and for a short while opposite the path they had marched down on the mainland side. Buda was a residential area of nondescript apartment blocks and bland deserted streets, until the cobbled road veered to the left and opened out to an immaculately sculpted open space between housing and river, complete with saplings, sward, and a blend of white gravel and tiled pathways artfully inserted. Dominating the scene was a graceful pedestrian and cycling bridge that curved and soared up over the river and then back down into Kortrijk's northern suburbs, suspended by an intricate cat's-cradle of grey steel tubes and struts. As he approached the bridge and surveyed under it, Sterling could see the scene completed by a large, well-tended expanse of pampas grass and even an artificial sandy beach.

Here the column stopped and spread out across the whole area, like a deluge of water across a flood plain, the cannon fodder cajoled and directed by the organising cadre. Haversacks were deposited, and flagstaffs thrust into the ground. The appearance of tents made it look as though an encampment was starting. Sterling looked up at the windows of the apartment blocks, curious about residents' reactions, and saw people, generally older and probably retired, staring down at the drama unfolding beneath them. Since neither he nor Willem, nor the girl, had received specific orders and directions, he motioned them to join him as he detached himself from the throng and edged off, goedendag in hand, haft over his left shoulder, down the northern side of the island, following one or two other small detachments. In the distance he thought he could again see the bridge that he, Angela and Becky had stood on earlier in the day, which might be the eastern extent of the island. As they walked beside the river, they passed knots of goedendag bearers at intervals looking outwards. Opposite, a monolith of glass and concrete, Guldensporencollege dominated the skyline, and it was next to this that the cat's cradle bridge curved down to a graceful conclusion. Looking up, there was a heavily fortified checkpoint just beyond the middle of the bridge on the 'mainland' side, and when they reached the other bridge at the east, a similar concentration of barricade and spikes, fortification increasing all the time.

Sterling had seen enough. A full circuit of Buda wasn't necessary. As he'd thought, the arrangements would be the same at each point. The odd trio turned around and started back to the encampment. 'What's all this about?' he said to the girl. 'It's not a very big island, and a well-equipped army of 20,000 or so soldiers could defend it – maybe blowing up the bridges, setting up snipers and preparing for a new Stalingrad. But ordinary people with goedendags and makeshift checkpoints... Even a determined group of riot police from Brussels or somewhere could find a weak point. They could break through the barrier on the footbridge and abseil down onto the beach, or paddle across in dinghies at a quiet point before reinforcements could be called up... establish a bridgehead backed up by teargas and water cannon... What happens when we all get hungry? Or were you told to bring ham sandwiches and Coca Cola? None of it makes sense...'

The girl shrugged. She was cannon fodder. 'I don't know. We have got food and drink though.'

Sterling laughed shortly, and without mirth. 'That's alright then.'

Chapter 32

It wasn't tension exactly, that strange afternoon on Buda island in a small town in southwestern Belgium. Sterling tried to think of a word or phrase for it. The best he could come up with was "organised recklessness". The festival atmosphere only seemed to fuel the carefreeness.

The quartermaster contingent had set up a marquee-style structure on the road next to the open space. It was long and narrow, with entry flaps at one end and the exit at the other, from which members of the invasion force emerged with plastic cups and hotdogs in grease-proof paper. Not everyone, then, had brought sandwiches and cola. The canvas was in bold red and white stripes with the Flemish black lion and other flags festooned on the sloping sides.

Sterling and Willem had finally been deployed as watchmen halfway between the Broeltoren bridge and the one down river and had taken up their positions opposite the Guldensporencollege. A few residents had joined the Liebaarts' hotchpotch army, mainly elderly folk while the younger ones were at school or work, or even at the college opposite. A white-haired couple was enjoying a different kind of afternoon from the regulation one and engaged cheerfully with the invaders. Others wandered about confused and anxious. An angry

woman holding a plump, long-haired cat in her wrinkled arms was given short shrift by another contingent
– enforcement, security, perhaps even secret police. She
retreated back into the building, shaken and white-faced.

On the raised part of the cat's cradle bridge, midway
across the river, in front of the huge barrier of barbed
wire, goedendags and Liebaarts soldiers, the roadies
were back, reassembling the dais, or, more likely, a
larger, more dramatic one, with loudspeakers and lights,
in jarring contrast to the absence of technology in the
army below. On the artificial beach, other technicians
were scurrying in and out of another covered structure,
like a large crime-scene tent, arranging something else
whose detail Sterling couldn't see.

The activity on Buda island wasn't going unnoticed
on the mainland. Cyclists looked over as they went
about their afternoon business. Students from the
college, at break time or with classes finished for the
day, lingered around the entrance and stared over.
Because the island was now effectively a no-go area,
north Kortrijk had been cut off from the old town at the
western end, and traffic was building up at the east.
Fumes began to drift across the river. And at last, police
squad cars were beginning to appear, the first presence
of law and order since a solitary, bewildered police
officer at the Groeningeveld Arch, as the column had
made its way down to the river. Between the college and
footbridge, another officer in a glengarry cap was in
deep and animated conversation on a mobile phone.
The complicated array of equipment on his belt, including a black holster with pistol butt protruding, pepper
spray and handcuffs, made a stark contrast with the
simplicity of the goedendags.

Next to Sterling, Willem straightened up from his slouch against his own goedendag. His eyes narrowed as he looked westwards towards the main bridge. Sterling followed his eyes and put a restraining hand on his friend's arm. They weren't the only sentries on this stretch, and he didn't want complications. Walking briskly along the river promenade towards the college were the unmistakable figures of Angela Wilson and Becky Strange, and as they walked they were scanning Buda island. A moment after Willem spotted them, they made their own sighting. Sterling ostentatiously turned away, back towards the preparations continuing behind him, his eyes and a slight incline of the head telling Willem to do the same. The older man understood instantly, evidenced by his own swivel to the open space. When Sterling glanced cautiously back to the college, he was gratified, but not surprised, that the women had taken his lead and also shown no signs of recognition. They sat on the college steps, not too out of place among the students and one or two older people who might have been members of staff.

A few metres further down, another watchman from the Dendermonde group brandished his goedendag and shouted, his greasy young face twisted with hatred. Willem's face reddened. He muttered under his breath and shook his head imperceptibly, looking at Sterling with a face of discomfort and apology. Angela was oblivious, but Sterling was pretty sure she'd been abused. Willem had been changing, and now he'd virtually reached an epiphany. He still seemed proud of his Flemish origins, but now it was inclusive. He had taken to Angela and had no time for racism. The Liebaarts' prospectus was familiar to him, but much of it, and the

movement itself, was now distasteful. He had easily rec-
onciled himself to his double agent role – because of
Christina. And there was something else. Sterling realised
that Willem, walking up and down on Buda, holding his
goedendag, talking with the girl from Dendermonde,
looking after Sterling, taking everything in, was enjoying himself.

The cadre responsible for security beyond the packed
checkpoints had been diligent enough in stationing
Liebaarts foot soldiers at regular intervals all around
Buda island, but less competent in recording, checking,
and supervising. Content that now contact with Angela
and Becky had been re-established, and that Angela's
savviness and Becky's fieldcraft would guarantee that it
wouldn't be broken, Sterling mimed drinking and eating.
Willem gave a thumbs up, and they edged casually away
from their position. It didn't look likely that there would
be an invasion, imminent or otherwise, from across that
stretch of water, and anyway, what did they care?

The coffee was weak and the hotdogs greasy, but
Sterling felt restored after they'd had a drink and eaten.
The marquee had been lively and noisy, and Liebaarts'
catering corps focused and efficient. The hum of a generator and large boxes of supplies suggested enough
provisions for a day or two, but then Sterling thought of
the invaders' numbers and revised the time down. He
was still puzzled about the final outcome.

He and Willem walked down to the water's edge.
There was a commotion on the cat's cradle bridge above
them. Two policemen had walked up from the college
and were approaching the checkpoint. There was a
rumble of voices and stamping of goedendags on the
asphalt surface, and the policemen stopped ten metres

away from the ramshackle initial barrier of barbed wire. The bridge swayed gently. Next to Sterling, the girl, separated earlier by a different deployment, had quietly rejoined him and Willem.

The white-faced younger policeman had his hand on his holster. The older, portlier one put his thumbs in his belt, splayed his feet and called out to no one in particular.

'He's asking what's going on,' said the girl. 'He's sure that things can be sorted out. Someone on this side has told him to...' – she looked slyly at Sterling – 'fuck off.'

The policeman held his ground. He looked as if he had enough years of service to have seen everything. His colleague stayed back.

'Now he's saying what offences are being committed – carrying dangerous weapons, blocking the path, bad language.' The girl's English was good, but it wasn't surprising that she didn't know the hackneyed English phrases.

From behind the barricades, two goedendags poked out and jabbed the air, but the portly policeman was able to maintain his composure as they were well out of range. He ostentatiously turned away and started speaking into his phone and listening. Then he cocked his head and motioned to his colleague that they should withdraw. Jeers and cheers followed them down the long bridge-ramp off Buda and onto the quay next to the college.

The first round had gone to Van Leuven.

And it seemed subsequent rounds too. The early-established impasse was continuing when the sun started to go down in the west, bequeathing the scene a glow of translucent golden light after six hours of bustle,

boredom and weak coffee. On the Buda side, the barricades were complete, and traffic of any kind over any of
the bridges and access points had completely ceased. On
the mainland side, the police had chosen to concentrate
around the college, where a dozen public disorder
response vans, complete with protective shields across
the windscreens, were lined up facing the insurrection.
Roadblocks had been set up either side, but that hadn't
stopped the hundreds of curious observers and bystanders, who milled around and chattered excitedly.
Something was bound to happen, and it seemed that
people didn't want to miss it when it did. The chip-and-
hotdog sellers and ice cream vans, perhaps the same as
the ones that had appeared in the Groeningeveld earlier
in the day, were once more doing a brisk trade. By this
time, Sterling, Willem and the girl had entirely abandoned any notion of guard duty and were wandering
freely about the island, and completely by coincidence
were approaching the Broel Hotel as a cheer went up.

Once again, Van Leuven and his entourage were on
the move, now leaving the hotel lobby with the Kortrijk
Chest and proceeding eastward from the Broel Towers
along the quay. Spectators on the other side of Buda
pointed and conferred as the procession continued.
It followed the northward curve of the island until it
arrived in front of the pampas grass and open space. A
small barrier at the beginning of the cat's cradle bridge
on the Buda side was opened, and Van Leuven and the
group moved up to the middle, exactly over the river.
There was a sliver of space between the stage Van
Leuven mounted and the main barrier separating Buda
from north Kortrijk. A surge of former marchers moved
up to the bridge as Van Leuven took his place at the

microphone and stood like a prophet, arms outstretched as he seemed to absorb the sun's fading rays. Even the police and people with no clear idea of what was going on across the river looked up in a kind of awe. Lighting on stalks attached to a trellised frame enhanced the eerie atmosphere.

Van Leuven began, his reedy voice low-key and almost matter-of-fact in the first few sentences. A regretful man having an intimate conversation with his supporters, the still river underneath him having a curious amplifying and distorting effect on the loudspeakers, as his words echoed along the water.

Once more, the girl fell into her role as proud translator. '"Why are we here?" he's saying. "We're here because we're dutiful citizens at the end of our tether. We are compelled. We have no choice." And so on.'

Van Leuven's voice changed and grew louder and more urgent as his rhythm developed. Now anger replaced regret.

'History lesson,' murmured the girl. 'We must right the wrongs of seven hundred years of oppression. The French bullied us in the south. The Burgundians controlled us through inheritance and marriage alliances. Our lands and people have been controlled by the Spanish Habsburgs and by the Austrian Habsburgs. From 1830 our statehood has been entwined with the Walloons, who have always tried to dominate us.

'No one asked the Flemish people what our wishes were. In the Great War, no one asked us permission to fight on our land. Why should the war dead of others be buried in our soil? Why didn't Churchill ask us when he wanted to make Ypres an English island in our territory?'

The girl's voice was monotone as she frowned with concentration and fervour. 'And our own people? Our own politicians? The Flemish Bloc. The Flemish Interest. The New Flemish Alliance. The mealy-mouthed centrists – now more interested in hanging on to power than advancing the federalism they so desired – no matter how pathetic that is.' Van Leuven's voice dripped with scorn, and the girl's began to mirror it. 'Failures. Only interested in themselves. Betrayers. Above all, betrayers. They are not the only enemies. Now we face new threats too – threats to our entire way of life – from the hordes of Muslim migrants flooding into Flanders, happy to take our charity while seeking to change us forever. Where are our elites when we need someone to protect us?'

Van Leuven paused for a long moment and looked down the river in the fading light, as if he was reflecting and asking his listeners to reflect as well. His voice dropped to an amplified whisper.

'He's saying that it doesn't have to be like this. We can have an end to domination – by the Walloons, by Europe, by Muslims and terrorists, by our own rotten elites. We can decide our own future. We can have our own destiny.' Van Leuven's voice rose to a crescendo. The girl ploughed on, concentrating even harder as she gave her translation. 'We must have change. To achieve what we need to achieve, we must be brave. You have been magnificent, but this is only the beginning. Go back to your towns and communities. Light the flame of liberation. We can never return to how things were. No sacrifice can be too great. And realise, truly realise, that some of us will become martyrs...'

'... Here in this city in 1302, our ancestors defeated the might of France at the glorious Battle of Kortrijk. Now, on this anniversary, we will defeat anyone in Europe who defies us. Our own borders, our own society. Our own manifesto. Flanders for the Flemish! Here, on Buda, in Kortrijk, the free, independent County of Flanders is born, and will last forever!'

Chapter 33

The crowd erupted. Whoops and cheers and the stamp of goedendags saturated the evening air. Van Leuven beamed and waved as he surveyed the masses beneath him. Even from across the quay, there was a ripple of applause, whether for the sentiments and declaration expressed, or the performance, or both. Amid the ecstasy, affecting almost everyone on Buda, Sterling noticed that towards the end of the speech, the crime-scene style tent was being removed from the artificial beach. A shadowy figure in dark clothing moved in with a device like a small blowtorch. Then the beach and the sky were lit up by a huge, golden-flamed stationary firework in the same shape as the entwined spurs in the Groeningeveld.

The figure moved on with his lighting stick, and as Van Leuven continued to drink in the acclaim and adulation as if from a pulpit looming over a congregation, other fireworks crackled, dazzled and exploded in a dizzying display. Resolutely un-mesmerised, Sterling looked around in a three-hundred-and-sixty-degree sweep. At the windows of the flats behind him, more people looked down. The sentinels along the quay had turned their attention from the opposite side to the fireworks that were adding ephemeral new stars to the heavens. Next to him, Willem, epiphany temporarily suspended, was fully engrossed in the passion and intensity of the moment, next to the spellbound girl. Even the gatekeepers on the barricade at the beginning of the cat's-cradle bridge had their eyes locked on the vividness of the evening sky.

Then Sterling thought he caught a movement among the throng. A small figure was edging towards the bridge in a slow but determined zigzag movement, zigzag because of the clumps of small groups that prevented any direct approach. From forty metres away, there was something familiar in the shape of the head, which was draped in a scarf that covered the hair completely, and the slight, well-proportioned female body. Sterling's ex-copper's gut stirred. He too, from a ninety-degree angle, started zigzagging towards the barricade, keeping out of the sightline of his quarry and arriving a few seconds later. The barrier, consisting of gatekeepers and a motley assembly of conventional road barriers and opportunist additions, looked formidable, but the woman took full advantage of the distraction generated by the fireworks to slip through the small, inadequately supervised gap at the side. Sterling stole through two seconds later, sentries' eyes focused upwards into the night. There were plenty of people with legitimate Liebaarts business among the equipment and other bits and pieces between the barrier and Van Leuven's platform. Having penetrated this small bastion, Sterling quickly realised that the same legitimacy had been conferred on him and the woman in front of him.

No one made a challenge, and no one showed any interest in two more nationalists, especially at the climax of the excitement. And no one noticed the woman clambering up onto the dais. Sterling edged silently along behind, benefiting from her single-minded focus amid the commotion.

Van Leuven seemed to sense activity behind him. He turned just as the woman drew off the headscarf with her left hand and a riot of tight, curly hair cascaded out. Now Sterling was transfixed as Griet Planckaert drew out a gun from the folds of her light peasant blouse. Van Leuven held out his arms and opened his palms.

Sterling didn't need to know Dutch to understand the exchange that followed, but the word 'bastaard' seemed to recur. Griet's face was twisted, her pain and rage palpable. But while Griet's fury intensified, serenity fluttered over Van Leuven like a cloak. He spoke softly, and Sterling detected a challenging, inviting quality. '*Komaan, schiet me dan maar neer.*' he said. '*Ik zal een martelaar zijn.*' Go on, shoot me, Sterling speculated for the first bit, the second obscure. But Griet wasn't finished yet. She ranted on until Van Leuven put up his hands. He nodded past Griet's face towards Sterling standing in the shadows. 'Who's your friend?' he seemed to say, changing tack.

Griet tried to look behind her, while still keeping an eye on Van Leuven. Below the platform, the danger had only just been identified, and a group was assembling to go up the steps. *Jesus,* thought Sterling. He couldn't think of a good outcome. Assassinating Van Leuven and making him a martyr would escalate and inflame the current face-off, and Griet's momentary insanity would earn her a life sentence, or, if not that, summary justice from a frenzied mob. And he, Sterling, would be collateral damage.

A goedendag thudded into a loudspeaker next to Griet. Her startled look and loss of focus gave Sterling the small opportunity he needed. He sprang across the two metres that separated them and enveloped her in a bear hug, lifting her off her feet. The gun went off, and the bullet whined into the night, the report masked by the continuing fireworks. Van Leuven looked shaken. Perhaps martyrdom wasn't such a good thing after all. Sterling manhandled Griet to the edge of the stage, which itself was only a foot away from the railing of the cat's cradle bridge. Normally, clambering on to the railing would have been difficult, but the stage's elevation brought the rail closer and lower. Sterling wrestled with the writhing woman and dropped her feet first into the river. He glanced back across the stage. An all-male cluster surrounded Van Leuven, full of caution and concern, with perhaps a measure of sheepishness as well. After all, an armed woman and probably a henchman had penetrated security and almost finished him off. The Hero of Buda himself was pressing his palms down to indicate that he was unscathed and that everyone should remain calm. Impatiently, he shook off solicitous hands on his shirt.

The cluster didn't trouble Sterling. It was the separate trio of rapidly approaching goedendag holders who prompted him to launch himself after Griet. He kept as vertical as he could after vaulting over the rail, with his arms to his sides. Down and into the water was further than he'd calculated. A sudden roar filled his ears as water filled his nose. He went deep before the downward momentum petered out and he struggled to the surface, coughing, spluttering and remembering how much he hated swimming.

Who can explain the intricate workings of the human brain? Even for the neurologists, much is still the subject of speculation. Long afterwards Angela suggested that shock may have played its part in the 'eureka' moment Sterling reported as he flailed around in the river Leie. Enlightenment came from nowhere, but somehow everything began to click. As he floated downstream under the bridge, following Griet and her Medusa-hair, obscure, misused words, the fag-end of a conversation, a policeman's gut and a dream analysis all combined with sudden clarity. And one thing above all was certain. The whole affair was not just about a foredoomed putsch on an obscure, urbanised island in a small Flemish town.

But the insight would have to wait. Right then, there were more pressing concerns. Griet must have heard him splash into the river behind her. She spotted him almost straight away.

'Griet, stay under the bridge,' he hissed urgently. Goedendags were poking and stabbing weapons, not spears, but they would be sitting ducks as soon as they moved into the open. As he spoke, a missile was thrown down, missing Griet by a hair's-breadth. She needed no second instruction to do as she was told.

'We stay under the bridge for as long as we can. It curves down to the college on the other side. Obviously, the river bank arrives before the bridge ends, but it should take us beyond the checkpoint, and then we'll be able to get out. While I've got the chance for a quiet word, where's the gun?'

She pointed downwards with a white finger.

'Good. Right, we're almost at the bank. We should be safe from spears, and there doesn't seem to be much in the way of modern weaponry. We'll edge towards the college and get someone to fish us out. Griet, listen. I can't be delayed when we're out. I've got stuff to do. I don't need an ambulance, and I don't want to be taken away for questioning by the police. So...' – fuelled by adrenaline, his mind was racing and his speech was struggling to keep up – 'I'm an English tourist and you're my Belgian friend, showing me around your hometown. I think two of my friends will be around too – Angela and Becky. They're visiting with me. They're quick on the uptake and they'll play along. The four of us got separated for half an hour. You were showing me Buda when it got taken over and we were stuck on it. When I protested to someone, a fight started and we were chucked off the bridge. It's not too hard to believe because they were rough with a cyclist and some motorists at the Broel Towers. No one on this bank will have seen you try and shoot Van Leuven and the fireworks covered the noise of the shot. You'll be in the clear for the moment. We'll sort the rest of it out later. Got it?'

Griet nodded.

Even though the river was no more than fifty metres from side to side, and he and Griet had dropped in it at the half way point, Sterling struggled with the twenty-five metres to the bank, pulled down by his sodden clothes and having to work against the sluggish current to stay under the protection of the bridge. In the end, Griet comfortably reached the bank first. As Sterling floundered, she grabbed the goedendag that had earlier come so close to skewering her, as it drifted by, and held it out for Sterling to catch. The bank was too sheer to clamber up, so they drifted down to a point opposite the college, where a young woman and her children, part of the gawping crowd, spotted them and called for help.

Sterling thought he recognised the young policeman from the bridge checkpoint who hauled Griet and then Sterling himself from the water, using a combination of the goedendag and his hands. A certain cockiness had crept into the policeman's manner, and his face had gained some colour. He had been first on the scene, and now he was centre stage. He guided them away from the bank, through the curious onlookers and bystanders and around the hoses, cables and apparatus of the fire service, the police service and recently arrived TV and media companies. They soon reached a restricted area that included the steps of the college, which had been turned into a command post. Sterling sat down heavily, the murky river water pooling around his legs, backside and feet. Griet joined him. On the other side of the police barrier, he spotted Angela and Becky, giving them a nod that no one else would have noticed unless they had been looking.

A senior policeman appeared, bare-headed but in a smart, well-cut uniform of a wool and cashmere blend, perhaps a little heavy for the time of year. A medal ribbon was incorporated into the breast pocket of the jacket. His grey crew-cut was pimpled with perspiration.

He spoke Dutch to Sterling, who looked blank and turned to Griet. She launched off into a torrent of indignant Dutch of her own, and when she'd finished she put up her hand to stop the policeman replying, before speaking in English. 'I've told him' – loud enough for Angela and Becky to hear – 'that you are my English friend and that we got caught on Buda when this stupid event started. We were separated from our other friends over there' – she waved at Angela and Becky, who waved tentatively back, like the demure and bemused tourists they had become. 'When we couldn't get off Buda because of the checkpoints, we went up to the people in charge to complain, and they threw us into the water.'

Griet was playing a clever game. She knew the odds were high that the policeman spoke English, and at the same time, her explanation gave Angela and Becky their cover story.

The policeman asked some questions and Griet replied. She summarised her answers in English. 'I've told him we know nothing about what's happening on Buda. I've said you're staying at the Hotel Accor.'

Sterling allowed his teeth to start chattering, not difficult in the circumstances. 'Tell him I'm going to catch my death if I don't get a change of clothes.'

'Catch your death? I don't...'

'He means he's going to get a cold,' said the policeman. He ruminated for a moment. Police officers were putting on riot gear and fastening shields. Reporters were shouting out questions. A group of firemen were conducting an animated debate about a turntable ladder on the back of a fire engine facing the river. Underlings were vying for the chief's urgent attention. The scene was chaos. Hapless tourists and their Belgian guide were a minor distraction. The chief addressed Griet. 'Give my inspector your name and address, his name' – pointing to Sterling – 'and the names of your friends over there – and passport numbers and addresses so we can check. No one should leave town before this is over. My inspector will get you a squad car.' He looked directly at Sterling. 'On behalf of Belgium, I'm sorry for your bad experience.'

'Thank you,' said Sterling.

The officer whose car was designated to return the 'tourists' and their guide to their hotel was not best pleased with the mess Sterling and Griet introduced to the back seat. He could barely suppress his tutting as they emerged with Angela and Becky at the glass doors of the hotel. Griet was not ready to go home, so the arrangement was for her to shower in Angela and Becky's room and borrow whatever clothes of theirs fitted. Then there would be an urgent meeting in Sterling's room fifteen minutes later.

'Yes, we're going to get rumbled, sooner or later,' he said when they'd reassembled. 'But it doesn't matter. We'll be finished by then.' He outlined his plan and faced down Angela's objections. 'It's me and Becky, with you and Griet as back up. You know why,' he said bluntly. Then the quartet moved off to the Grote Markt. Sterling was on tenterhooks. He'd kept much of what he'd worked out to himself. Even so, he'd still look silly if he was wrong.

Chapter 34

The Grote Markt. 9pm. Sterling listened to the faint screams from high above. There were still one or two swifts darting and swooping for a late supper through the fading blue sky. The square itself was almost deserted, the drama playing out at Buda. There was hardly any traffic either, which showed that the stand-off was continuing. He wondered what Van Leuven would be doing, and what the next step would be. An attempted assassination, if there was footage, would play well for the media. Perhaps negotiations were going on to have reporters and cameras across the bridge. Talk of surrender was unlikely. What could be better for the cause of Flemish independence than riot police in all their twenty-first-century paraphernalia battling with plucky nationalists armed only with their goedendags?

Not Sterling's concern. Now, in the Grote Markt with his team, he was standing in front of the building swaddled in plastic sheeting framed on scaffolding. He hadn't paid proper attention to the neighbouring buildings before, but now he noted the bank on one side and a restaurant-brasserie on the other. The bank was of gracious late nineteenth-century pedigree, all great stone blocks, long tall windows and wide stairs splaying like a duck's webbed foot on to the square. It looked dark and lifeless and probably had been from Saturday night and through to the evening of this public holiday. Angela and Griet, who had quickly established an easy rapport, took up a casual position at the base of the steps as Sterling and Becky carried on to the far corner of the square, turning left towards the building site behind the façade, where Sterling had lost the Big Man and his mystery sidekick what seemed like a lifetime ago.

Becky took his hand as they passed down the street, lovers out strolling. In the middle of the site's perimeter panels was a human-length turnstile to monitor and restrict pedestrian comings and goings. Becky squeezed Sterling's hand as they went by. Forty metres further on, they stopped.

'Right,' said Becky, 'the look-out is at a second-floor window back there on the other side of the road from the site. There are apartments above the cafés and shops. I expect we'll need the buzzer to get in.' But as the pair approached, a young woman with a nose-ring and purple-blonde hair already buzzed and the catch on the door clicked back. She held the door and spoke a few words of Dutch. Becky nodded and smiled, and the girl started up the stairs. Sterling looked at the name slots above the letter boxes in the drab hallway. One slot, for a flat on the second floor, was empty.

'When we get up there, don't knock,' said Becky. 'Even someone speaking fluent Kortrijk Dutch making a mistake with a pizza delivery address will be suspicious to a look-out.' She got out a lock pick set. 'This should work if I'm quiet enough. Look-out work is boring. A pound to a penny he'll have ear buds in.'

Sterling nodded. Talented as Angela was, she didn't have the same wide-ranging skillset as Becky, so his team deployment had been sound.

There were two doors on the second floor, and Becky approached the one on the left. Sterling slouched against the landing rail and kept watch. Becky looked both ways and then set to work, not kneeling but standing close to the door as if she was about to knock. She worked carefully and with focus, but quickly as well. The lock resisted for no more than three minutes. Sterling stopped his slouching when he saw a sliver of weak light appear at the open door, and almost instantly, he and Becky had slipped into the flat. Becky eased the door silently shut. There was a musty, unlived in smell about the hallway, and it was cool despite the warm summer evening outside. They edged down the narrow passage, the yellow and brown patterned linoleum curled at the sides and pitted over the years. There were doors on each side, and it was obvious that the living room would be at the end of the hall and located over-looking the street, where the light and view would be most favourable. The door was slightly ajar. When Sterling looked into the room, it was entirely bare and unfurnished, and harshly bleak except for the nest built up in front of the main window. There, a young man with poorly cut curly blonde hair, virtually a pudding basin, sat in a canvas director's chair looking out into the street. On a matching small foldable table on the left, probably from the same leisure and camping shop, sat a pair of binoculars and a mobile. Strewn around on the right were pizza cartons in garish red, white and blue colours, cola bottles and other, similar detritus. The large room smelt of stale smoke from roll-ups whose production equipment covered the rest of the table, with wispy short strands of tobacco sprinkled widely.

Becky had been right. The young man seemed alert enough, with a perfect view over the building site opposite and up and down the street, but the music playing in his ears ensured that he was utterly unaware that Sterling and Becky were approaching. Zip ties and masking tape appeared from somewhere else about Becky's person, and by the time the young man caught a reflection in the glass of the window it was too late. Sterling's restraint training from the job kicked in, and in a few relatively painless moments the look-out was completely silenced and immobilised, trussed hands and feet, mouth generously taped. His blotchy pale face indicated fear and surprise rather than anger and defiance.

Sterling put his forefinger up in a shushing gesture. 'We're not going to hurt you if you cooperate, but we're going to ask some questions. No shouting. OK?'

English didn't seem to be in the young man's repertoire, but he understood the warning. Becky peeled off the tape.

'How many in the building site?'

The response was a blank face. Sterling pointed to the site. 'How many?' he repeated, raising his fingers in an exaggerated mime. The look-out nodded when the count reached five. Sterling couldn't think of anything else useful to ask. While a crackpot on Buda was declaring the independent County of Flanders, the perfect diversion, a bank raid was taking place in the town.

They left the hapless criminal in the far corner of the large bare room, taking his phone as they went. Even if he was able to get free in the next hour it would be too late. At the turnstile, Becky went to work again with her lockpick. Her hood was up, and so was Sterling's, but it seemed likely that the raiders would have disabled the security cameras anyway, and if not those, then certainly any alarm. The turnstile click-clicked as they slipped into the site. There was a damp smell of concrete and plaster in the dusty atmosphere, mingled with a faint reek of diesel. Piles of granite slabs, lines of timber and all the other material required and assembled for the complete transformation of a gutted building dotted the ground. There was barely any difference in atmosphere going from outside to inside, with gaping holes in the roof and a patchwork of beams and tiles. The two trespassers penetrated further in, and soon found a door on the skeleton ground floor wall that gave on to a rickety, temporary staircase going down into a cellar area from which a glimmer of weak light emanated.

Sterling looked at Becky and she nodded. Gingerly, he eased onto the top step and started downwards. He could feel Becky's breath on his neck and the vague warmth of her body behind him. Down here, the air was close and dusty. At the bottom, they edged left towards the bank building. The light was leaking through a jagged hole bashed out of a thick partition wall of brick and plaster.

When they reached the hole, they stooped down and looked through. As their eyes grew used to the gloom, they could make out a scene of utter disorder. Somehow, the raiders had managed to lug in a small generator, no longer running, but which accounted for the diesel smell on the site next door. Scattered around and discarded was equipment for drilling and oxy-acetylene, and a large cache of tunnelling and digging tools. Shadowy figures were silently moving back and forth into a large vault, the ransacked contents, mostly wads of cash, being transferred to large holdalls. It might have been noisy earlier, but now it was largely silent apart from light footfalls and the thud of cash hitting plastic and leather. The raid had reached the endgame.

For Sterling that should have been that. He'd seen enough. He counted four men beyond the hole, one certainly the Big Man – Janssen – from the sheer size of him. It was time to slink away and get the police involved, if there were any left who were free from dealing with the Buda insurgency. But then a loud crashing boomed from the top of the staircase and the site next door. Janssen and his fellow raiders, and Sterling and Becky in the next compartment, froze. Janssen dropped the cash and the hold-all he'd been carrying and said something to the men behind him. Sterling was astonished to see a Taser appear in Becky's hand. His mind was spinning. The conclusions that kept flashing in his head were utterly clear, and all involved craziness. It was crazy to have come this far, just himself and a 110lb woman, no matter how well-armed and skilful in close combat. It was crazy to expect to come out on top against a determined group of desperate criminals, led by a giant. It would be crazy to consider anything other than swift withdrawal. If there was ever a time to be cautious rather than bold, this was it.

'Come on,' he whispered. Angela might have argued. Becky moved to the staircase with the lithe swiftness of a big cat, closely followed by Sterling. Janssen, on the other hand, was an angry rogue bull elephant as he crashed through the hole from the vault room, roaring as he came. Sterling and Becky were quick up the stairs, but so was Janssen, surprisingly for a man of his bulk and age. Becky was almost through the door, but Sterling was only four steps from the top when he felt a huge fist close around his right ankle, bringing his momentum to a juddering halt and causing his hands to slap on the concrete landing to soften his fall and protect his face. Janssen started hauling him back like an angler wrestling with a shark.

'Becks,' gasped Sterling.

Now a fist had closed over his other ankle. Becky stepped forward and two-handed pointed the Taser at Janssen's chest, which presented a clear target as his arms tugged at Sterling's legs. The darts sprang out and hit, causing the Big Man to shudder and quake, like someone having an epileptic fit. With a few grunts soon tapering into silence, he subsided into a wide, motionless sprawl, his huge body draped over the staircase.

Panting heavily, Sterling looked back to the bottom of the cellar. The three other vault raiders had emerged through the hole armed with an array of spades and picks but were temporarily blocked by the prone body of their leader. The escape window was tiny and Sterling had seen enough. He followed Becky though the door, to which there was no lock and no key.

'Help me,' she said, as she started erecting a barricade, using material around the building site. 'It won't hold them up for long, especially as they have all that tunnelling equipment, but it will give us the breather we need.'

In two minutes it was done, and still quiet on the other side of the door. Presumably, the gang members were having to remove their stricken leader and revive him before mounting an assault.

'Can you go around to the square and find Angela and Griet, Becky?' said Sterling. 'It's time for the police, and Griet will know how to make the emergency call.

I need five minutes to check something here and then I'll join you.' He struggled to hold eye contact.

Becky said nothing and lingered.

'Don't go all Angie Wilson on me, Becks. I'll follow shortly, I promise.'

Abruptly, she nodded, turned and padded off out of the building. Sterling came to the edge and watched as she clacked through the turnstile. She had an inkling of what was happening, he was sure, but she was letting him get on with it.

He stood stock still and listened. There was a small mixture of noises – a creak, a scrape, a shuffle. 'Hello, Yves,' he said.

Chapter 35

Albertin emerged from the shadows, holding a grip bag in one hand and what looked like a small hand gun in the other. 'Hello, Frank. I should be surprised to see you, but I'm not.'

'What are you going to do? Shoot me?'

Albertin didn't give a direct answer. 'We've got a few minutes. As your little blonde friend said, Janssen won't get through for a while with the job you've done. But equally, she'll struggle to get the police because of Buda. That was the whole point. Doing the bank while there was chaos elsewhere. And it was working until you turned up just now.'

'We found the look-out across the road, and he said there were five of you. There were only four in and around the vault. You're the fifth man. Probably keeping an eye on things on-site. I see you've got some of the cash...'

Albertin gave a small, rueful smile. 'A bit of insurance... just in case... sensible of me I reckon. And you're right, I'm the on-site, ground-level security. I heard you come in and I wanted to see who it was. But what about before all this? You didn't just turn up out of the blue.'

'There were some things that didn't click – things you said that told me that the University of Warwick probably wasn't where you'd spent time in England. "Diesel" – not a little vocabulary error but a slang word for tea used in the prison estate. Same with "blag". "Nick", "went down", "took the rap". Where was it, Yves?'

Albertin smiled again, his face lopsided. 'HMP Standford Hill, on the Isle of Sheppey. You probably know it. Fraud. I was always getting myself into scrapes. Never have been able to resist short-cuts to making some cash. I've got habits I can't break.'

'Marie the code-breaker in Comines also tipped me the wink, indirectly. She hinted that I should be careful. When I was having coffee in the square, I saw Janssen from a distance with somebody outside the bank. I only realised it was you later, when everything else was fitting together. The thing is, I think my subconscious didn't want me to recognise that it was you. Then Angie made me analyse a dream, funnily enough. The clincher. About betrayal.'

Albertin winced.

'I'm thinking and hoping that when we started out – when you and Willem and Agnes joined Angela and me – nothing was going on, and that you spotted an opportunity when you saw Janssen in action with Guy.'

Albertin was looking for absolution. 'You're right. When we began, I just had Christina's best interests at heart, like Willem. But it was too good a chance to miss. I've known Leo Janssen for years, and when I saw him I knew what he'd be up to. He's an old-fashioned blagger. Him working for the Liebaarts was a blind. I knew it would be. You should have heard him slagging off Van Leuven and his mates while he was using them and pretending to work for the cause. But as I said, the Buda thing, and everything leading up to it, was a perfect red herring for his plan – rob a bank when the police are completely overrun. He had the weekend to do most of the work, and today being a public holiday was a bonus. Anyway, I made contact and joined the… project.' He smiled thinly. 'I didn't give Leo much choice. But I can still help Christina.' He held the bag up. 'There's plenty of money here.'

'Sounds like bullshit to me,' said Sterling. 'I think you're going to have to disappear, and if Christina finds out what you've been up to, the last thing she'll want is your money. So back to it, Yves. What are you going to do now?'

'Well, I'm not going to shoot you, Frank, unless you give me no choice. You've messed things up for me, but I enjoyed our adventure, and I'm fond of you. Besides, Christina would be devastated. I reckon every option is dangerous. I can't let Janssen and the others out. My job was to stop anyone getting in. And when the police come, they'll know I let them down. I'll be a marked man then, a grass as they'd say in the nick. So I agree with you – it's time to vanish. Tell Angela… well, tell her I'm sorry. I was glad to have met her. Tell Christina…' He trailed off. 'Tell my granddaughter that I'll see her again, but I don't know when. Give her my love.'

There was a loud thud at the door to the cellar – by the sound of it a test blow. The gang had regrouped. Albertin aimed high and let off a shot into the wood. Sterling was stunned by the report in the narrow space, and by Albertin's decisiveness. There was no immediate second blow.

'Give me a minute and then get out yourself,' said Albertin as he backed into the yard. 'Goodbye, Frank.'

When Sterling, his ears still ringing, pushed through the turnstile, he saw the last of Albertin just before he disappeared around a corner down the street. Going in the opposite direction, to the Grote Markt, Sterling spotted Becky, Angela and Griet by the belfry, sensibly distanced from the bank, and made his way towards them just as two police vans, blues and twos flashing and whining, swerved around the corner.

'All sorted out?' said Becky.

'Yep. You've managed to get an armed police squad, not just a single- or dual-officer patrol car. Good work. We need to go and retrieve Willem from Buda. But the old bloke was comfortable enough back there, and I got the strong impression that he can look after himself, so let's go back to the hotel to recharge our batteries first. With luck, Aurélien will be around, and we can have a drink and something to eat. It's about 10 o'clock. It's going to be a long night. We can go out again as soon as we've re-fuelled.'

In the hotel lobby, the atmosphere was highly charged and volatile. People talked with loud voices. There were arguments and finger-pointing. A young man marched around draped in a black lion flag, like an athlete who's won a race. Outside in the street too, it was like when a football crowd could go either way – off relatively peacefully into the night or erupting into a long fit of violence. The late evening dog-strollers and insomniacs, and those local citizens without dogs or sleeplessness, mingled curiously with the large contingent of nationalists and Liebaarts who had somehow not been corralled on Buda. When Angela went up to Aurélien to get more coffee and Becky went off to phone an update to her husband Mike, Sterling took his chance quickly.

'Griet, we need to get back to what happened on the bridge. I don't think anyone knows apart from Van Leuven and some of his cronies that you tried to bump him off up there. The fireworks were going and people couldn't see from the other side. Angie and Becky don't know. They just think we were escaping.'

'Bump him off?' said Griet with a smile.

'You know what I mean. What on earth were you thinking? You could have lost everything.'

'You know what I was thinking. And I have lost... not everything, but an awful lot.'

'What went on between you and Van Leuven?'

'Not much.' She scowled. 'I didn't have much chance. You picked me up and threw me in the river. I called him a bastard. He invited me to shoot him – he said he'd be a martyr.' Then she smiled at a particular memory. 'He changed his tune when the gun went off though.'

'I noticed,' said Sterling. 'Well, in the end, no harm done. We'd better fix you up with an alibi just in case. Luckily, Van Leuven's got loads more on his plate than you. This whole stunt can't end well for him, and you'll have your revenge, I'm sure – or at least, some kind of payback.'

'It's funny,' said Griet. 'I feel better for having tried something.'

Ten minutes later, the quartet of irregulars was heading back towards the river. Griet had been disinclined to do anything but remain with her new acquaintances. 'It's different from my normal night-time routine,' she'd said ruefully.

'Tell me about it,' Angela had replied.

Having a Kortrijk resident on board turned out to be useful. The main action was taking place at the north-east corner of Buda, and all the bridges across from the south had been closed by the Liebaarts. There was an ever-increasing police presence too, blocking the streets and turning traffic and pedestrians away. 'We can go to the west,' said Griet. 'There's a new bridge down there, beyond Buda. If we cross there, we can then go east on the other side. It will take us opposite the north of the island. If the police are blocking the quayside, we might be able to get into Golden Spurs College from the back, where the car park is.'

After a mazy back street journey, it was as Griet described. The police were focused on the drama in front of them. Security and supervision at the opened-up college were lax to the point of invisibility at the back, aided perhaps by groups of adult education students and their teachers protesting assertively at the disruption. Sterling wasn't surprised. For all the impression of power and efficiency, police organisations were just as prone to cock-up as anyone else. He knew that from personal experience. Telling his companions to act as if they were exactly where they should be and for all the right reasons, they strode through the frantic lobby area and mounted the main staircase up the tower block that dominated the college and the skyline. The first three floors were busy. The third floor, in particular, had a cohort of senior police officers with binoculars trained across the river.

The fourth floor had been colonised by the gawker contingent – like that segment of the population attending strangers' funerals or random cases in the law courts. Sterling and the three women jostled for position at the improvised viewing area. If action was what they were expecting after hours of deadlock, their timing was immaculate. Before their eyes, searchlights came on from locations they could not see below them, raking Buda and its occupying army with brilliant light. A curious, squat, military-style armoured vehicle appeared from nowhere and started edging up the cat's cradle bridge towards the barrier halfway across, behind which Van Leuven's stage was still set up, even if Van Leuven himself was probably elsewhere. Down river, similar assaults looked to be starting at the western bridge, and simultaneously inflatable dinghies were whipped out from behind cover and tossed into the river at regular intervals.

'Bloody hell,' murmured Angela, riveted. 'History in the making.'

Hard-nosed Becky offered her own appraisal. 'Classic assault. Good timing. Good strategy. Pros versus amateurs. Men versus boys, the equivalent of. This won't take long.'

From long habit, drummed into him by training and supervisory officers when he was on the job, stressing the importance of linking events to timelines, Sterling looked at his watch. Midnight exactly.

He had no idea about Angela's comment – she was the historian in the crew, not him. He reckoned that it made a kind of sense – maybe. But Becky's assessment seemed spot on. As things unfolded though, even that fell short.

Chapter 36

It could almost have been a farce. The water cannon vehicle was almost the width of the cat's cradle bridge as it edged up and around the long curve to the middle of the river and the Liebaarts' barrier. If the proportions had been reversed it would soon have been hopelessly stuck well before reaching effective striking distance. As it was, the accompanying heavily armed and protected police squad had to stay behind it as there wasn't room to go alongside or get ahead. Twenty metres from the barricade, a jet from the water cannon burst forth. Behind the barricade, defenders brandished their goedendags, partially protected from the stream by the stone blocks, heavy-duty bespoke plastic screens that slotted together across the bridge and other supporting equipment. A loud, archaic chant went up, echoing the famous one of 1302. '*Vlaanderen de Leeuw, Vlaanderen de Leeuw*' – 'Flanders the Lion'. Clusters of Liebaarts crouched up against the screens to stop them being pushed over by the water, while others maintained the points of their weapons against the police approach.

Four inflatable dinghies full of armed and armoured police set off at regular intervals, from the cat's cradle bridge down to the Budastraat bridge to the west. Under the Buda streetlights and searchlight beams blazing out from the vicinity of the college, knots of defenders rushed to confront the dinghies with the same battle cry, thrusting down with the goedendags to resist the invaders. In response, the riot police banged their batons on their plastic shields. For twenty minutes, there was stalemate on all fronts. Sterling calculated that the same struggles would be going on at the Broeltoren and locations to the south of Buda. Like Angela and the other observers, he was transfixed by the battle unfolding before them. Under fierce assault, one dinghy retreated to the middle of the river, and the jeers and whoops of the defenders of that assault point drifted across to the college.

Initially taken aback by the fierce resistance, the attacking forces upped their game. From the dinghies, officers produced tear gas guns and fired canisters close to the river bank. Clouds of gas poured into the atmosphere as they slipped on gas masks. Suddenly, in a miasma of confusion, two officers from one of the dinghies had thrown out grappling irons and hauled themselves onto the quayside. Swiftly, desperately, their comrades followed, pouring and scrambling from their craft. A figure fell back with a splash into the water but was hauled out unceremoniously by eager hands. One bridgehead had been established, and the Liebaarts were driven back in disarray, disoriented by the gas and unused to the requirements of military discipline.

Sterling knew about crowd control and had participated in trying to quell the occasional riot. He found himself rooting for the police. They were getting paid, and it was their job, but it was dangerous. He knew that the success of one group in establishing a foothold would spur on the others. The defenders, faces wrapped in makeshift scarves and strips of cloth, tried strongly to stop link-ups between police squads, but the break-through had been made.

On the bridge, the water jet was having a wearing down effect on the barricaders. The chants died down as they concentrated on maintaining position. Along with the torrent of water, tear gas canisters arrived and shortly afterwards the police squad swarmed around the sides of the bridge and over the barricade aided by grappling hooks, assault ladders and gas masks – just as the defenders were forced to fall back.

On one side, small squads, perhaps in total a thousand strong, of dedicated, fully armed and trained riot police, equipped with batons, shields, tear gas, and possibly guns *in extremis*. On the other, twenty thousand Liebaarts, many with rapidly diminishing commitment to the cause. Van Leuven and his commanders clearly knew the score. As a large proportion of the throng drifted away, an air of sheepishness and interest in self-preservation palpable, the die-hards were forming themselves into squares, and performing with a determination and discipline of their own.

At that moment, half an hour from the beginning of hostilities, the battle lacked tanks and cavalry, or their equivalents, and of course using firearms on your own massed citizenry, no matter how lawless, was out of the question. The water cannon vehicle on the bridge had done a kind of job in establishing a second bridgehead, but couldn't for the moment go past the barricade, and it was probably the same story to the south and west. The Liebaart squares of grizzled veterans presented united fronts bristling with goedendags, and men, and sometimes women, darted out to kick away tear gas canisters before returning to group safety. The police feinted and probed but lacked the numbers and equipment to break the resistance in front of them.

'Interesting,' murmured Becky, her professionalism piqued. 'I may have spoken too soon, earlier. This might take a while.'

Sterling focused on the largest defensive square, to which the smaller ones were edging from along the quay and from the south. In the middle, he was certain, was Van Leuven and his leadership group.

A local man among the viewers, talking excitedly to a friend and including Griet, had stopped using his state-of-the-art binoculars, which hung from a strap over his large belly.

'Griet, can you ask him' – Sterling nodded towards the man – 'if I can borrow his binoculars for a few seconds?'

The man smiled and nodded, eager to be friendly and helpful if it ingratiated him with the attractive optician. Sterling fiddled with the focus adjuster and raked the quayside searching for a sighting of Opa Willem. He didn't see him in the first sweep but saw increasing evidence of ferocity in the islands of struggle before him – stabbing movements from the goedendags, savage baton attacks from the police. A young woman, possibly his interpreter from earlier, was trapped and dragged away after darting from a square and kicking out at a tear gas canister. An older man reeled drunkenly from a blow to his head, blood pouring from a wound.

Sterling returned to the largest square, his view perfectly magnified and sharpened by the powerful lenses. His instincts were right. Van Leuven was in the middle surrounded by determined lieutenants as an inner corps and by an elite cadre of Liebaarts ten deep with their goedendags, moving smoothly and methodically towards the open space of pampas grass and beach. The goedendags formed a smooth arc of spikes, the ones on the edges held out horizontally, and in the inner layers progressively to the vertical. Van Leuven seemed to be in a kind of trance, serene and still amid the mayhem around him and throughout Buda. *Van Leuven's last stand,* thought Sterling. *Crazy.* Then one of the lieutenants, facing towards the cat's cradle bridge from which the group had just shuffled down, turned full on to the college.

'Bloody hell,' muttered Sterling. 'Bloody, bloody hell. After all our trouble.'

'What is it?' said Angela.

Sterling offered the binoculars. 'Look at the group in the centre of the biggest square.' While Angela fumbled, he dug in his pocket for his phone. Dead. No wonder.

'Guy,' gasped Angela. 'How did…?'

'Christina probably tried to phone or text me, but the phone's out of juice. Well, he can take his chances as far as I'm concerned. We did our best. Sod him.' Sterling watched as a small company broke away from the square, dashed off with what was obviously the Kortrijk Chest and disappeared into the maze of flats in the middle of the island. To add to the sense of farce, the Chest, its linen stretcher, the poles and the men holding them looked like a scene from a pantomime – Widow Twankey's laundry basket being borne away by a couple of coolies, or Ali Baba escaping into a bazaar.

'Frank,' said Angela. 'I've just spotted Willem. He's left the battle and he's walking along the quayside towards Budastraat.'

Sterling looked down at both sides of the quay. Their side, the college side, was now relatively empty apart from vehicles and a few senior police officers. On the Buda side, the various skirmishes happening earlier had died away as goedendag squares coalesced into the single one that sheltered Van Leuven. By far the largest contingent of Liebaarts was simply throwing their goedendags aside and seeking to escape through Buda's inner streets and via the Broeltoren and other southern bridges. Even from a distance, Sterling sensed the mindset of those melting away. They'd probably expected to come to a protest, and for some excitement in otherwise humdrum lives, not a pitched battle with goedendags against armed police. Committed to the Flemish cause, yes. Up for a bit of disruption and delinquency, yes. Willing to face sustained spells of violence, danger and injury, actual and potential? A resounding "no". He wondered if they realised that Van Leuven and the hardcore Liebaarts had misled and manipulated them.

'Come on,' he said to the women. 'We'll go down, get his attention and take it from there.'

The college lobby was virtually empty, and they ran down the steps to the quayside without any challenge. As they rushed along, Willem's figure on the other side grew larger. They were able to catch up with him because he'd seen the blockage at Budastraat and stopped walking.

'Willem,' yelled Sterling.

The older man stopped and looked across the water, recognition spreading over his features. He smiled and waved, cupping his hands to his mouth as he shouted his reply.

Griet laughed.

'What did he say?' said Angela.

'Something like, "How come every new time I see Frank, he has another woman on the team?", which I assume means me.'

'Tell him I can explain when we get him back. Ask him if he can get off Buda.'

The two Flemings held a short conversation. Griet turned to her new friends. 'There's no easy way off. The police have turned the island into an open prison.'

'What's his swimming like?'

Griet shouted over and reported back. 'He's asking if he'll get a drink and a change of clothes if he dives in.'

'Of course,' said Sterling. 'At the hotel.'

Willem swam like a fish. Extracting him from the river with a stray, discarded floating goedendag, for some obscure reason seemed to add to his high spirits. Leaving the battle still raging, the quintet hurried through the warm streets of north Kortrijk, bypassed the bridge at Budastraat, crossed further down where they'd come over before, and zigzagged to the hotel. It was past one o'clock, too late for Griet and Willem to go home. Aurélien oversaw the extra arrangements – the women in one room, the men in the other. Before he fell into an exhausted sleep, Sterling thought the adventure was all but over. Wrong again.

Chapter 37

Buda looked woebegone, like a drunk the morning after the night before. It had hosted a march, a festival (of a sort), and then mass fighting. Now there was nothing except the forlorn, trampled pampas grass, the greensward pocked with huge divots from the Liebaarts' last stand, and the littered, pitted, ruined, artificial beach. A single goedendag had mysteriously survived, speared into the sand, or had been planted later, a solitary act of final defiance. The torn standard of one of the Flemish towns hung over the quayside and fluttered weakly. A tiny golden spurs brooch lay in the mud awaiting a scavenger or a council worker when the clear-up began, potentially a souvenir for generations to come.

Willem had gone home – still in high spirits. He'd told Griet, who'd told the others, what he'd learnt – that Flemish pride did not mean being against everything else, and he had no truck with Van Leuven and his bigoted message. Willem had taken a shine to Angela, and he was all charm, his curmudgeonly nature dissipated by his adventures. Griet, though, had still been reluctant to go home. Her children were coming over later, and she'd organised for her customers to go to another optician in the high street. The present company was pleasant, she said, and took her mind away from her troubles. Revisiting the scene of the attempted crime didn't seem to trouble her. She, Sterling, Angela and Becky were standing outside Guldensporencollege and looking across the river, curious to see for themselves the aftermath of the Battle of Buda.

The college was open, which indicated that the police had no further use for it as a command post, and students milled about in what was clearly the lunch period. There was a heavy police presence on the quay, however, and on Buda itself, and access on and off the island was still heavily restricted – but this time by a legitimate organisation and not insurrectionists.

Two police officers in glengarries barred them from the cat's cradle bridge. The woman spoke a few words, and Sterling turned to Griet. 'She's saying "Nothing's happening. Walk on".'

Sterling laughed.

'What did I say?' smiled Griet.

'It's what *she* said. I reckon police the world over have a dictionary of expressions they use, translated into every language. In English, it's "Nothing to see here. Move along". Come on, let's go and find some lunch. We'll follow your recommendations, Griet.'

It was crowded in the Café Rouge, the establishment opposite St Martin's Church, but a table for four had just been vacated and they were guided to it. The television screens were showing a news programme which was full of the events of the day before, a clipped, intense voice-over in Dutch providing commentary. First there was wobbly, amateur, mobile phone footage of the Golden Spurs march taken by spectators along the route. Someone had even captured blurred, dramatic images of the arming of the marchers from the garages and lorries. Then more sophisticated pictures appeared, almost certainly from one of the floors of the college – above or below where Sterling and his team had assembled later. As the insurrection had established itself, news teams had converged on Kortrijk and Buda and professionalism had taken over.

A shot panned over Van Leuven's stage, and suddenly everyone was ducking. Then a figure dashed across to the far edge, picked up a second figure, and dropped it over the side, following shortly after.

'You and Griet,' said Angela.

'Yeah. Luckily Griet's hair is wrapped up in a scarf and our backs are to the camera.'

Becky spoke, her expression cool and amused. 'You know what that reminded me of? Dallas. Kennedy. Other stuff like that. The sudden ducking and running. We never really knew why you were up there in the first place, the two of you.'

Griet looked down at the table. Sterling held Becky's gaze. 'Yeah, interesting. Quirky. I think I'm going to have a croque boum boum and a Hommelbier. What about you lot?'

'Look at this,' said Angela. Now the footage was showing the final police assault on the Liebaart position, after she and the others had rescued Willem. When the Liebaarts had first taken Buda over, it had been like a huge Sealed Knot-style enactment. Now the police were weighing in with their batons with ferocity as the final square of goedendags dissolved under a barrage of tear gas and finally an assault vehicle that had found its way in from the south. The cameras picked up the pain and distress of bloodied, dirty faces and the savage police charges.

Finally, there was a clear view of a battered Van Leuven and his lieutenants being dragged off to a Black Maria.

Sterling sipped his beer. 'What on earth was the point of all that? I kind of understand commemorating the original battle, but the rest of it – stupid.'

'Not in the slightest, Frank,' said Angela. 'You're just seeing it from the short-term point of view of a pragmatic ex-policeman who finds demos and protests and… politics… tedious. You're certainly not your father's son in that respect. I think Van Leuven's been clever and has studied his history. He's been playing the long game and he'll carry on with that. I'll give you two examples. There was an event in Dublin in 1916, during the First World War – the Easter Rising. A group of radical Irish republicans took over the General Post Office in O'Connell Street, barricaded themselves in, and tried to take over various other points in the city. The British sent in heavy reinforcements and there were six days of fighting – set pieces as well as sniping and isolated other incidents. In the end, almost 500 people were killed and artillery fire left parts of Dublin in ruins. Afterwards, people were rounded up, including some who weren't involved in the fighting, and sent to internment camps. Many of the Rising's leaders were court-martialled and executed.

'Originally, many Irish people in Dublin and Ireland were hostile to the Rising. But it was the heavy-handed, savage British response that changed public opinion dramatically. Of course, up to that point there'd been fifty years of constitutional nationalism working for Irish independence. But it was physical force republicanism that was the tipping point. Van Leuven knew he was going to lose – pikes versus the might of the Belgian state – no contest. But that didn't matter. He's started something. Getting beaten up on telly is even better.'

'And assassination would have been best of all,' murmured Becky. She had a dog-with-a-bone quality Sterling hadn't noticed before.

'Then there was the Beer Hall Putsch in Munich in 1923,' Angela continued. 'Hitler in his early political days. He and his group of Nazis marched into the centre of Munich and confronted the police. About thirty people died in the clash, four of them police officers. The putsch failed, but Hitler became known throughout Germany and there were headlines throughout the world. Better still for him, his trial lasted twenty-four days – twenty-four more days of publicity for his cause – and then the martyrdom of nine months in jail. After that, he turned to parliamentary politics. It wouldn't surprise me if Van Leuven wasn't planning a similar path.'

Griet turned her head from the television. 'You should be on that, Angela. The woman talking now is saying the same kinds of things. But you forgot to mention the Kortrijk Chest. It has been hidden somewhere on the island and is fast becoming a symbol of Flemish independence. The residents of Buda have been helping the Liebaarts keep the Chest hidden, and they are complaining that the police went too far. They were cursing all the inconvenience, but now they're enjoying the spotlight. There's been a surge of support for the Liebaarts in Kortrijk and the rest of Flanders. Someone has released a transcript of Van Leuven's speech, and it's being well received.

'The commentator's analysis is that the Battle of Buda, as they're calling it, is going to break the deadlock between the Flemish separatists and the rest. Van Leuven's been arrested, and there's a lot of anger about that.' She looked at Sterling. 'I'm angry too. He's going to get away with it, Frank. What about my Jan, Angela? Where does he fit into all this? Doesn't his murder count for anything?'

Angela cleared her throat and took a sip of her water. 'I can't imagine the upset you must be feeling. Credit to you for still being here and functioning. I'm not sure I could do it. But as far as Van Leuven's grand plan is concerned, your husband's murder seems like... collateral damage. That's not my view, so don't take it the wrong way – it's just from a strategic point of view. It feels like an aberration. Foolishness. An arrogant sense of invincibility. That's if Van Leuven did arrange it.

'Hopefully, he'll be brought to account and it will ruin everything for him.'

Griet shook her head. She could see the sense of it, but the relegation of her husband and his murder was distressing. Then a change on the screen drew her attention again. 'This is about the bank robbery. Now the presenter is saying that Kortrijk has had a busy night, and that during the disorder, police received an anonymous tip-off. Five men have been arrested and are in custody, four having tunnelled into the bank's vault from a building site next door, and one acting as look-out from an apartment opposite. A million euros have been recovered.

'Five men,' said Becky, gnawing away. 'That look-out told us five on the building site. With him as look-out, that makes six altogether. So one must have got away...'

Sterling's eyes swept around the café. It was one of Kortrijk's more upmarket ones. He could imagine Griet coming in here for lunch with her husband in happier days, a halfway point between museum and optician's. The atmosphere was vibrant and exciting. Now, and perhaps for days to come, Kortrijk was at the centre of the Belgian, maybe even European, universe, as Catalonia had once been. Buda would be remembered like 1302. Half the clientele's attention was on the television screen and half in animated conversation. An elegantly dressed woman was holding a fork of cake half way to her mouth, fascinated by the news, her husband in an earnest exchange with a man at the neighbouring table. Similar mini-scenes were playing out all through the cavernous room.

To avoid the current talk, he allowed himself to be mesmerised by a young mother, thick brown hair cut short into a practical bob, who'd just entered. Her baby was strapped in a sturdy but soft harness to her front. She manoeuvred various bags of equipment as she carried the baby. She went to the side of the room to get a high chair, which she lifted out of a stack and took over to her table. Easing the harness from her shoulders, she detached the child and slipped him into the high chair in one smooth movement. Having sat down and laid out the things she needed from her bags, she engaged the tiny bundle with a huge smile.

Sterling dragged his attention back to the women, their faces expectant. It was safe, he decided, to tell them about the robbery. He'd keep quiet about Griet's murder attempt though, and tell her to, since she was going to continue to be a pillar of the local community. Becky had an inkling, but she'd keep quiet.

'I was going to wait for a better moment, and certainly tell Christina first, but you've stuck by me, so in the circumstances... It was Albertin. Albertin was the sixth man.'

'The man you came to see me with, over at my house?' said Griet. 'Christina's other grandfather?'

'Albertin,' said Angela. She shook her head. Her eyes brimmed. 'Yves. My pal. My political soulmate. I wondered where he'd got to yesterday. But why, and how did you know?'

'We had a little talk while Becky went to get the police. The "why" is probably more difficult than how I knew. He saw an opportunity for a great deal of cash, and he was tempted. I think he's got quite a substantial criminal record one way or the other. When we started following Guy Verstraete and the Big Man came on the scene, Albertin knew him, though he pretended not to. He found out what Janssen (the Big Man) was up to and joined the enterprise. Maybe he had something extra to offer, or maybe there was a bit of blackmail involved. Somehow, before Yves came on the scene, Janssen had got involved in the Liebaarts, and he saw the march and the Buda thing as an opportunity as well, diverting attention completely from the bank on the Grote Markt. He'd have got away with it too, I reckon, if Yves hadn't joined up.'

Sterling repeated what he'd said to Yves about the various slips Yves had made, about Marie's warning, and about the dream. 'The dream and the dream analysis were good, Angela. I'm glad I worked on them. Everything slotted together when I hit the water with Griet.'

'Good about the dream,' said Angela. 'You realise that you completed the cycle when you confronted Yves. That was the ritual part, after the associations, dynamics and interpretation. It's going to help you a lot in the future with your trust issues.' But she was distracted. 'We can come back to that... God, how could I have got him so wrong? I thought I was pretty good at judging people... So all that stuff about Paris 1968, and the University of Warwick and the rest of it was just rubbish.'

Sterling shrugged. 'Looking back, I'm not sure what was fact and what was fiction. It might be true, or some of it might be, or none at all. He admitted to a spell at Her Majesty's pleasure at HMP Standford Hill, on Sheppey. It's Category C, so white-collar crime. Fraud, I think.'

'Where's he gone?'

'No idea. It's possible he's legged it to the south of France where he said his son lives. He's burnt his boats and not only with Christina and us. Janssen and his gang will probably think he's grassed them up. They won't forgive that in a hurry. He might have got some cash, but he's lost an awful lot.'

'When are you seeing Christina?' said Becky.

'Willem's relieving her at the hotel. She's coming over later this afternoon. Guy sweet-talked her and then hot-footed it back to Kortrijk to join in the fun. I imagine he got arrested with Van Leuven and the other senior people in the Liebaarts. She's our principal, so I report back to her before we do anything else.'

'Well, I've taken a knock about Yves,' said Angela, 'and that's going to take a bit of recovering from, but it's going to be worse for her. Her world's being turned upside down. Not as badly as yours, though, Griet.'

The food arrived. Sterling's croque boum boum, toasted cheese combined with bolognaise sauce, looked like the kind of concoction that would give a nutritionist palpitations. He took a long swig of Hommelbier and tucked in. Fortification was required, and this was it.

Chapter 38

It was just after the croque had been dispatched, and the food and drinks that had been ordered by the women, that Griet was finally overwhelmed. She had become very quiet during the lunch, and she was looking down at her plate again, only now for a much longer period. Angela put her hand on Sterling's arm and gestured with a tip of her head. Griet's shoulders were shaking, and although her face was entirely hidden below her thick unruly hair, tears were dropping onto the table cloth. Action and excitement, and her new friends, had sustained her through the worst days of her life, and Sterling had saved her from the perils of her misguided attempt at revenge. Perhaps Angela's analysis of the small role of Jan Planckaert's murder in the overall scheme of things was the trigger, and the business-like way, bordering on insensitive, in which she delivered it.

Becky looked on at the scene impassively. Empathy and emotion were not her strongest points. Sterling put his hand on Griet's shoulder. 'Griet, we haven't been very thoughtful. Let's finish up here and get you home as soon as possible. Your daughter's coming over, and she'll be in contact with your son. You need your family around you, and some rest, and time to… get over things. Now that everything's calming down, you're bound to be suffering a reaction. We'll get a taxi and wait with you at the house until your daughter arrives.' He tried a light-hearted note. 'Your coffee is far and away the best in Kortrijk. I wouldn't be surprised if you had biscuits to match.'

Griet looked up, sniffed, nodded almost imperceptibly, dabbed her eyes and cheeks with a napkin and blew her nose. A smile played around her mouth. 'Yes. Good idea. I'm sorry. I'm not usually like this.'

'You've been through a lot,' said Angela, as they all emerged from the café into the sunshine. 'Not helped by my thoughtless contribution.' She took Griet's arm in hers in a gesture of support and contrition.

Like the rest of Kortrijk, the area around St Martin's Church and the gates of the beguinage was crowded. But although there was still a general air of excitement, Sterling felt a shroud of anti-climax settle over him. He'd taken on the case, he'd solved it, he was about to report back to his client, and then it would be time to go home. Everyone in the small group was silent, preoccupied with their own thoughts.

The most dangerous time is when things are not quite over. Sterling felt a sudden twinge of unease. A recent memory image poked him, prompted by a ravaged face in his peripheral vision, and a faint smell redolent of leather. Time slowed down and his senses sharpened. Something similar seemed to happen to Becky at the same time. He saw her body stiffen and her step falter.

People milled around, seemingly without purpose – except for one. A man materialised from the crowd, striding doggedly forward, head slightly down. Becky buffeted sharply into Sterling but was a fraction too late. He felt a sharp stab of pain in his right side. Instinctively, his hand went down, and when he brought it up to his face, it was bright and sticky and red. Time wound on in slow motion, people continuing to throng, and a faint, faraway roaring assailed his ears, like a bout of tinnitus. His body moved into shock. His right leg began to crumple. Becky was shouting. He felt himself seized under the arms and gently laid down on the cobbles. The sun was bright, even when he closed his eyes.

Amid screams and sounds of panic around him, he could hear Angela's faint voice. 'Frank, hold on. Hold on. We've got an ambulance coming.' There was shade. He could tell from the darker colour on his eyelids. He could feel firm pressure on his side. He opened his eyes on Angela's frightened, anxious face. He coughed and smiled, then nodded. 'OK,' he tried to say, but it came out as a croak. Then he drifted away.

Chapter 39

A ngela didn't believe in divine retribution, or fate, or anything like that. But if she did, she would have been connecting her insouciance over poor Griet's plight – losing husband and livelihood in one nightmare week – with what happened next.

One moment Frank and Becky were a few steps ahead on their way to the taxi rank on the Grote Markt. The next moment, Angela and Griet were gently laying Frank down on the cobbles near the archway entrance of the beguinage, blood pulsing through his shirt from a wound in the side of his stomach. Angela knelt down and cradled his head in the crook of her arm, while Griet, shocked into a new round of action, pressed on the wound with a light summer scarf she'd retrieved from her handbag.

Angela realised that an earlier blur of movement she hadn't initially been able to interpret was Becky somehow deflecting the knife thrust from even more damage. In the crowd around them there were gasps and stares as Becky expertly swayed beyond the arc of the knife now being deployed against her. In the same smooth motion, her hands pounced on the wrist of the assailant, using his momentum and her outstretched leg to whisk him onto his back.

He cried out when the knee hit his groin, and the knife span away across the cobblestones. Angela turned back to Frank, telling him again to hold on, and when she next looked up, the thug was lying prone with zip ties pinning his wrists and arms behind him. He moaned softly.

'Griet,' said Becky sharply. She was panting lightly. 'Call an ambulance. Angela will keep the cloth on the wound.'

'I've already done it,' said a tall man emerging from the crowd. His accent was heavy and his ears stuck out.

Angela wasn't a bad judge of character – or at least, not until Albertin – and she had the sense that this was a man born to command, but only in his own imagination.

'I saw everything and heard you speaking English. What's going on?' In his hand he held the bloody knife, wrapped in a handkerchief.

'We don't know,' said Becky. She glanced down at Angela and Griet and gave them a look that screamed "Leave this to me". 'We'd just had lunch. We're sightseeing.'

The man raised his eyebrows. 'Sightseeing,' he repeated. 'In Kortrijk with all this excitement. Those judo skills against a knifeman. Special things to tie him up with.'

'We haven't got time for this now,' said Becky. She crouched down next to Angela. 'How is he?'

'I told him to hold on. That an ambulance is coming. I got a little smile...'

'His pulse is OK at the moment,' said Griet, her practicality welcome.

The women could hear the ambulance for a good while before it swung into the narrow lane, and the paramedics moved swiftly into action, one of the young men with a volley of rapid-fire questions in Dutch that

Griet fielded. Gently, they eased Sterling's head from Angela's arm and she watched, hollow and devastated, as they lifted him onto a stretcher and then into the vehicle, a drip and an oxygen mask hastily manoeuvred into place.

'I'm going with him,' she said, rubbing her arm vigorously to restore the circulation.

'No,' said Becky. 'He's in good hands now. There's nothing you can usefully do at the moment.'

'I'm going,' Angela repeated, moving towards the vehicle.

But the decision was taken out of her hands by the paramedic ministering to Sterling. He put up his hand and swung the door shut, shouting out a short reply to Griet's clipped question. The siren started abruptly and the ambulance disappeared around the edge of the Grote Markt.

'The hospital is "Our Dear Lady",' said Griet.

'Madonna. Good,' said Becky. She cocked her ears. There were two sirens now – one going, and one on its way. 'Listen, Ange, we're not abandoning Frank. We're living to fight another day. He's out of it, and we're illegals. We need to get out of here and get to Griet's as quickly as possible so we can re-group. That thug is obviously going to be arrested, but we can't get involved in a crime scene. We've been lucky – the police response is slow, not surprisingly, and' – Becky tilted her head at the large man standing proprietorially over the figure on the cobbles – 'Sticky-out Ears is taking charge.'

Blended in among the bystanders, the women watched his back as he barked orders to a gathering overcome with a curious docility. Angela was thinking that the incident had been like a firework, flaring up and then petering swiftly out, and the crowd as passive as a cinema audience. No one commented or resisted as they slipped unobtrusively away. The man himself had lost interest in them, assuming that they'd simply hang around to face the music.

'The taxi rank in the Grote Markt is out,' said Griet. 'We'll go up to the shopping centre and get a taxi from the glass market. Wiping Sterling's sticky, now rust-coloured blood on her skirt just sharpened Angela's unease. The taxi driver was talkative – full of the "Battle of Buda" as he called it, but Becky had told everyone to wait till they got out before they tried to sort things out, and by the time they'd got to Griet's house he was as silent as his passengers.

The women crowded into the bathroom together, in a hurry to clean up and get settled. Griet produced towels, and then coffee. If Sterling had been right about its quality, Angela was too preoccupied to notice.

Then Becky started speaking. 'We do things on our own terms. The police are going to start piecing every-thing together when they finally get on top of things. We need to contact Christina and get her to the hospi-tal. If you think about it, Christina's virtually the only innocent in this whole thing. She and her family can keep us in the picture.'

Anger surged suddenly through Angela, like an electric charge. 'I shouldn't have listened to you. We shouldn't have left him. We should go to the hospital and to hell with the consequences.'

The skin around Becky's nostrils turned white, and her whole body quivered, something Angela had never seen before. 'Do you think I'd be suggesting this if I didn't think it was the best way to go? Don't you think

I feel the same as you about Frank? You haven't got the monopoly on affection for him. And think for a moment, a tiny moment, about what Frank would want. He'd want us to protect ourselves. And he'd want to tie up the case himself, when he recovers. You know exactly what he's like. So we're only leaving him temporarily. And likely we're following what would be his wishes.'

'Ladies,' said Griet. She rubbed her eyes.

Angela too felt overwhelmingly tired. 'Sorry,' she said. 'Sorry, Becky. It's just that…'

'… I don't have feelings. I just go around bashing people and blowing things up. Action woman.'

But Angela detected a small smile. 'Well…,' she said.

Griet had picked up on it as well. 'So next we contact Christina. Good. Let me have her number.' She dialled and spoke in Dutch, then handed Angela the phone.

'Christina?'

'No, it's Agnes. Is that Angela?'

'Yes. Is Christina there? It's urgent.'

'Because of everything that's been happening, she's resting at the moment. Exhausted.'

'I understand. But can you put her on the line? It's about Frank. Not just urgent, an emergency.'

'Wait a few moments.'

'Hello?' The girl's voice was listless.

'Christina, some bad news.' There was no point in sugar-coating it, and Angela knew enough about Christina, recently and from her earlier adventure with Frank, to be sure that she was a robust and feisty character. 'Frank's been stabbed. He's been taken to' – she looked at Griet, who said "Onze-Lieve-Vrouwhospitaal", which Angela repeated carefully. 'We couldn't go with the ambulance, and we can't go now, as we're not here legally, so you have to.'

'Of course,' said Christina. Her voice reflected the surge of energy she must have experienced. 'How is he?'

'We don't know,' Angela replied. He lost consciousness and lots of blood. It didn't look good, but the paramedics came quickly and knew what they were doing. Becky and I are going to have to go back to England, but not by any usual route. As soon as I get home I can come back if necessary. We're at Griet Planckaert's' – she read out the number – 'and we'll wait here till we hear from you.'

'OK. I'll go to the hospital now, with my mother or Opa Willem. I'll tell you what's happening as soon as I know myself.'

'Thank you, Christina.' Angela paused. This part was difficult. 'One last thing before you go. Frank had some news for you – about your case – I can…'

'Never mind about that, Angela. I don't expect it's anything I want to hear, and I can guess what it is anyway. I'll speak to you soon.'

Christina was as good as her word. Over two hours later, as Angela and Griet sat and fretted and drank coffee, and Becky spent time on a burner phone in the hallway, making arrangements for the clandestine crossing back to England, Christina was getting to Kortrijk and catching up on Frank's condition. Angela started as Griet's landline phone rang.

'Hallo?' Griet said and listened. She handed the phone to Angela and mouthed "Christina".

Angela's legs wobbled and her heart fluttered as adrenaline surged, like the feeling at a sudden dip on a rollercoaster. 'Christina?'

Christina's voice was measured and even. She was picking her words carefully so that there could be no misunderstanding, given that English was not her first language. 'Frank is fine. He has been given some blood. His heart is beating strongly. He has been sent to sleep with drugs. He is calm and in good condition. The doctor told me that it will take time for him to get completely better, but he is not in any danger. He is not going to die.'

Angela's eyes filled up and she blinked.

'Are you still there, Angela?'

'Yes, Christina. Thank you. That's such good news. Let me tell Griet and Becky.'

Griet grimaced and put her thumbs up. Becky smiled broadly, which jarred with her usual laconic manner.

'Will you stay at the hospital, Christina?'

'Yes, my mother, Opa Willem and I will take it in turns. It will mostly be me, though.'

'And you'll give us regular updates?'

'Certainly. I have your details. I've also managed to find out that the man who stabbed Frank is safely locked up in the police station. He's a criminal, but they say he's strongly linked to the Liebaarts and Flemish nationalists. The police think it was some kind of revenge attack.'

'Good. Griet would like to visit Frank too. She has helped us and knows about you. And I'll come back as soon as I can.'

Angela and Becky left Griet as her daughter arrived from Poperinge. After that, in daylight and darkness, the return journey to England involved the same elements as the outward one: taciturn men, in a white van and then on a motor launch from a deserted French beach; a choppy Channel crossing; landfall and collection near Sandley Yacht club; and finally Sandley.

Angela's emotions veered from relief and satisfaction to the lingering sense that, despite everything, she had still deserted her friend. And for all the new-found efficiency, crisp decision-making and accurate communication of Frank's remaining team – in contrast to much of the casual, ramshackle nature of what had happened before – she'd come to realise that, without him, they were rudderless.

Chapter 40

Disinfectant. Its pervasive smell was the first thing Sterling was aware of when he woke up. After that, it was soon apparent that he was propped on pillows in a hospital bed. A drip had been inserted into his wrist, and the tube looped up to a transparent bag on a stand by the bed. He was in a quiet room with sunlight streaming through the window to the left of the bed. On the right was a high-backed hospital armchair, and next to that a small, portable table on which rested a small pile of recently published women's magazines in Dutch, which told him he was still in Flanders, and various other items that suggested a vigil – pens, a crossword book, a romantic novel (judging by the cover), a pillow and some fruit.

He tried to piece together what had happened, and it came back quickly, his last conscious image Angela's face as she cradled him in her arms. Apart from a head-ache, he felt all right. There was a dull pain in his side, and he was hungry and woozy. A complicated array of machines was charting his progress, their individual purposes obscure, except the heart monitor. The line on that was showing healthy peaks and troughs rather than beeping and flatlining, as it would do on the cop shows, so that was a good thing. Presumably.

After about fifteen minutes of swirling thoughts with his eyes closed, Sterling felt a presence. He opened his eyes and the nurse, a slender woman whose ruddy face was somehow out of proportion to the rest of her, jumped. 'Sorry,' said Sterling, almost as a reflex.

The woman recovered and bustled about cheerfully, chattering in rapid Dutch. She went through the equipment, plumped his pillows, fussed around his sheets and ran a cool flannel across his face. There was more rapid Dutch accompanied by gesticulations, including the mimed use of a stethoscope that suggested that she was going to summon a doctor. The gestures signalled that she was aware that he was not Flemish.

Sterling pointed to the armchair and opened his palms, triggering more rapid Dutch, but this time she shrugged and gave up, leaving Sterling no wiser about who his visitor was. Minutes later, a young doctor of Asian extraction arrived and said "Good afternoon" in English. The same performance with the equipment followed, and a note made on the small computer at the end of the bed.

Then the woman sat in the armchair. 'I'm not sure how much you remember, Mr Sterling, but you were stabbed.' She got up and checked something on the screen. 'Four days ago, now. You lost a lot of blood from a stomach wound and we had to knock you out and do a transfusion. You've been very ill. At one point we didn't think you were going to survive. It was reported that someone bumped into you before the knife went in. That might have saved you. A little bit higher and it would have pierced your heart.' The doctor's English was so precise and faintly accented that it was almost stilted, and unlike anything an English person might have produced.

'Permanent damage?' said Sterling.

'None,' said the doctor, 'but you'll need to be careful for a while, and real progress won't be until after six months.'

'Good. Well, thank you very much for the care you and your colleagues have given me. How long do you think I'll have to stay here?'

'About three more days, I would estimate.'

'And who's been keeping me company in the chair you're currently sitting in?'

The doctor smiled for the first time, her delicate features losing their professional mask. 'I don't know her name, but she's about my height and build, with red hair in a ponytail. The nurse's station has the details. I'm told that she's been very... attentive. She's gone for a break now but I expect she'll be back soon. There have been plenty of others in and out. People have been worried.'

Christina. Good news. Sterling wondered where Angela and Becky were.

'The other thing... we've been asked by the police to notify them when you are awake. I expect they'll want to talk to you as soon as possible. We'll make sure they don't tire you out. I'll leave you now. It's never much of an idea to get stabbed, Mr Sterling, but you're lucky it wasn't worse.'

Sterling stared at the ceiling. A hairline crack ran jaggedly in a diagonal from one corner and then out of sight. The police. Inevitable. An Englishman injured on the most violent night in Kortrijk's recent history. He'd need to get his story straight. If it came down to it, he'd tell them as much as he could, while protecting those who needed protecting – Angela, certainly. Griet. But he'd be grassing people up too. He'd have to check stuff with Christina. His head was clearing quickly. Four days of sedation was wearing off, and he was even beginning to feel perky.

It would be handy to run through people and match them to possible crimes, a kind of reverse process, he reflected, to the one the police would be following, who would be looking at the crimes they knew about, and then for the perpetrators. He'd been guilty himself of a bit of trespass and perhaps withholding evidence, and that would apply to everyone else who'd been helping him. Angela had sneaked illegally back into Belgium, and likely back out the same way. Her sins, and Becky's, and the team's, were the same as his without some of the overlap. Sterling didn't know Belgium's laws or legal system, but Willem was guilty of unlawful assembly or riot. Goedendags were offensive weapons. Griet had attempted murder, but even if Van Leuven wanted to make something of it – from a prison cell or in the dock – it would be hard to prove – no bullet, no death or wounding, gun at the bottom of the river Leie, and no confession. Albertin – bank robbery at a minimum. Van Leuven – murder, conspiracy, treason, an endless list. Guy Verstraete – theft, assault, demanding money with menaces, and many of the crimes that could be laid at Van Leuven's door. Sterling's mind was beginning to boggle. The list was long. The only person coming out of it smelling of roses was Christina, and perhaps her mother.

But the Belgian police would be like police forces the world over. If Sterling gave them enough wins, they wouldn't bother too much with the gaps and discrepancies. He'd need to see Christina before he embarked on his story...

Boredom had set in when the nurse returned with two men, one in his thirties, handsome, thick black hair, sallow skin and dark eyes, the other shorter and thinner, intelligent, keen air. Detectives. Lead and offsider. This was going to be tricky.

'Good afternoon, Mr Sterling,' said the older man. The younger one nodded, not friendly but not hostile either. Interested but detached. Professional. The older man continued in Dutch, introducing himself as a detective sergeant and his colleague as a detective constable. The younger man interpreted. 'My colleague is saying that "Good afternoon" is the limit of his English, so I'm doing the translating. He's saying that we're glad to see that you're awake. We've been temporarily posted from Ostend to Kortrijk police station to help during the current state of emergency. The doctor says that you were very ill but have pulled through. We know you're English and your identity. We'd like to ask you some questions if that's OK.'

Sterling nodded. He didn't have much choice, he reckoned. In fact, never had an audience been more captive, but he didn't have to act as alertly as he was feeling.

'That's fine, but I'm still feeling groggy, to be honest, so I might not be much help for a while.'

The offsider nodded and reported back. He didn't acknowledge Sterling's condition with any sympathy. The detectives wanted answers and not flimflam. Sympathy would deflect from the task at hand. The usual speak-interpret-speak cycle geared up.

'We'd like to know what you are doing in Kortrijk, Mr Sterling, at such a... busy time.'

'Visiting,' said Sterling.

'So, a tourist, then.'

'Not really. I've got friends in this part of Belgium.'

'Witnesses say that there were three women, one black, two white, who were with you when the attack happened. While the black woman and one of the white women tended to your wounds, the other one disarmed and apprehended the man who stabbed you. They were astonished that such a small woman, could be so... brave and effective. To take a knife from a thug like that, without getting stabbed... Unfortunately, for reasons we don't understand, the women disappeared before our officers arrived at the scene. Tell us about these remarkable women.'

Angela, Griet and Becky. Out of it. Good. Tell the truth, just not all of it. Christ, this is going to be tricky. 'Two were visiting, like me. The doctor says I've been here four days. They'll have had to go home because of the hotel and their tickets. I expect they made sure I was OK before they went.'

'And their names...'

'Angela Wilson and Rebecca Strange. As I said, just visiting friends...'

The detective doing the interpreting actually tut-tutted. The questioning intensified. Who was the other woman, the one with red hair? Why were you all together?

Sterling pushed back. 'This feels like an interrogation. Aren't I the one who was stabbed? Aren't I the victim here?'

'Of course, Mr Sterling. It's just that it wasn't a random act by a mad person. The man in custody has a long history of crime and violence, and strong right-wing sympathies. The attack happened in broad daylight, so it's doubtful that the motive was robbery. It seemed... vindictive. So you were a *specific target*.'

Sterling saw the pock-marked face and smelt the leather from two encounters. The memory induced a prickling of sweat on his forehead and palms. So did the relentless questioning. The detective sergeant reminded him of Andy Nolan again, this time uncomfortably. Andy Nolan always got to the bottom of the most complex investigation with his intelligence and determination.

Sterling needed to see Christina. 'Surely, if you've made an arrest, the case is over. I'm getting very tired.'

The detectives gave no sign that they'd heard. 'Just a few more questions. We really want to get everything properly tied up. I'm sure you'd like us to as well...'

Sterling's smile was a rictus. It was still fixed when the door opened. The nurse with the large face entered and began her customary bustle, plumping the pillows, checking drip and line, and entering data at the end-of-bed terminal. She was one of those professionals who wielded little power in any usual circumstances. Ticket inspectors were another. If your ticket was in order, then the inspector moved on to the next person, but if not... IT helpdesk technicians... parking enforcement officers... And when these people had power, they wielded it ruthlessly.

Sterling was lucky. The nurse looked up from the terminal as Sterling sank back, red-faced and perspiring. Discreetly, he held his breath. The nurse glanced at her watch. An exchange in Dutch started with the DS. "A few more questions" or "just a little longer" he seemed to be saying, and her tone oozed disapproval and disagreement. Assertiveness segued into anger. 'Nee, genoeg,' she said distinctly.

Both detectives looked at Sterling, who worked hard to resist a smirk. Instead, he arranged his face in apology.

'We'll come back soon,' threatened the offsider. Sterling nodded. *And I'll tell you as much as I can then,* he promised silently.

*

Coming out of the lift at the main reception, the DC sneaked an appreciative glance at the rear of a pretty, shapely, red-haired young woman in figure-hugging blue jeans and T-shirt as she passed in the other direction. The DS noticed but didn't comment. In the car, they stared out over the visitors' car park.

'What did you make of that?'

'He knows much more than he's saying. I got the impression that he wanted to help but something was holding him back. I don't think he was scared. I think it was something else.'

The DS nodded approvingly. 'I was thinking along those lines.' They hadn't worked together for long. 'What's your degree in?'

'Psychology and communication.'

'Useful. Mine was in economics and economic history, but I was never going into those fields. Police work is more appealing. But I was thinking of the Scotsman Adam Smith's theory of the invisible hand. Or *The Lord of The Rings.* We all read that as teenagers – about one ring to bind them or some such.'

'All that was a bit passé when I was that age,' the offsider said. 'Saw the films though.'

The DS smiled. 'Well, neither the invisible hand nor the binding ring is the right analogy really. One is related to markets, and the other to magic. But we have all these events and crimes – the firebombing of that optician's, the riot on Buda, the murder our colleagues are investigating at the 1302 Museum, what turns out to be the violent theft of the Kortrijk Chest from Oxford in England, the bank robbery, and most recently the stabbing of an "innocent" tourist whose companions have disappeared. There's probably stuff we don't yet know about. We haven't had a general briefing meeting for days because of the chaos. There's talk of further agitation for the uniforms to deal with, and they're still chasing after so-called Liebaart ringleaders. All our teams are running around in the dark, following their own lines of enquiry, and everyone we've arrested is keeping shtum or lawyered up.

'But my distinct impression is that Mr Frank Sterling from England is the key to our full understanding. Everything is connected, I reckon, and he links it all together. He's the invisible hand. He's the ring. Obviously, he's a victim too, but we need to make sure he doesn't do a runner.'

'I'll get on to it,' said the younger man.

Chapter 41

Christina smelt fresh and fragrant as she leaned over Sterling and kissed him delicately and tenderly on each cheek, continental-style.

'My first break today, and when I'm away, you wake up,' she chided.

Sterling smiled wanly. 'Sorry,' he said. He felt gritty and at a disadvantage, much more so than with the detectives. He was being well looked after, but blanket washes, a catheter and a colostomy bag did not make for a feeling of cleanliness and well-being. An army of ants marched across his skull, which he was unable to scratch, and his hair was lank and greasy.

'Don't be,' said the girl. 'I'm so pleased you're getting better. We've been so worried. My mother and Opa Willem have been to see you as well, while you were asleep. The young man from the hotel and his friend...'

'Aurélien and Denys,' said Sterling. 'Good of them.'

'And Griet,' – the face that had launched, if not a thousand ships, then a high degree of... turbulence, betrayed something – irritation, possibly jealousy – 'who Opa Willem knows a little, and who you helped, like me. She and I spoke on the phone when you were first brought here.'

Sterling pretended not to react in any significant way to the last piece of information, and hoped he was successful. He'd become fond of Griet, who was from similar feisty, Flemish origins, he supposed, as Christina herself. 'Not just them,' he said. 'After the nurse and a doctor today, two detectives arrived.'

'Already. That was quick.'

'Yep. And what about Angie and Becky? They were with me and Griet when it happened.'

'Angela and Griet looked after you while Becky dealt with the man who stabbed you. They got the ambulance that brought you here. Because Angela and Becky had both come into the country illegally, they couldn't get involved with the police. So they went home with Griet, contacted me and I came to the hospital straight away. I phoned them back when I knew you were out of danger. They went home the same way as they came.' She smiled at a memory. 'Becky is nice, but you know when not to ask questions. I've phoned them every day, and I promised to look after you.'

'And you are, Christina. Thank you.'

She took Sterling's un-intubated hand and squeezed it. 'They also thought it might help you if they weren't here. "It will keep things simple", Angela said. They send their love.'

'Good.' Sterling cleared his throat. 'What about Opa Yves?'

Christina made a moue with her dainty mouth but could not keep up the show of disapproval. She put palms to the tears that sprang from her eyes. 'It's been a difficult time for me... Angela told me what happened – at the bank. She was very kind about it. She said you'd have wanted to tell me yourself.'

'He asked me to say he's sorry,' said Sterling. 'He was upset. He sends his love.'

'My mother told me something about his past, so part of me wasn't surprised. He was always good to me, and I didn't ignore him like the rest of the family.'

'And he appreciated that, Christina,' said Sterling. He and Albertin had never actually discussed it, but embellishment could do no harm, and it wasn't as if Albertin was going to turn up to contradict him any time soon.

'I expect he's gone off to find my father. Two bad pennies – isn't that what you say? – together.'

'Should I leave him out of my conversation with the detectives when they come back? He's going to be punished in a way – losing you – and his fellow robbers will think he's informed on them. I'd say he's a marked man.'

'I suppose so, if you can. He didn't hurt anybody, did he?'

'No, he didn't hurt anyone. I liked him. He was a rogue, but I liked him.'

'A rogue. I can guess what that is.'

'How are Willem and Agnes?'

'Busy with the hotel while I'm here. All this has done Opa Willem good. He enjoyed the excitement. He's been less bad-tempered – in fact, not bad-tempered at all. He's become more easy-going. He has contact with Angela. They're friends.'

'What about Van Leuven and the Liebaarts, and the Kortrijk Chest?'

'You know I'm not interested in all those things, Frank. I don't bother with the news. But Opa tells me that Van Leuven and some others are under arrest but they're getting lots of support from around Belgium. Opa says things are getting interesting, politically. Not that I care.' Then she brightened. 'The story about the Chest is funny, though. Lots of the people in the apartments on Buda island have become Liebaarts supporters and they're hiding it, passing it secretly from place to place. The police can't find it, even after four or five raids…'

'The pantomime continues,' Sterling muttered softly to himself.

The nurse came and went, smiling conspiratorially, even though there was no conspiracy. A drink and food trolley appeared. Christina made some phone calls to update interested parties about Sterling's return to consciousness. The whir of machinery overrode all the other sounds of a busy hospital and had a lulling effect. Sterling dozed and woke up. There was further conversation about the events of the last few days and what should be public and what should be withheld. Then it was time to get to the heart of the matter, curiously avoided up to this point. The time for beating about the bush had run out.

'So, we've sorted Angie and Becky out, and Opa Willem and Opa Yves. The detectives said that the man who knifed me is in custody. I reckon I can tell them that he probably murdered Jan Planckaert too, authorised by Pieter Van Leuven, and they can investigate that.' Sterling did not mention Griet's wild spell, since only Becky suspected the assassination attempt on the cat's cradle bridge. 'That leaves…'

'Guy. My fiancé.'

Sterling lay quiet.

'Well, we both know most of what happened. He came with me back to Ypres the night of the murder – the night before the so-called "Battle of Buda" – and he

was his old, charming, loving self, which he demonstrated with such...' She struggled for the right English
word.

'What, you mean you...'

Christina laughed wryly. 'Yes, Frank. We made love.
We had sex. It was exciting too. More exciting than it's
ever been. After that, when I was asleep, he sneaked
back to Kortrijk and you saw him at Buda with your
own eyes. When Angela told me that, it was the end. I
was so angry. He made his choice then and I don't owe
him anything now. The big hero of the Liebaarts is not a
big hero of mine.' She gulped. 'And he's not my fiancé
anymore. Maybe we could have had a future of some
kind after everything he did. Maybe we could have been
happy again, but not now. He escaped from the battle,
but the police will get him eventually. So, tell the detectives your story and put Guy in it. It's not me punishing
him. It's what he decided, and I'm certainly not waiting
around while he's in prison.'

Sterling said nothing, but it did feel as if it was punishment. It felt like revenge.

Now that Christina had started, the words poured
from her. 'It's been a horrible time. I've lost Guy. I've
lost Opa Yves. We thought we might lose you. But it's
not just the last few months and the last few days. I've
lost four years of my life. I've been wasting time.
Everything had become so boring and ordinary. Thank
you for what you've done. I never expected anything
like this when I came to see you in England, but you and
the others have given me freedom. I'm going to have
some fun. I'm going to do some proper living.'

Since Sterling had first met Christina, he'd always
had a soft spot for her – her beauty, her spirit. His

throat was thick and dry. Among the bank of machines, the ECG strip on the heart monitor started showing a different, more complex and agitated pattern, accompanied by beeping. They looked at it for a long moment.

'The fun,' he croaked. 'When I'm better, I can help with that.'

Christina took his unencumbered hand again, in both of hers. Her smile was glorious. Her green eyes sparkled. 'Good,' she said. 'I was hoping you'd say that.'